The Book Guild Ltd

First published in Great Britain in 2016 by
The Book Guild Ltd
9 Priory Business Park
Wistow Road, Kibworth
Leicestershire, LE8 0RX
Freephone: 0800 999 2982
www.bookguild.co.uk
Email: info@bookguild.co.uk
Twitter: @bookguild

Typeset in Aldine401 BT

Printed and bound in the UK by TJ International, Padstow, Cornwall

ISBN 978 1911320 067

British Library Cataloguing in Publication Data.
A catalogue record for this book is available from the British Library.

For Alan

- Part One -

Flo

1943-1945

Chapter One

Flo looked across an unfamiliar airstrip to a row of hangars, which were gaping open to reveal mechanics working on fighter planes. Beyond the hangars, the branches of leafless trees made a lacy pattern against a leaden sky. She shivered in a chill wind and wished that she had thrown her coat on before leaving her new office and losing her way. She had been posted to RAF Burghfield, near Reading in Berkshire, only the day before and didn't yet know her way around her new station.

By the spring of 1943, the war was over three years old and seemed to Flo, at twenty-two, to have lasted forever. Burghfield was her second posting and she was now a corporal in the Women's Auxiliary Air Force. She had started work that day as a secretary to a senior officer. He had asked her to take some documents elsewhere on the station, gabbling directions she had barely understood, although his message about speed had been clear. She had left their Nissen hut in a hurry, quickly losing her way.

Flo was a slight young woman, with straight brown hair worn in a roll secured by grips. Lively brown eyes sparkled from her fresh face and a smile was rarely far from her lips, although she was frowning now. She asked a passing mechanic for help, but he didn't seem to know where she was trying to go and scurried past her.

She was looking around, unsure of which way to turn, when a loud voice surprised her from behind.

'You shouldn't be here. Women can't be air crew. Where do you think you're going?'

Flo span round. A young man was facing her with a confident expression. He was strongly built and brimming with energy. Despite the regulation short back and sides, dark hair was threatening to curl across his forehead. Sergeant's stripes showed clearly on one arm. The sharp words caused her some trepidation, but she relaxed when he smiled.

'I'm trying to find Air-Vice Marshal Manston's office. I'm taking these papers to him, but this place is so confusing that I've no idea where I am.'

'Let me show you… it's this way.' He strode off back in the direction of the Nissen huts, from where Flo had come. Flo trotted after him and he slowed down as if suddenly conscious of her shorter legs.

'I haven't seen you before. You must be new here,' he said, glancing down at her. Not for the first time, Flo wished she were taller. She had often found that 5 ft 3 ins (two and a half if the truth were known) were not quite enough.

'I came yesterday, from RAF Debden in Essex, in Fighter Command. I work for Wing Commander Grant. He did tell me where to go, but when it came to it, I couldn't remember all the directions.'

'Never mind. It's not that far,' her guide said. A few minutes later he stopped beside one of several Nissen huts that now surrounded them. 'Here we are. Now, how will you ever find your way back to your office?' The smile was back, teasing now.

'Oh, could you show me?' Flo's smile was pleading.

'All right, I'll wait, even if it means we lose the war!'

Once Flo had delivered her papers, they set off and then he spoke again. 'Look, head down here and turn left at the end, then you're there. See you around.' He was gone, barely giving her the chance to thank him.

In later years, when Flo looked back on that small incident, she saw the beginning of lasting changes in her life, but at the time, she was thinking only that she was lost.

At lunchtime the next day, she came into the NCOs' mess, where rows of bare, wooden tables were occupied here and there by people eating their midday meal. On one side of the hut, a queue for food wound towards the serving hatch where kitchen staff stood wielding large spoons. The sound of chatter rose from the tables and a smell of boiled cabbage hung in the air.

Flo was with Ellen, a friend from before the war. They had first met at Selfridges in London's Oxford Street, where they had both started work after leaving school. They had lost touch during the war, but Flo had been delighted to find Ellen at Burghfield on her arrival. She was showing Flo the ropes. At that moment, this involved facing a pile of lumpy mash, watery cabbage and boiled mince.

'Well, we'd better get it down us, if we're to survive the day,' Ellen said, picking up her knife and fork. She was a pretty woman with masses of brown, curly hair and a capable, friendly manner. She tucked in, but Flo, who normally had a good appetite, was quailing before the unappetising food and began her meal slowly, looking around her, eager to familiarise herself with her surroundings.

'Oh, hello, Bill,' Ellen said, pausing between forkfuls. 'Still organising supplies are you? We seem to need so much stuff here that I'm surprised you have time to eat.'

The sergeant who had helped Flo find her way the day before was sitting down beside them with a plate piled high.

'This is Flo, who arrived on the station a couple of days ago. Bill – he's a genius with finding uniforms to fit the oddest shapes,' Ellen said, by way of introduction.

'Hello, again. Flo – short for Florence?' Bill said.

'Yes, but everyone calls me Flo. Hello, Bill – is it short for William?'

'Yes, but everyone calls me Bill.'

He laughed at the way Flo had echoed his question to her and then turned to Ellen.

'We met yesterday. Flo was lost. I thought she was about to take a ride on a Spitfire. I stopped her just in time. You can't get away that easily, you know. You're going to have to learn your way around first,' Bill said, turning back to Flo with a smile, and beginning to wolf down his lunch at the same time.

'Yes, I know.' Behind Flo's answering smile was a desperate wish for a witty response to come to her aid, but she could only manage, 'Thank you for helping me out. I'm sure I'll get to know my way around soon.'

Ellen was already finishing her lunch. 'Well, I'd better get back to my desk, talking of work, or they'll be sending out a search party.' She stood up to leave.

Flo gave her a quick smile. 'Don't forget, you're going to take me on a tour later.'

'Oh, I meant to say that I won't be able to this evening. My desk is stacked high today and I'll be there till I drop. Another time,' Ellen said as she left, taking her plate and cutlery to a hatch, as everyone did.

Flo, keen to lose her newness to the station, felt let down. She was deciding she would have to learn her own way around when Bill spoke. He had finished eating.

'I'm an old hand here – that is, I've been here long enough to know my way, so I'll take you round the place, if you like.' His tone was casual.

'Well, after yesterday, I couldn't imagine a better guide. But are you sure you have the time?'

Flo ceased to struggle with her unfinished food and prepared to leave the table and return to her desk.

'Yes. See you here at 6 pm? Don't get lost on the way!' He was pulling a pipe and some tobacco out of his pocket.

'Fine. I won't.' She smiled at him in gratitude as she left him to smoke.

That afternoon, Flo found herself looking forward to the tour of the station and she finished her work in good time. Bill met her as arranged in the NCOs' mess, but they didn't linger there. He whisked her outside and pointed to where the gathering dusk just allowed them to see a large, old house that she had noticed on her arrival.

'Of course, it's a bit of a come-down now,' he began. 'If you'd come here a few weeks ago, you'd have been billeted in Sulhamstead House over there. It was requisitioned for us. Unfortunately, we've all moved into Nissen huts now.'

'Oh, my dreams of the high life are in ruins then.' Flo was pleased that he laughed.

'Keep them for some other day!'

He led the way to the stores, where he worked and then on to the other Nissen huts set out in neat rows. There was one for the officers' mess, another for their sleeping quarters and ablutions, with similar, but more modest accommodation for other ranks.

'The airfield is used largely for training purposes,' he said as they neared it. 'Now, if you feel like walking, I'll show you what there is to see nearby.'

The countryside immediately around the airbase was level, with grass underfoot. They were in the grounds of Sulhamstead House, near Burghfield Common. Bill explained that the RAF station included an explosives factory, an anti-aircraft battery, a series of pillboxes, an anti-tank ditch, a fortified house and a searchlight battery, but that they were too scattered for them to see everything on a walking tour. After the Nissen huts, he took her to see a pillbox, which still meant plenty of fast walking, so that it was dark by the time they had finished and Flo was ready to sit down.

'Thanks very much. I hope I couldn't get lost now,' she said, as they headed back to the NCOs' mess from where they had started.

'I'm sure you won't. Look, I've got things to do, but I'll see you around,' he said quickly.

Flo watched him stride off, thinking what a helpful person he was. He sat next to her in the mess at lunchtime the next day and after that she ran into him frequently and found that she was always pleased to see him. He brought life to any conversation and Flo's world began to feel a little flat when he wasn't there.

In the weeks that followed, she learned to find her way around the station and she renewed her friendship with Ellen. The moments when the war seemed far away and it was as if they were all scurrying around in a closed world were few. Most of the time, Flo moved at the double, even when she was simply at her desk. She had plenty of work to do and there were always other girls to talk to in spare moments, so time passed quickly. Radio news or newspapers kept them in regular touch with events beyond the station.

Flo was keeping a scrapbook of newspaper cuttings on the progress of the war. She was trying to stay abreast of the action and to gauge when the war might end, but it was nowhere in sight in the spring of 1943. London news was of particular interest to her as a Londoner, and the most recent entry in her scrapbook was about the terrible crush at Bethnal Green tube station in March that year. Nearly 200 deaths had resulted from panic at the unaccustomed sound of new anti-aircraft rockets.

Flo was full of admiration for the pilots who were training at the station. They were like young gods to her, and she was glad she wasn't allowed near the planes because the thought of fighting in the air was terrifying, even though she would have loved a joy ride. She had never been in a plane.

One way or another, she saw Bill most days. He was usually ready to stop for a few words and she found herself thinking that she was glad that he wasn't a pilot because of the danger they encountered. She wondered whether he might already have a girlfriend or might be posted away suddenly and she didn't like the idea of not seeing him again. She didn't know how he felt about her.

One evening, Bill suggested that Flo come out of the station with him for a drink in the nearby village of Burghfield. She accepted with pleasure, but was secretly worried that he might find her lacking, away from the camaraderie of the station. It wasn't as if she were a code-breaker, a secret agent or even a pilot, like some women she had heard about by this stage in the war. She wouldn't be stupid enough to say so, though. She desperately wanted to impress him.

They met at the main gate, both making sure in advance that they had passes. Flo felt shy to be leaving the station with Bill. It was one thing to be shown the way by him or to talk casually on the station, but outside their common base, she felt she was starting again with him. His accent showed that he wasn't from her sort of background and even though it must be written all over her, it was important that he shouldn't know how much she liked him until it was clear that he liked her. Bill was relaxed, as they started walking.

'You didn't just appear on this earth out of the blue, did you, Flo? You must have a family somewhere,' he said.

Flo found herself describing her family home in Plaistow in East London, her parents, Alf and Mabel, her brothers Bobby and Jeff and her sisters Rosie, Joan and Annie, their ages and likes and dislikes.

'And what about your life before the war? What did you do?' he asked.

'I started my first job in 1937, in the finance office at Selfridges, and that was when I began to listen to what people were saying, on the underground and on the wireless. I read the paper. Even then, people were talking about war with Germany.'

'It was building up for a long time. I was born at the end of the Great War, but you're right. By 1937, another war was in the air we breathed.'

'Yes. Everyone was expecting it and buying food, blackout cloth and sticky tape for their windows. And the next year we were given those gas masks. I felt like suffocating when I tried mine on. It was so tight around my face. I carried it around for a few months, but then I stopped bothering,' Flo said. 'How I wished the war would come or go. I hated the uncertainty.'

'What were you doing on the day it began?'

'I was at home with my family, listening to the wireless. It was my nineteenth birthday, 3rd September 1939. I remember wishing the war had waited a few days, because no one was thinking about my birthday at all, apart from my mum.'

War had broken out in the same year that nylon stockings came on the market. Flo had been desperate for a pair to replace the thick lisle of every day and, because the Phony War didn't seem real, the nylons had at first commanded almost as much of her attention as the war. She didn't say that to Bill, nor did she mention being disappointed by her mother's present of a square headscarf that day, when it was the nylons that she craved. She didn't know him well enough.

'Where were you when the war broke out?' Flo said.

'Still living at home. I was out cycling with Gerry, my brother. It was a Sunday and we had both decided to miss church and go out for the day because the weather was nice. My mother would normally have thrown a fit about missing church, but the war had put everything else out of my parents' heads.'

Like many other women, Flo had felt it was her duty to help with the war effort. She had continued with her job knowing that it would not be for long and that her life would soon change considerably. By the summer of 1940, when the Blitz began, her brother Bobby had left home. He had been called up for National Service in the RAF at the age of eighteen. Flo and the rest of the family were frightened by the noise and bombing of the war once it began in earnest. Night after night they had been woken up and had fled to the nearby shelter. Flo had hated the blackout, especially in winter with so many more hours of darkness.

'Dad was too old to join up when the war began, but when the age of conscription was changed, he was called up and he joined the RAF. He's in the north of England now. I wanted to help with the war effort and I was keen to leave my job. I'd been there for over three years by then. So when I was called up, I joined the WAAF and was stationed at RAF Debden in Essex where I learned shorthand and typing. My sister, Rosie, stayed at home with Mum and found a job working for the NAAFI, feeding the troops. Jeff followed Dad and Bobby into the RAF.'

Flo's shyness with Bill left her as they walked along. It was early evening and it was easier talking to Bill in the twilight than it would have been in the full light of day. It was thoughtful of him to ask her about what she knew best, rather than starting on a subject she might find it hard to contribute to, like his interest in photography or his knowledge of fighter planes. He had never trained as a pilot but he was keen to see action of some kind.

'My brother Gerry and I see things the same way. He's in the RAF too, in Devon at present. My mother tends to breathe down our necks and we've sometimes had to join forces against her,' Bill said as Flo finished her family story.

They had arrived at the pub, which was noisy and crowded. Flo was relieved that no one she or Bill knew seemed to be there. She wanted Bill to herself. They found a quiet corner, where no one disturbed them. Bill fetched drinks, then he entertained her with stories about some of the officers and NCOs on the station and she laughed more than she had done since her schooldays, when everything, especially in the adult world, had seemed funny to her and her friends.

Flo watched Bill light his pipe. She liked the way he packed in the tobacco and lit the pipe with the quick flare of a match. She breathed in the mild scent of the smoke, observing the way he gestured with the pipe to emphasise a point, the comic realisation that it had gone out, the lighting again. She felt at home with him, but it wasn't a dull kind of feeling at all.

They walked back to the station in darkness made deeper by the blackout, with Bill ahead and Flo just behind him on the path, which seemed narrower in the dark than it had in the daylight. Bill talked to her over his shoulder. When they arrived back at the station, just before the curfew, Flo was disappointed that Bill didn't try to kiss her and they parted with another *See you around* from him. Previous boyfriends had sometimes moved more quickly and Flo found herself feeling uncertain about Bill's intentions, although she felt increasingly that she liked him.

She hoped that no one had noticed her going out alone with Bill. Gossip raced like wildfire through every RAF station, often far ahead of the truth. She looked in the mirror in the ablution block at her shining eyes that night and Ellen, who was creaming her face nearby, turned to Flo.

'What are you grinning at, then, Flo?' she said and laughed knowingly.

Flo smiled, but said nothing about where she had been. She wanted to keep it private, even if privacy on the station was hard to come by.

The next day was Friday. Flo had to work into the lunch hour and Bill had finished lunch before she came into the mess. She was disappointed to see that he was leaving as she joined the queue for food, but then he stopped and spoke to her.

'Come for a walk on the common with me on Sunday afternoon, if you're free,' he said.

'All right,' she said, 'if it's not raining.' Afraid her pretence at being casual sounded grudging, she added 'I'd love to,' and smiled at him.

'Good. I'll meet you by the main gate at 3 pm. See you then.'

Flo worried all that Sunday morning that the grey clouds that darkened the sky might let rain fall, but it stayed dry, although the afternoon was chilly. She didn't tell anyone where she was going and found a quiet moment to slip out. She didn't have a watch, but she made good use of the station clocks. By about five past three, when there was no sign of him, she had begun to worry that he had stood her up. She hunched her shoulders against a cool breeze as she waited. When he appeared as if from nowhere, her worries collapsed like a balloon losing air.

'Oh, there you are,' she said, with relief.

'Sorry to be late! I was held up by a warrant officer who wouldn't stop talking. You look cold. We'll warm up if we move. Come on,' he said, beginning to run.

Flo was wearing civilian clothes for the date and her tight skirt wouldn't run with her. She was beginning to think that she should have kept to her uniform for a walk on the common. Bill, several steps ahead of her, turned round.

'Oh, of course, you can't run dressed like that.'

He looked at her as if to see how much fuss she might make about being cold.

'Honestly, I'm all right walking,' she said.

'Take my arm. That's better. That'll help to warm you up,' he said. They started walking towards the common, talking about life on the station. Flo found out that Bill was two years older than she was and had done National Service before the war.

Bill's teasing manner made Flo laugh. They even played a game of trying to name some of the flowers that had braved the cold.

'I'm testing you now. What are these?' he said, pointing at a mass of yellow flowers.

Flo laughed. 'You must know what daffodils are!'

'Well, maybe, but I don't know anything about flowers. All right, now I'm testing you properly. I bet you don't know what those are.' He pointed at some tiny blue flowers.

'They're speedwells,' Flo said. She had learned the names of some wild flowers from holidays hop-picking in Kent as a child and from her father, for whose country childhood she felt grateful at that moment.

She couldn't believe how the time had flown. An hour shrank to minutes and they had soon crossed the common and were wandering along nearby lanes, talking and observing, Bill teasing her when she was too solemn. When it was time to go back and Bill asked her to meet him again, she found it easy to look pleased. If her excitement over Bill could have taken a shape, it would have been bigger than she was.

Chapter Two

It became a Sunday afternoon habit for Flo to meet Bill when possible, no matter how often they ran into each other on the station. Bill told her about his passion for photography. He owned a camera and liked photographing people. One Sunday, he brought his camera along and showed her how it worked, taking her picture in her WAAF uniform. A week or so later, he gave her a copy.

'Thank you. It's like a proper portrait,' she said, thrilled.

'You look pretty, smiling like an angel.'

'Smiling at you,' she said and blushed.

Flo wasn't certain whether she was pretty, but the photo made her think that she was, especially if Bill said so. Increasingly she hoped that she mattered to him. She didn't mention her hobby of knitting, when they talked about likes and dislikes. It was too homely an interest to discuss with a man she was trying to impress. Instead, she told him that she loved reading and had wanted to stay on after matriculation at the grammar school she had attended. Her father, who had unfortunately lost his job just when Flo had been pleading to stay on at school, had insisted that she must leave school and find a job. He couldn't support her any more. Bill had had a more comfortable childhood. He had stayed at school until he was eighteen, exactly as she had wanted to do.

How slowly time moved in his absence, compared with how it flashed by when they were together. She thought about him a great deal when they were apart and looked forward to seeing him. She didn't say how she felt about him, because she was waiting for him to take the lead, but she tried to convey it in other ways, by her attentiveness and her manner.

When Flo received a letter from home with troubling news, she thrust it into her uniform pocket, but kept sneaking a glance at what it said, in case she had made a mistake in reading it. She couldn't put it out of her mind all day, even though Wing Commander Grant kept loading her with work.

'What's the matter, Flo? You're not your usual cheery self today,' Ellen said, after only a minute or two, when they met that evening in the NCOs' mess.

'It's my sister. I had a letter from home this morning. My sister Rosie is ill. She's working at the NAAFI headquarters in London and sometimes if she can't get back home at night, she sleeps in the underground. She's had a cough lately and she can't seem to shake it off. When she started coughing up spots of blood, Mum went with her to the doctor. She had some tests and the doctor says it's TB and she probably caught it in the underground.'

'I'm sorry to hear that. TB is no joke. It must be worrying for you and your family.'

Ellen didn't tell Flo not to worry or say that Rosie would be all right. Everyone knew about TB. Flo felt better for talking to her and the shared confidence bound the two friends more closely together.

Yet it was Bill's laughter and jokes that chased away the cold spring breezes for Flo and did the most to help her to live with her fears for Rosie. She told Bill about the letter as well and he comforted her with words and an arm around her shoulder. It was the second time he had touched her and Flo hoped afterwards that her sister's plight hadn't been the only cause. She wanted him to touch her again.

On Burghfield Common with Bill, released from the bustle of the station and even sometimes from the war, she could be herself, more than herself, she thought, because she had never smiled so much. She laughed a lot and her cheeks were flushed by more than the fresh air. They could joke for ages about anything, no matter how small, an insect or a leaf, but they had conversations about things that mattered too, what they wanted from life and what they cared about. Fascinating as the common appeared when Flo was with Bill, it was quite different if she ever walked over it on her own or with anyone else. His absence made it look empty and lifeless.

It wasn't long before their walks ranged further and one Sunday afternoon, about a month after the first walk on the common, they became lost amongst a network of country lanes. They didn't have a map, and signposts were few and far between. They had been talking and laughing so much that they hadn't noticed where they were going and weren't sure whether they were walking towards Burghfield or away from it. No one was within sight to ask. They went on, becoming more and more lost. Then it started to rain.

'I wish there was someone to ask. It sounds stupid, but I don't like being lost. I'm not used to these big open spaces. It's not like hop-picking, when there are always lots of other people around,' Flo said. She and her family had always gone hop-picking in Kent in the summer, returning to where her father had grown up.

When they came to a fork in the path they were following, Bill stopped, uncertain of which way to turn.

'I'm getting wet,' Flo said.

'I know. So am I. We're going to have to guess which way to go. I think left is probably best.'

'Don't you know?' She couldn't help the sharp question.

He looked at her and laughed. 'No more than you do, but we'll find ourselves, don't worry. We're only mildly lost.'

'You shouldn't have brought me, not knowing the way or anything.' She hated herself for complaining, so she tried a diversion.

'It reminds me of once when I was a child of about six, out shopping with Mum and my brothers and sisters. I looked round at one point to find myself alone. Strange people were all around and the street seemed to tip and wobble as I searched. I was frightened without Mum and so relieved when the family appeared. They had gone into a shop and Mum had thought everyone was with her until she counted heads. When she saw me, she gave me a sound ticking off for lagging behind, but I was so pleased to see her that I didn't mind at all,' Flo said.

Staring at the empty fields, she felt like a child again, but this was a different sort of lost. There was no mother to find and reassure her and she was going to have to play her part in finding the way. Grow up a bit, she told herself sternly, determined to be cheerful.

Bill seemed unconcerned. 'Well, you're not on your own now. Where's your spirit of adventure? It's only a common, not Dartmoor. We're not far from anywhere and the wild animals won't get you yet!'

Flo couldn't help looking around at the mention of wild animals and he laughed.

'Look, I know it was my idea, but I don't have a map and I don't think we've gone far wrong. Don't be upset! And it's not fair to blame me. You were happy enough to come along.'

He put his arm round her to comfort her and then hugged her more tightly. She put her arm around him. He kissed her then, beginning with her cheek but not lingering there. She had to stand on tip-toes, and they turned around and around as the kiss lasted longer and longer. It was magical, all the warm, tasting, caressing, exploring length of it, as were all the kisses that followed. She almost forgot to breathe and started to feel faint. She was swimming, flying, dancing, melting. She didn't care anymore about being lost and was glad no one was around. She had never been kissed like that before and she no longer minded that it was raining.

Afterwards, gleeful, they pinned their hopes on Bill's choice of footpath. It led eventually to a road and a signpost directing them to Burghfield, which was nearer than they had thought. They arrived back on the station minutes before their passes expired.

Flo didn't escape Ellen's questions.

'Where have you been all afternoon, Flo? You're not usually out as long as this.'

'Curiosity killed the cat,' Flo said, but then relented. 'It was just a Sunday afternoon walk, that's all.' They were getting ready for bed and their beds were adjacent.

'Sounds innocent enough.' Ellen was yawning and losing interest.

Flo didn't mention being lost and certainly not what it had led to. She was full of the sweet excitement of falling in love and she was asleep within minutes, dreaming of being lost with Bill in warm rain.

Bill and Flo began to see each other as often as they could. After the episode of getting lost in the countryside, it was as if a bubble had burst and everything was out in the open between them. They talked about their feelings for each other, which they had never done before.

'You were kind, helping me when I was lost and giving me a tour of the station,' Flo said.

'I couldn't resist you,' he said, ruffling fingers through her hair.

'We have got something in common,' Flo said, when she was absorbing the idea of the big house in Epsom where Bill had grown up, a house that seemed further away from her family home in Plaistow than the mere width of a city. 'We've both been to a grammar school.' It mattered to Flo that she had won a scholarship to the local grammar school at the age of eleven.

'Do you think you could come and meet my family, if we can take leave at the same time?' she asked one day over lunch. The others had left them to themselves as happened these days. Her father and brothers and sisters might not be there, but her mother at least would be at home. They had finished their meal and Bill was smoking his pipe. He took it out of his mouth to speak.

'We can try to fix it. What would your family think of me?'

'Oh, they'd love you!' She was in no doubt. Apart from his friendly manner, he was in the Forces, an RAF sergeant like her father. However, she noticed that he held back from suggesting that she might meet his family. She asked him about his parents.

'They're rather stiff and I have to be careful about introducing a girlfriend to them,' he said. Flo wasn't sure what he meant by that. She wondered if Bill's parents would think she wasn't good enough for him and the thought made her feel angry, but she held her tongue for the present.

Bill and Flo made the most of snatched moments together. They found the best places to be undisturbed on the station and outside it, despite the demands of their work and the roar of the planes flown by the trainee pilots. The haste and constant fear of discovery made their explorations of each other all the more intense. Bill soon learned that Flo wouldn't let his hands go below her waist and when they strayed, Flo removed them smartly.

'Let me,' he always said.

'No.'

'I want you, dearest Flo.'

'It would be nice, I'm sure, but I'm saving myself,' she said one day, feeling pushed into an explanation.

'But I love you.' This was said with a kiss and the gentle touch of a straying hand.

'I love you too. No!'

He never insisted.

In the heightened atmosphere of war, the few weeks they had known each other felt like much longer. One summer's day, Flo watched Bill picking a little posy of wild flowers, such as buttercups, daisies and cornflowers, on one of their walks on the common. He didn't need to be able to name the flowers in order to hand them to her.

'Will you marry me, Flo?'

'Yes. Oh, yes, yes, yes!'

The posy of flowers was under threat of falling to the ground in the kisses which followed. She held onto the little bunch tightly all the way back to the station. They were drooping a bit by then, but Flo was ecstatic.

The next time his hands strayed, she still said, 'No.'

'But we're going to get married.'

'Wait until we do.'

For the present, he had to be content with that. He explained that they couldn't get married yet because his parents would need time to get used to the idea. Without his saying so, Flo now felt certain that they were snobbish and would dismiss her as common. She knew that her accent, despite her grammar school education, still hinted at her East End London background. Flo would have liked the wedding to happen sooner rather than later, but Bill was adamant about waiting for the right moment, even though it meant his hands had to stay above the waist for longer.

Being in love was such fun that Flo thought life would be easy from then on. The war would surely be over one day, even though it had been going on for years, for so long that it had become a way of life. Like everyone else, she looked forward to peace and she was full of confidence that nothing bad was going to happen to her with Bill at her side.

Flo and Bill stayed at Burghfield for the remainder of 1943 and through the winter that followed, conscious of how fortunate they were not to be separated by a sudden posting elsewhere. During home leave, Flo visited her sister Rosie who had gone into a sanatorium. She was upset to see her favourite sister so ill and their parents look so worried. She was afraid of what might happen to Rosie with her persistent cough.

Flo gave in to the straying hands as the months went by. It didn't make sense to keep on saving herself when she and Bill were going to be married. Besides, he had awakened strong feelings in her that she hadn't experienced before and she wanted him more and more. She was soon convinced that she and Bill were the happiest couple on earth, despite the secrecy of it all. They went up to heaven together as often as they could find a place where they would be undisturbed, making up for lost time and not always using a French letter.

Flo had known something of what to expect. She knew what little boys looked like, but her brothers had soon learned to cover up and a grown man was different. At the age of eleven, she had asked how babies were made, and her mother had tried to explain, but despite her experience as a mother of six, she had become so tongue-tied that she didn't get far. Flo had felt that her mother was silently begging her to stop asking questions.

She had learned more from girls at school and women at work, as well as films, magazines and newspapers. Young men she had been out with during her time as a WAAF, although strictly above the waist, had helped. There had been no one in her life she liked enough to think of marrying until Bill came along.

In the spring of 1944, when she had known Bill for a year, there were rumours of a big push and Bill thought it likely that he would be taking part. At the beginning of April, all military leave was cancelled and rumours abounded about troop movements to France. When Bill told Flo that he would probably be going away, she was alarmed.

One warm afternoon in the middle of April, shielded from passers-by by some convenient bushes, with red poppies blooming around them, they went up to heaven on the common, even though they had no French letter. Flo was particularly joyful that day. Bill called her Poppy after that, when they were alone together. After that, they took more risks. In the fevered atmosphere of mounting military preparations, and with people around them most of the time, moments had to be taken when and where they could be.

Flo was deeply in love. She wanted to spend her life with Bill and to have his children, to belong to the world together. An ambition of bettering herself that she had breathed in as a child at home would be fortunately achieved along the way, by marrying a grammar school boy from a respectable background. When the order came for Bill to join the British Liberation Army, there was a tearful parting.

'No matter what my parents think, we'll get married when I come back,' Bill said as he prepared to leave RAF Burghfield.

'I can't wait. I'm going to miss you so much,' Flo said.

'We'll write to each other. Wait for a letter from me and then you'll know my address.'

'All right. Here, I've got a keepsake for you.' Flo handed him a small package wrapped in tissue paper.

'Thank you, dearest Flo. Oh, strike a light!' Bill said with a laugh, unwrapping the package to find a matchbox.

'It was all I could find for a box, but look inside.'

He slid the box open to see a tiny silver heart on a chain, nestling on a piece of cotton wool.

'It's a heart from a charm bracelet that I've had since I was a child. I found a chain to go with it.'

Bill kissed her lovingly and wore the heart round his neck from that moment. A day or so later, he gave her the gold signet ring that he wore on his little finger. It was too big for her little finger, but it fitted the third finger of her left hand, like a wedding ring, as he said. It would do for the present and he would buy her a real wedding ring when he came back. He promised again that they would marry on his return.

On his last day, he was busy packing and with briefings, but they found a few moments in which to say goodbye. In the gloom of the stores where they had often gone up to heaven, they had only time for a few last kisses. They clung to each other. At the last minute, Bill tore himself away, fearful of being late for the departure. Flo watched him go, before returning to her desk.

There was a long silence after Bill left to take part in the Normandy landings and Flo missed him badly, as well as being anxious about what was happening to him. Ellen and some of the other girls had young men in the British Liberation Army as well, and they didn't hear anything at first. Flo relied on thinking that Bill wasn't in any real danger, because the news was that the Nazis were on the run in France by the summer of 1944, but she couldn't help worrying, just as she was afraid that her family might be hit by one of the flying bombs which were being fired at London now. She found it hard to concentrate on her work.

Then she missed her monthly. Day after day, she waited anxiously for the sign of its arrival, but there was nothing. Her mind went back to the times when they hadn't used a French letter and she was afraid that she was pregnant, but she kept quiet because she knew that she would be thrown out of the WAAF in disgrace if it were true and anyone official found out. This was linked to a larger fear. Even though she had given him her home address before he left, she was afraid that Bill might never find her if she left Burghfield.

Chapter Three

Every day for months, Flo searched the pigeon holes where the post was left, in vain. At last, a letter arrived addressed in Bill's handwriting. Her heart leaped at the sight of it and her fingers scrabbled to open it.

British Liberation Army
HQ No 24
Sat 12 Aug 44

My dearest Poppy,

I miss you so much and my thoughts turn constantly on our times together. How I wish I could be with you, my hands everywhere that used to be forbidden!

I'm sorry you've had to wait so long for news of me but I couldn't send you an address earlier. We waited days before we could embark, but the journey was extraordinary. You will understand I can't say anything about where I am or what I'm doing.

The food is terrible – nearly all imported from England and nothing like the butter, eggs and cheese the villagers have in plenty. Despite that I'm in the best of health.

I worry most about whether you are safe with stories of flying bombs at home and long to be with you.

Your ever loving Bill

Flo wrote back immediately, telling Bill that she thought that she was pregnant. She waited anxiously for the reply, and tore it open when it came.

BLA
HQ No 35
Fri 25 Aug 44

My dearest Poppy,

I'm writing to you sitting outside my tent in a meadow full of the wild flowers you love, but how I wish I were by your side.

I can't write much because I don't have the time. I have your letter here and your news that you might be expecting. It's not what we intended. I suppose we weren't careful enough. I hope you're feeling better now and not so sick. Please keep our secret.

I hope all the time that you're safe and that none of the flying bombs have dropped near you.

I'm fit and well and sleeping like a log. I cannot, as you know, tell you anymore, but let's hope that it'll all be over soon. There is talk of Paris being liberated!

Your ever loving Bill

Reading this letter, Flo didn't mind what Bill said about keeping the secret, because he had said it before and she knew why, but what upset her was that he didn't seem to want the baby. She wrote back immediately. She didn't talk to anyone else about being pregnant, but tell-tale sickness in the morning didn't escape Ellen's sharp eye.

'Admit it, Flo,' she said one morning as they stood at sinks in the ablution block. 'You've got a bun in the oven, haven't you?'

A green-faced Flo nodded, relieved at last to talk to someone. She had been scared to say anything, as even whispers could grow.

'It's Bill, isn't it?' Ellen said.

'Yes, but we're going to get married,' Flo said. Excited as she was about Bill, she still thought that she had done wrong. Then she realised she had revealed the secret and put her hand over her mouth.

'That'll be all right, then. And don't worry. I won't tell anyone, but you're in trouble. You know what they'll do, don't you?'

'Yes,' Flo said. 'When they find out. I'm not saying anything until I have to. Bill will come back soon and it'll be all right then, even if I have to leave here.'

Flo didn't know quite what she meant by saying that it would be all right when Bill came back. She and Bill hadn't talked about how they would live after the war or about babies, except in a general sort of way. Ellen was a forgiving sort, but from a stern background, and made it clear that she was heartily glad that she had not allowed her young man below the waist without a French letter before he went away.

A further letter came from Bill. Flo opened it immediately, as ever, and read it so many times, as she always did, that she almost learned it off by heart.

BLA
HQ No 47
Sun 10 Sept 44

My dearest Poppy,

Here I am again, grateful for your letter, which I've just finished reading and can't resist replying to straightaway. I miss you terribly and think of you all the time. It must be so difficult for you on your own and I wish I were there so we could face the world together. I must admit that it was a surprise, when you first told me about the baby, but I'm getting used to the idea now.

I hear the flying bombs are bad and hope all the time that you're safe. I'm glad you're not in London because it must be worse there. My parents often have to go down into the shelter. If they knew about the baby, they'd probably explode, but everything will be all right, you'll see.

I visited a town the other day and found it shabby, but the people are looking well, as they do here, if not so well fed. Education has suffered from the war and there are children of eight or nine who can't read.

The news is good as the Americans are near Amiens and the flying bomb bases will soon be cut off. We've got them on the run!

I know you'll keep our secret until I return. Be safe.

Your ever loving Bill

Flo felt joyous when she read what Bill said about the baby. She could face anything now. Everything was going to be all right. She replied fulsomely, but Bill wrote again before receiving her letter.

BLA
HQ No 47
Thurs 14 Sept 1944

My dearest Poppy,

I haven't heard from you for a few days now but I know you've written and that your letters will catch up with me. You're such a good correspondent and I hope you're safer now. The speed of the German retreat leaves us no time to sit and write but I've seized these few moments. The food continues to be terrible, also the coffee which is ersatz and needs brandy to be drinkable, but these are small things compared to our advance.

My dearest, I'm sorry you're still feeling unwell and I hope you're safe and that you and the baby are all right. I think all the time of seeing you again and when I miss you most I kiss the silver heart you gave me and that I wear all the time on its chain around my neck. I'm looking forward to the little creature now, although it was a surprise at first. I'll tell you more when I come back and until then I am, my dearest,

Your ever loving Bill

Flo's eyes shone as she read and the ink flowed from her pen as she replied in her square, upright handwriting. She had always loved writing and she covered every inch of paper because there was so much to say to Bill. It wouldn't be long now. He would be home soon, the war would be over, they would be married and their baby, who would be born in January, would be legitimate. It was going to be all right, she kept telling herself.

By late September, Flo was over five months' pregnant and afraid that she was beginning to show to more eyes than Ellen's. However, something even more important was on her mind. She was beginning to wonder when Bill's next letter would come.

'It's ten days now and no letter,' she said to Ellen over lunch one day. Bill wrote at least once a week and sometimes more often.

'Yes, but they can't always write regularly. He's probably had to move around. He'll be all right, you'll see,' was the brisk, consoling answer.

Flo wasn't sure how Ellen could be so definite, although she clung to her friend's reassurance. Yet, with each passing day of no news from Bill, her concern grew.

'It's two weeks since I've had a letter,' she said to Ellen one morning and then, a week later, 'Ellen, it's three weeks now. I'm sick with worry as well as everything else.'

Neither Bill nor Flo had thought seriously about how she would find out if anything had happened to him, because she wasn't his next of kin and neither of them had liked to think about the fact that he might not return.

'It is a long time as he's been writing so often,' Ellen said. 'Look, why don't you ask Wing Commander Grant to see if he can find anything out? Explain that Bill is your intended and you haven't heard for three weeks when usually he writes every few days.'

Wing Commander Grant, Flo's boss, was an older family man, openly glad not to have been sent to France with the British Liberation Army. Flo was too worried by then to let any natural timidity stand in her way of requesting a favour from a senior officer. She explained the problem to him. She said nothing about being pregnant and only hoped that he hadn't noticed. He warned Flo that he was busy with far more urgent matters and that it might be difficult, but promised to do what he could to find out. Every morning after that, Flo looked at him with hope in her eyes, but he said nothing about Bill.

One morning, two weeks or so after her request, when she had heard nothing from Bill for about five weeks, Flo came into the office to find Wing Commander Grant staring out of the window. He turned towards her, clearing his throat.

'A fine autumn day,' he said. It was almost the middle of October and a mild sun was coming in through the windows of the Nissen hut. Leaves were turning, but many were still on the trees. Flo thought immediately that Wing Commander Grant didn't usually make small talk, even about the weather.

'Sit down, Haldon. I have something to tell you,' he said.

Flo sat obediently at her desk. He remained standing and she looked up at him.

'I'm sorry, but it's bad news.'

Say it then, get it over with, Flo thought, but she said nothing. She wasn't going to help him say what she couldn't bear to hear. He spoke slowly.

'I've managed to find out what happened… I heard last night, too late to tell you. Sergeant Martin is missing and presumed dead.'

'Dead,' Flo said, mechanically, as if the word meant nothing. She stood up. She had to move.

'I'm afraid it doesn't look good.'

Everything was coming towards Flo at once, the floor and the walls, the kindly October day outside and the wing commander himself, as her head span and she fell. The others in the hut clustered round her and helped carry her to the sick bay.

The nurse on duty saw at one glance that she was pregnant and treated her with some sympathy at first when she heard of the bad news that Flo had received. Flo lay on a bed, numb with shock, scarcely moving and saying nothing for half an hour. It was then that the nurse, a tall, bony woman with dyed blonde hair piled on top of her head, who was trying to attend to several people at once, showed a hint of impatience.

'When is it due, did you say?'

Flo had worked this out as well as she could and answered 'Early January, I think.'

'Well, you can't stay here, you know. We're not running a nursery. You'll have to leave the station.'

Flo heard the sharpness of the tone and flinched. 'I can't go home,' she said, alarmed at the threat of having to leave the place where she had been so happy, the place where Bill had known her, and dreading turning up, unmarried and pregnant, at her parents' home. Her joy at being pregnant, once Bill had accepted the baby, collapsed and she felt only shame.

'You'll be discharged from the WAAF on compassionate grounds,' the nurse said briskly. 'It will be up to you where you go after that. There's a war on and girls like you aren't helping.'

Flo didn't like the sound of *girls like you,* but she was too weak to argue. The nurse moved on to tend another patient. Flo climbed off the bed in the sick bay and went numbly back to her office, where Wing Commander Grant gave her the rest of the story. Sergeant Martin had been in charge of a small group of men entering a village in Normandy. He had been ahead of the others and there had been a confused exchange of fire. When the others grouped together afterwards, he wasn't with them and no amount of searching had found him.

Listening to the even tones of Wing Commander Grant, Flo felt as if she had been there at the time, observing the small group of servicemen approach the village, watching carefully for snipers, but not able to have their eyes everywhere, and then hearing shots ring out, with everyone dashing for cover and later searching for their leader and not being able to find him. She wept as she heard the story and did her best to thank the wing commander for the trouble he had taken. Then she stared blankly at her desk, unable to work. Wing Commander Grant told her to take the rest of the day off.

Flo had more than a day off. She was discharged from the WAAF, as the nurse had threatened. The day after she received the news about Bill, she was summoned to the desk of a brusque WAAF officer and given her discharge papers. She didn't have time to say goodbye to the girls in her Nissen hut, except for Ellen, who had left her desk to help her friend to pack. Flo turned a distraught face to her friend.

'I don't even have a photo of him.'

Ellen didn't even have to ask who Flo meant. She rummaged in the locker beside her bed. 'Here, take this. Remember that someone took it with my camera? I can always get another copy,' she said, thrusting a small, black and white photograph at Flo. It showed Ellen, Bill and Flo and three others standing in a row, in uniform. Bill and Flo were smiling at each other, oblivious of anyone else. Flo remembered the occasion and took the photograph gratefully.

Carrying a small kitbag which contained all her possessions, Flo left Burghfield and was lucky to catch a lift to Reading, where she took a train to London. She was twenty-four and, apart from visits on leave, had been away from home for nearly four years, since being called up early in 1941. She had fallen in love and been happy until she had started to worry about Bill's silence. Throughout the slow journey home, punctuated by the delays due to wartime conditions of travel, Flo felt numb with shock over the news that Bill was missing, presumed dead. How could she ever believe it, when his face was in front of her, smiling and full of life, every time she closed her eyes?

Despite what she had said to the nurse, she had no choice but to go home. She feared what her mother, Mabel, might say when she turned up on the doorstep evidently expecting a baby.

Florence Jane! You're in trouble. Think of the shame of it. What will the neighbours say? Our daughter, the grammar school girl, with all her upbringing and her good start in life, couldn't wait to do the decent thing.

That Flo was going home in disgrace was bad enough. There had been no time to warn her mother of her arrival, and she had no idea what she would do if her mother, seeing her condition, slammed the door in her face.

Reaching Plaistow at the end of a warm, October afternoon, Flo walked the familiar route from the station to the house where she had grown up. She was tired. The kitbag, for all the few possessions that she had, had become heavy and unwieldy. She knew that she had travelled from relative safety into danger. London was now under attack from V bombs, nicknamed flying bombs or doodlebugs, which struck terror into people's hearts because, unpiloted and in uncanny silence before they exploded, they did horrendous damage to people and property. Yet Flo knew from letters that her mother, Mabel, was here, living in danger and steadily refusing to go and stay with relatives in Kent. It was just as well that she hadn't gone away because the family home in Plaistow would probably have been looted or requisitioned by now.

Flo walked part of the way down her street before she stopped, puzzled. Something was wrong. A terrible gap yawned where houses belonged, as if a tooth were missing in a mouth. A bomb had exploded and her house had taken a direct hit. The street had been cleared of debris, but where the house had stood was a jumble of bricks and floorboards, broken furniture and torn wallpaper. Finding it hard to breathe, Flo sank down onto a low wall in front of the intact neighbouring house and put her head in her hands to shut out the sight.

'We got Mabel out, but it was no good,' a voice was saying beside her. 'I'm sorry love, but no one knew where you were. It was only three days ago, in the middle of the night. She's down at the morgue. Her budgie didn't make it, either.'

It was Jessie, from next door. Flo gasped as she took in what Jessie was saying, but in that first moment, her mind pictured not Mabel, her mother, but the budgie, always so full of life, even if confined to the small cage that Mabel kept in a corner of the dining room and over which she threw a cloth when she wanted silence.

Jessie's house looked oddly untouched and Flo could see the outlines of the rooms of her own house on the adjoining wall. There was the girls' bedroom, which she had shared with Rosie, Joan and Annie, until she had joined the WAAF. Rosie had gone into the sanatorium and Joan and Annie had been evacuated. Flo stared at the familiar flower-patterned wallpaper. Ribbons of it were fluttering in a slight breeze.

'I'm expecting a baby,' she said. It was what she had been going to say to Mabel.

'You'd better come in.' Jessie led the way. She was a large, untidy woman whose four children had left home some years previously and whose husband, Flo knew, was away in the armed forces. Flo complied, too weary to argue.

'Didn't Mum go to the shelter? Flo asked, when they were sitting down inside. She was glad not to be gazing any longer at the heap next door, even if she wasn't in her own home. Jessie's home was at least familiar to her.

'No, I called for her, but she shouted something I couldn't hear through the letterbox and I had to get on.'

'She didn't like going there. Maybe she thought she'd give it a miss as she was on her own. Oh, how terrible!' She began to cry.

'It was a direct hit. She would have gone out like a light,' Jessie said. Flo nodded. She knew it was meant to be comforting and she wanted to think that her mother hadn't suffered.

Flo was reminded of the beginning of the war, when her father, Alf, suggested that Mabel take the younger children to his mother in Kent for safety and stay there with them.

'I'm not going anywhere,' Mabel said, hands on hips. 'I was born and bred in the East End of London. I've lived through one war and I'm not moving out for another one. I'd rather be bombed out of my own home than live in the country and I'm certainly not going out to Kent.' She made it sound as if Alf had said Australia.

'Joan and Annie would be safer there,' Alf said, going on to argue that the older ones would have to take their chance at home, while Flo could run the household.

'All right, we'll send Joan and Annie to your mum. She's a tight-fisted old woman and she'll take what she can for looking after them, but I'm not going and I don't want to send them to strangers. There's no telling what they might turn into.'

Flo could hear Mabel's voice and feel her presence as if she were in the room with her. Jessie's voice broke into her thoughts and she looked up, startled.

'You can stay here for your leave, there's plenty of room.'

'I'm not on leave. I've been discharged because I'm expecting. I was going to live with Mum until the baby's born.'

On the journey home from RAF Burghfield, apart from thinking about Mabel's reaction, Flo's thoughts had been mainly of Bill. The life she had expected to lead with him was hard to shrug off and it was impossible to accept that the joy of the eighteen months of knowing Bill was over. She didn't want to replace it with the cold emptiness of life without him. She didn't want to think ahead. She could hardly take in the fact that her mother, the one person she had relied on to help her survive now, was dead and her childhood home destroyed.

'You can stay here, anyway. Of course, I can't feed you. You know that, don't you? You're going to have to get your own ration book,' Jessie said.

'I know. There's a form in with my discharge papers.'

'Here, I'll put the kettle on. You look dead beat,' Jessie said next and Flo nodded. She knew that she should be grateful, but she was too sad and exhausted to say more than necessary. If only Mabel were ticking her off now or even slamming the door in her face.

Chapter Four

Flo's father, Alf, and her brothers, Bobby and Jeff, were away, serving in the RAF. Rosie had been admitted to a sanatorium and the younger sisters Joan and Annie were living with their grandmother in Kent. No one in the family yet knew, Jessie said, about the bombing raid that had killed her mother and destroyed their home.

Unpacking her kitbag in Jessie's house, Flo was reminded of an incident during the Blitz when she was at home with her family.

Mabel had gone next door to borrow a cup of sugar from Jessie. She came back with the full cup and cradling a paper bag.

'Look what I've got! Jessie owed me a favour and she's given me these fresh eggs. We'll have them for tea tomorrow night, when your Dad gets back from work. I didn't like to ask where she got them from.'

The following evening, Alf was home and the eggs sizzling in the frying pan, when the air-raid warning sounded. The dreaded sound was familiar and inescapable.

'Oh, God, I'm about to dish up. We can't waste the eggs,' Mabel said, holding a loaf of bread against her chest to slice it. 'We'll go to the shelter in a minute, when we've eaten.'

The family sat round the table, with the budgie twittering in its cage in a corner of the room. Flo was worried that Mabel was taking the air raid too lightly, but she was looking forward to a fried egg. Like everyone else she knew, her family had been eating dried eggs, with fresh eggs so scarce because of the war.

The moment they picked up their knives and forks, a loud explosion occurred nearby. Abandoning the eggs, everyone scuttled under the dining room table, terrified. They waited, saying little, until they heard the long wail of the all-clear. Rosie was the first to crawl out from under the table. She gave a cry of dismay as she stood up.

'Oh, look at all the pepper on the eggs! I don't want pepper on my egg.'

Standing up and glancing at the table, Mabel groaned.

'For crying out loud! That's not pepper, you silly goose! Them eggs are covered in dust. I can't even try heating them up. They'll all have to go into the bin.'

'What's for tea, then, Mum?' Flo asked.

'It'll have to be bread and scrape and a tin of pilchards. That's all I've got in.'

Mabel's face was weary.

The house had been shaken by the blast and there was dust everywhere, even in the budgie's cage, although it wasn't hurt. Alf went out to see the damage and ran back with news of a number of deaths and a gaping hole on their street. The loss of fried eggs was nothing compared with that and the family, chastened by the news, ate their pilchards without complaint.

After coming back to Plaistow, the numbness that had initially protected Flo from the news about Bill retreated. She refused to believe that he was dead and clung to the fact that he was missing and could still be alive. She hadn't seen him for nearly five months, but she still felt his presence. She missed him terribly, forced herself through the days in Jessie's house and went to bed thinking about him at night. At times she felt abandoned and empty, but at other times she was almost herself again, although never as blithe as she used to be. In her better moments, she half-expected Bill to turn up on her doorstep one day. He had her address and surely, seeing the bombsite, he would knock on surrounding doors, to find out what had happened to her.

Should she go to Epsom to find him? More than the increasing weight of her pregnancy stopped her. He had always referred to his parents, and particularly his mother, as difficult and Flo knew she would not be welcomed. Her arrival on his doorstep could cause problems for Bill. No matter the agony of waiting, it was better to let him find her.

She wrote to him in Epsom, several times, just as she had from RAF Burghfield, telling him about the bomb and her mother's death, where she was living and what she was doing now, telling him also about the baby, but most of all saying that she missed him. There was never any reply.

She grieved for her mother. It seemed unfair that she should lose both Bill and Mabel at once. *Life isn't fair* had been Mabel's stock response to any child's wail of *it's not fair,* but Flo expected some fairness. Life without it wouldn't be worth living.

She couldn't ignore the baby, even as she missed Bill. Thanking Jessie for letting her stay and promising to pay her what rent she could afford, Flo settled in to her new home. She went to the local authority clinic, where she arranged for a hospital birth, as was now common for a first baby. She was greatly relieved that she wouldn't have to pay, even though she had no health insurance and didn't pay into a club that provided health care.

She felt a glow of satisfaction when the baby moved inside her, almost the only pleasant feeling since Bill's disappearance and her mother's death. The baby began to seem like a person, and when Flo was on her own, she talked to her baby. Apart from Jessie, who was blunt, but not condemning, she shunned local friends and neighbours out of a feeling of shame. Talking to the baby, as well as talking to Bill, helped to take the edge off her loneliness and grief.

She ignored the pile of bricks next door. She didn't have time to think about it, or know what to do. She wrote to her father, Alf, and to Bobby and Jeff and her sisters in Kent, whose addresses she fortunately had with her, to tell them the dreadful news about Mabel and the house and she went to see Rosie in the sanatorium. She arranged a funeral for Mabel, with the benefit of her burial policy, and Alf was able to get compassionate leave and return for a day. He and Flo represented the family at the funeral and Jessie and a handful of neighbours came for the street.

In her years with the WAAF, Flo had only earned a pittance, which had paid for her mess bills. However, with few expenses, little need for nice clothes, nylon stockings or makeup and no rent to pay, she had managed to save a small amount. If she could find a job locally and eke out her savings, she could manage until after the baby was born. She couldn't think beyond that.

She found a typing job, part-time, in Plaistow, working for a solicitor, a Mr Tressall. She told him she was pregnant and would need time off for the birth, but he was desperate to replace a secretary who had left without warning and he was willing to overlook her shortcomings as an employee. Otherwise, she stayed at what she now called home, waiting for her baby to arrive. Jessie, who missed her children and had known Flo all her life, was happy to have the company.

Her weekly visits to Rosie led to making a confidante of her sister. Rosie was flattered to be told about Flo's baby and wanted to hear all about Bill. In the quiet of the sanatorium, Flo found herself spilling out her story in much greater detail than she had done to Jessie. It helped to take Rosie's mind off being ill and Flo felt the relief of confession.

She and Jessie had to go out to the shelter on many nights as the flying bombs continued to attack London, often falling short of their target of the centre. Given the bomb that had destroyed her home and killed her mother, Flo was vigilant about going to the shelter immediately she heard the siren. Luckily, it was winter now and she was well-wrapped up and able to disguise her pregnancy sufficiently to avoid open remarks. People were sorry for her loss of her mother and she was grateful to those who didn't pester her with questions about herself.

Flo undertook to do some of the housework, cooking and shopping for herself and Jessie. She had hated housework as a child and had resented the way that Mabel had foisted it on her in their large family, but now she was looking for something to do and undertook it more willingly. It was less of a chore in different circumstances.

She made a habit of walking past the nearest shops and going to those further away, where she was less likely to meet inquisitive neighbours. One Saturday, armed with her ration book, she joined a queue at a butcher's, where she was hoping for an end of bacon to use in soup, and some tripe to make a stew. Looking up from her shopping list, she saw that a woman ahead was staring at her. She looked familiar, but Flo couldn't place her immediately.

'It's Flossie, isn't it?'

'Hello... oh, of course... Betsy.'

It was Betsy from school, an unpleasant girl who had mocked her accent, but whose own accent wasn't so different, Flo thought, hearing it now. She was less than pleased to see Betsy.

'What are you up to, these days then?' Betsy said. Her tone of voice was inquisitive rather than friendly.

'Oh, I've been in the WAAF. What about you?' Flo said, as vaguely as she could, hoping that her winter clothes would be sufficient protection against Betsy's curiosity. She was to have no such luck.

'I'm in the Land Army. It's hard work, but I'm home on forty-eight hours' leave. I see you're expecting. When's it due?'

'January,' Flo said shortly, wishing the conversation would end so that she could get out of there and never see Betsy again. She had so far avoided meeting anyone from school, because most of them were away serving in the armed forces. She was now desperately wishing that she had done her shopping nearer home. Fortunately Betsy's attention was claimed by the butcher and then it was Flo's turn to be served. To her great relief, Betsy vanished with a quick nod as soon as she had paid for her meat.

Walking home, Flo feared that Betsy would gossip about her, wherever she could find someone to talk to. At least Betsy hadn't forced her to say she wasn't married or to lie and say she was. Had she noticed Bill's signet ring, which Flo still wore on her ring finger, and assumed she was married? It was fine to be pregnant if you were married. If only Betsy would assume that and forget all about meeting her.

Meeting Betsy took Flo back to her schooldays. How desperately she wanted to go to the grammar school. She had taken the entrance exam at the age of eleven. Weeks had passed and she had heard nothing. Then a letter had arrived in the post one morning. Alf had already left for work and Mabel had opened it, screwing up her eyes to read.

'Oh, crikey! You've won a scholarship to the grammar school, Flossie.'

'Oh, mum, I never! Let me see,' Flossie said, her eyes huge and a wide smile breaking out as she reached for the letter, while the budgie sang as if it understood the news.

'I knew it,' Mabel said. 'There's not much gets past you, Flossie. Now, don't get too big for your boots. See those beds are made before you go off to school.'

Alf read the letter that evening when he came home.

'Yes, but must you go? You're a girl, after all. You don't need so much education when you're only going to get married. I left school at twelve and it ain't done me any harm,' he said.

'Oh, Dad, please let me go, please.' Flossie wore him down with her pleading. There was help from a charity with the cost of the uniform and, in any case, Mabel bought Flossie's uniform at least two sizes too big for her, so for the first year it was hard to find her inside it. Alf was only out of pocket for the bus fare, counted in pennies, so he had no strong objection in the end to Flossie taking up her place.

On the first day of term in the autumn of 1932, Flossie went off proudly to catch the bus to the girls' grammar school, wearing her new grey, blue and gold uniform. She had recently had her twelfth birthday and she felt important and special.

Girls were seated in alphabetical order by surname for their lessons, but in the playground, they mingled as they pleased. Despite the uniform, Flossie was aware that some girls were posh. She could tell as soon as they opened their mouths. Girls who spoke like her ganged up together and sometimes the posh girls mimicked them. Betsy, a big girl with a heavy face, took it upon herself to be particularly unpleasant to Flossie.

'Look at the slum girl, common as muck, dropping her aitches everywhere!' she said more than once. Flossie tried to keep out of her way, but didn't always succeed. Luckily, she found an ally in Carol, who lived only a couple of streets away from her. The two friends walked to and from school together.

One morning, at break-time, a group of girls started giggling and pushing each other around. Coming from behind, Betsy pushed Flossie over.

'Mind what you're doing!' Flossie said, stumbling and falling awkwardly. When she got up, she screamed at the sight of her right hand at the wrong angle more than from the pain. The teacher on playground duty took one look at her and marched her up to the hospital as soon as the bell rang for the others to go back in. Flossie didn't know what to expect. She had never been in a hospital before, but by this time her arm

was hurting badly, although she had calmed down. She and the teacher trudged along corridors and breathed in the smell of disinfectant before seeing a doctor who diagnosed a broken wrist. He set Flossie's arm in a plaster up to her elbow and made a cotton sling for her to wear.

'How old are you? Ten?' he said, tying the sling in place.

Flossie drew herself up to her greatest height.

'No. I turned fourteen in September.' She tried to sound grown up.

'Well, you're small for your age.' He looked at Flossie as if it were her fault.

The thick material of Flossie's school uniform hid the changes that her body had started to make – little buds on her flat girl's chest, hair under her arms and down below. She had started her monthlies. She was growing all right, but not much upwards. She was certainly not going to tell the doctor about any of that, even though he made her feel small in more ways than one. She wanted to be tall, because people took more notice of tall girls and they could do more for themselves, but she despaired of her height. Mabel was small, she realised, and she was eye to eye with her now.

The teacher waited at the hospital and afterwards took Flossie home. Mabel pulled a face when she saw the plaster, but when the teacher had gone, she tapped it lightly with her hand.

'All right, Flossie. I know you don't like housework, but do you have to break an arm to get out of it?'

Flossie burst out laughing and Mabel's normally grim face cracked into a smile. Bobby was impressed with Flossie's plaster and insisted on writing his name on it. Rosie drew a picture of a cat on the plaster to cheer Flossie up.

Betsy might have thought she had got away with pushing Flossie over, but Carol had seen what had happened. When a teacher, looking at Flossie in plaster, asked the class about the incident the next day, Flossie kept quiet, not wanting to be a sneak, but Carol spoke up.

'It was Betsy, Miss. I saw her do it. She pushed Flossie over from behind.'

'Betsy, come and see me after class,' the teacher said.

Flossie and Carol found out afterwards that Betsy had to stay in after school and write a hundred lines. Betsy kept out of her way after that, but Flossie had made an enemy. Betsy always scowled at her and Flossie and Carol called her Beastly Betsy, as if she were a character in one of their comics.

That afternoon, Carol invited Flossie to come to her mother's teashop after school. It was a shop front on Plaistow High Street, not far from Flossie's home. Inside, wooden chairs and tables occupied a floor covered in lino. Cakes, buns and sandwiches were laid out on a counter along one wall and Carol's mother reigned behind it. The air was thick with smoke when Flossie and Carol came in.

The eyes of Carol's mother widened at the sight of Flossie in plaster. She served both girls with lemon barley water and added two iced buns. Flossie dared not stay long because Mabel expected her to go home straight from school to help with housework, but she enjoyed the snack. Carol's older brothers, Joey and George, who went to the boys' grammar school, came in as Flossie was licking the last of the icing off the fingers of her free hand. They, too, were impressed by the plaster and wrote their names on it. Flossie's eyes shone at such attention from older boys. She became so proud of all the signatures on her plaster that she was reluctant to see it go when the time came.

In the autumn of 1935, aged fifteen, Flossie started a Saturday job working in Carol's mother's tea shop, clearing tables and washing up, to earn some pocket money. Carol was there on Saturdays as well and Joey and George sometimes came in and teased the girls.

'We've got paper rounds. Waiting at tables is girls' work,' George said, but his smile showed he wasn't sneering.

Reaching Jessie's house and digging out her key, Flo came back to the present day. She was worried about Betsy. She wasn't sure quite why yet, but she wanted her pregnancy to be as much of a secret as possible. Now that Betsy, her one-time enemy, knew about it, she might talk. She might easily remember disliking Flossie at school and getting into trouble for causing her a broken wrist and make the best of what she had found out now. The news could pass around old school mates who would know Flo's shame in having a baby on the wrong side of the blanket.

Flo gave up her typing job in Mr Tressall's office at the end of November. He was sorry to see her go and promised to take her on again after the baby was born. She planned to live on her savings until the baby was born and then think again. She knew she would have to get a job to keep them both. There was no one she could depend on and no money for unmarried mothers like pensions for old people.

At Christmas, the men in the family were unable to get leave, and Joan and Annie stayed in Kent, while Rosie was too ill to come home. Flo was deeply relieved not to be seeing anyone else in the family for more reason than that there was no home to come back to. The shame of her condition was bad enough without everyone knowing about it. As the winter wore on, she sat by the fire in the evenings, shovelling on a lump of coal now and then and listening to the wireless with Jessie.

Like Flo, her brothers and sisters had all been born at home and she could remember Annie's birth. She had woken up several times in the night, aware of strange noises and scurryings up and down stairs as the midwife assisted at the birth. In the morning, she had crept into her parents' bedroom and there had been a baby to see, with such tiny hands and feet. She waited for her baby to come, knowing that it would not be long now.

Chapter Five

One cold evening in the New Year, Flo's waters broke and it was clear that the baby was on the way. Jessie pulled on her coat, ran to the nearest phone box and called for an ambulance to take Flo to Charing Cross Hospital where she was booked to have the baby. It was a long time coming. Bombs were still raining down on London and ambulances were busy with war work.

The baby was in the breech position and couldn't be turned in advance. By Flo's reckoning, the birth was several days late. She was desperately missing Bill and wanted his arms around her, their future with their baby safe. Yet Bill had been missing, presumed dead, for three months now.

The birth was long and exhausting, but when it was all over and the midwife handed her a baby boy, wrapped in a piece of flannelette sheeting, Flo was surprised by a new feeling, of a miraculous arrival in her life. She felt an overpowering love for her baby.

It was Friday, 12th January 1945, only months after the liberation of France, which may have cost Bill his life. She would call the baby William. That much was easy, but what really worried her, as she began to recover from the birth, was how to support him.

Flo and her baby returned from the hospital, with Flo glad to leave. She hadn't felt comfortable in the maternity ward, surrounded by married women with their new babies, even though some of the husbands were still away in the armed forces. She was grateful for the offer of a lift by another new mother whose father was driving her home. Jessie welcomed her back. She was joyous over the baby and lent Flo a cradle, as well as nappies and baby clothes once worn by her own children and which she was keeping for their children. Although she was working, she helped to look after the baby when she was at home, while Flo was recovering from the birth.

Four years in the WAAF and the bombing of her home had left Flo with few clothes and personal possessions and she was conscious that she and her baby were, in a sense, both starting afresh in the world. She confessed her worry to Jessie on her first evening back at home.

'Why don't you come down to Tate and Lyle's with me when you're a bit stronger? I could get you a job packing sugar,' Jessie said.

Flo's heart sank at the thought of a trained secretary packing sugar.

'Thanks, Jessie, but no, I couldn't manage on that. Not with having to pay someone to look after the baby. I'll try for a secretarial job. I must, because I'm down to my last few quid.'

After a week back at home, Flo felt she was getting to know the baby, to see tiny changes in him. Her eyes shone as she gazed at him, her face framed by her thick roll of brown hair, pinned up with metal grips. He was a little person in his own right already, judging by the way he closed his fists with his thumbs between the first two fingers, his sounds of satisfaction as she fed him, or the way his surprisingly thick hair promised curls like Bill's. She even liked the way he cried, because it showed he wanted her attention. She would feed him or change him or cuddle him and he would stop crying. She loved him more and more. He was a heavenly baby and her determination to overcome the difficulties of caring for him rose by the day.

She registered the birth of William Haldon at Plaistow Town Hall later in January. She wanted to put Bill's name on the birth certificate, but a clerk refused to let her because they hadn't been married.

On the way back from the Town Hall, she had the idea of asking for help from Bill's parents. She still didn't want to go there, but she could write to them. However difficult they were, she was now desperate. She put her idea to Jessie that evening.

'If Bill were alive, surely I would have heard from him by this time. I'm losing hope, but I've been thinking of writing to his parents about William. He wanted me to keep all our plans secret, but things are different now.'

'You've got nothing to lose. They might give you something for the baby to tide you over and from the sound of it, they're not short of a bob or two,' Jessie said.

That evening, Flo sat down and wrote the letter. It was a hard letter to write, but William's presence in her life gave her the strength to try any means to keep him.

Thurs 25th Jan '45

Dear Mr and Mrs Martin,

You don't know me, but I was engaged to be married to your son Bill. I was told he was missing in action in September, but I now fear the worst because he hasn't been in touch with me.

Our baby, William, was born in Charing Cross hospital on 12th January and weighed 7 lbs. He is a lovely baby and I thought you would like to know that you have become grandparents.

However, I'm afraid that I'm not going to be able to keep him. There are so many difficulties. I should be grateful for any help you could give me at this time.

I look forward to hearing from you.

Yours sincerely,

Flo Haldon (Miss)

When Bill and Flo had exchanged home addresses at RAF Burghfield, Flo had learned his address by heart in a flash. It was extraordinary how good her memory was for anything to do with Bill. She didn't need to check the address before she wrote it on the envelope and posted the letter to Epsom in Surrey. The birth certificate went into a drawer in her bedroom for safekeeping.

She leaped on the post every day when it came, hoping for a magic wand to solve all her problems at a stroke. Exactly what form the magic would take she was not sure, but it was something to do with money.

She didn't have long to wait. One morning, a letter was lying on the doormat and Flo tore it open.

Monday 5th February 1945

Miss Haldon

Whoever you are, it is outrageous that you have written us this begging letter. That's what it is, even if you don't say so. You want money, don't you? How dare you write to us in the midst of our grief for the loss of our son with your story about a baby fathered by him? You are a slut who has got herself pregnant and is now trying to hoodwink us into paying for your child. It's disgraceful. If you ever contact us again, I will telephone the police.

Winifred Martin

The words of the letter from Bill's mother burned through Flo, especially the phrase *in the midst of our grief for the loss of our son.* This was proof of what she had long feared, but refused to believe. Bill was dead. The letter came in the first post and Flo alternately cried and seethed all day with the words running through her head, until she seemed to know the whole letter off by heart. Bill's parents had given her an answer to an unasked question, unasked because she had feared the answer.

Yet surely it was better to know definitely about Bill than never to be certain. It was easily the nastiest letter that she had ever received. It was so wrong that this woman should say such dreadful things about her. Yet she cried far more for the loss of Bill than the manner of finding out the loss.

That evening, she showed the letter to Jessie, who swore copiously on reading it, which made Flo feel slightly better.

'You should have him adopted,' Jessie said, handing the letter back. Flo blanched.

'Oh, I couldn't possibly.'

'What will it be like for him to grow up without a father, with everyone knowing? Kids at school would never let him forget it. And what about you? Would you ever get married with a baby in tow? Not many men want that. You've got to think of that, Flo. No, give the baby up. It's easy. Plenty of women want a baby. You can't give him a family life like yours, or stop people looking down on him as a bastard. Kids are cruel and he'll grow up with a chip on his shoulder, because his parents never got married, even though his father's dead.'

'People wouldn't have to know I wasn't married. They would just have to know his father was killed in the war,' Flo said.

'They would know, unless you're going to buy a ring and call yourself Mrs Whatsisname. And even then, they'd know, you mark my words. The other thing is the cost. You'll have to work all the hours God sends to support yourself with a baby.'

Flo didn't want to argue any more. In the days after receiving the letter from Bill's mother, she felt drained. The confirmation of Bill's death, even though she had expected it, was a severe blow. She thought constantly of Bill. Her loss, which in some ways she had avoided until now, was in the air she breathed. If she forgot him for a few moments, then something would happen to remind her, some minor incident or thought would cast her down as if she were on a see-saw. It was within her that it was happening, so a see-saw wasn't the right image. It was a sea with tides that rose and fell and there was no pattern to it.

She allowed herself to imagine that he might come back to life, turn up one day on her doorstep, or that she would run into him on the street. You're mad, completely mad, he's not coming back, she told herself unsparingly at first, but at other times, she indulged the thought that he might. She wanted him to come back so much that she felt that she could almost make it happen, if she closed her eyes and wished enough. Bill alive was so near to her that she could almost see and hear him, as if she were looking at him through a net curtain. The only problem was that she couldn't reach out to draw the net curtain aside. She began to have conversations with him in her head, about all sorts of things, and made of him an invisible companion. She searched for him among people on the street and was always disappointed, although a facial expression, height or build or colouring in some total stranger would remind her of him.

Alone with William at home, Flo had plenty of time to think about Bill, but the need to find a job drove her to go and see Mr Tressall. She took William with her, as she had no choice. Jessie was out all day at work and there was no one else to leave him with. She knew that Mr Tressall had taken on someone else while she was having her baby, but she was hoping that he would keep his word about taking her back and even extend her hours from three days a week to five.

Entering the rundown shop front on Plaistow High Street where the solicitor had his office, Flo saw Mr Tressall bent over her replacement's desk, ostensibly correcting some work. Judging by the embarrassed laughter when they both looked up and saw her, more was involved. Flo felt unwelcome, but she introduced William and made the speech she had prepared, asking for a job. It was unfortunate that William chose to punctuate the moment with a cry more forceful than Flo had known he could make and she had to beat a hasty retreat with the pram.

Convinced she had wasted her best chance of finding a job, Flo was still determined. At home, she began scouring the local paper for secretarial posts. She needed a local job in order to leave William as little as possible, so she dismissed any thoughts of trying to return to Selfridges, in the West End, where she had worked after leaving school.

Flo applied for several jobs, but, as soon as the employers realised that she had a baby to support on her own, they retreated. Then, a month after she had made the visit to Mr Tressall's office, when she barely had a pound left in her Post Office savings account, she received a letter from him to say that he had thought about her suggestion and was willing to take her on, provided that she didn't make a habit of bringing her baby to the office. She was delighted. Here at last was a way through.

'There's Bertie. I dunno what he'll say when he comes home, but he might not be too pleased to find you here,' Jessie said, when Flo told her about the job offer that evening. Bertie was her husband, a humourless man who might well have views about unmarried mothers. People were increasingly certain that the war would end soon, which meant that Bertie would come home.

Flo ignored what Jessie had said for the present. She would deal with Bertie's return home when she had to. Her father, Alf, would take her in when he was demobbed. He would have to find somewhere for himself and Joan and Annie, Flo's two youngest sisters, at the very least. Surely he would take Flo and her baby in as well?

She telephoned Mr Tressall to accept his offer of a job, wondering as she did so, why it had taken him a month to reply to her request. There was something fishy going on, but for the moment luck was on her side. He was open with her.

'Your replacement wasn't up to much. Spent all her time on the phone to her friends and couldn't type to save her life,' he said.

Flo wasn't sure about that. After all, they had been getting along well on the day of her visit to the office with William. She wondered if Mr Tressall had expected his secretary's duties to extend beyond the secretarial and been turned down. She said nothing about that. If he tried anything like that with her, she would give him short shrift. He needn't think she would be an easy touch because she already had a child. In the meantime, he was offering a full-time job, with reasonable pay and she was going to accept it.

She arranged to start on the following Monday and that evening she and Jessie drew up a shortlist of three women in the neighbourhood who might look after William. The next morning, Flo went on a round of visits and met Maureen, a young mother on their street whom Jessie knew and who welcomed the job. Her own baby was a year older and she needed some extra cash.

The first two weeks of the new routine went well. Every morning, Flo delivered William to Maureen and every evening, she collected him. At the office, she typed all day, answering correspondence, preparing legal papers and managing Mr Tressall's diary.

Yet each day seemed longer than the previous one. After two weeks, Flo had to admit that she was tired all the time and she felt low. She couldn't quite remember afterwards when it became all too much, but it wasn't long before she began to drag herself through the long days. She missed Bill dreadfully and her mother and her home and family. She barely had the strength to go and see Rosie in the sanatorium. One day she couldn't get out of bed and Maureen, a kindly woman, came round to see what was wrong when she didn't arrive with William. Mr Tressall, told from a call-box that Flo would not be in that day, was distinctly grumpy.

The next day, Flo managed to take William to Maureen and do a day's work, but she was white-faced with exhaustion by the time she and William arrived home in the evening.

Matters came to a head over Rosie. She wasn't getting any better. Flo went to see her at weekends, leaving William with Jessie. The two sisters had grown closer than they had ever been and Rosie, without knowing it, helped to fill the emptiness in Flo's life. She was sad about Bill's death and delighted about William.

'Look at this. I've made a teddy bear,' Rosie said on the Saturday, two weeks after Flo had started work. She held out a small brown bear to Flo. 'It's for William.' Her smile turned into a coughing fit.

'Thank you, Rosie. It's lovely and how clever to make it yourself.'

Flo took the bear back to Plaistow and showed it to Jessie, who took it gingerly, holding it by one ear.

'Oh dear. What if it's carrying disease? But it's hard to say no to it, when Rosie made it.'

Flo was now uncertain that it was safe to give the bear to William. She left it in the living room. It lay there untouched for the rest of the weekend. When Flo came into the kitchen on the following Monday after work, parking the pram in the hall and leaving William to sleep there for a moment, Jessie was taking the bear out of the oven.

'What are you doing?' Flo's eyes were wide.

'It's the teddy bear that Rosie made,' Jessie said.

Flo stroked the bear with a finger. Its fur was darker and crisper than before.

'I can see that, but it looks burned. Why have you cooked

it? Surely it's not for tea? I know a lot of food is still on the ration, but we're not starving.'

Jessie's smile at Flo's joke faded quickly.

'No, of course not. It's just to be sure. I had half a mind to wash it, but the water might not have been hot enough to get rid of the germs.'

Anger flared in Flo like a lit match.

'That's a terrible thing to do. You're trying to kill it! And it's my teddy bear. It's nothing to do with you!'

She snatched up the bear and ran from the kitchen and up the stairs to fling herself onto her bed. She knew, in her heart of hearts, although nobody ever said so, what was going to happen. Why didn't anyone ever say it? If it wasn't bad enough that she had lost the man she wanted to marry, as well as her mother, her favourite sister was going to die. It was too much. Flo sobbed, raw with grief, pouring out her feelings for all those she had lost and for Rosie. Only a cry from William brought her downstairs. Later, she apologised to Jessie, who wasn't to know that the bear stood for Rosie in Flo's mind.

'Flo, you're cracking up. Go to the doctor tomorrow. You're exhausted. I know what it is – childbed fever.' Jessie said.

'If you know, why do I need to see the doctor?' Flo said.

'Because he might be able to do something for you. You never know. If you go on at this rate, you're not going to have the strength to keep William,' Jessie said.

Chapter Six

Flo didn't dare take a morning off work to see a doctor, but she called into the nearby clinic after work one evening when it stayed open late, taking William with her. This was the clinic she had attended while pregnant and where she now brought William to be weighed and checked.

The clinic was brightly lit with neon lights for the winter evening and Flo blinked from the harshness of the glare as she came in. She sat on a hard chair to await her turn, parking the pram against a wall where there was space and lifting William out as he was awake. The hall where the clinic was situated had other uses as well and the nurses brought all their equipment, like weighing scales, with them, so the room looked bare and inhospitable, but Flo knew that the nurses were competent and sensible women.

The nurse she saw was a familiar face, an experienced, middle-aged woman used to dealing with new, young mothers and not disapproving of Flo's single state. Flo explained that she was tired all the time and often felt close to tears. The nurse was in no doubt what was wrong.

'It's quite normal to feel low after having a baby. You need some proper rest. Looking after a baby takes a lot of time and energy and you're not giving yourself time to recover from the birth. Can you give up your job until your strength comes back? You've been through too much recently, from what you've told me and on top of everything that's happened to you, you're trying to work full-time.'

'But I can't give up my job. How are we going to eat? And I can't ask any more of Jessie,' Flo said.

The nurse looked sympathetic, but she was firm.

'You'll collapse if you don't slow down and then where will you be?' she said.

Flo couldn't see a way round the problem and began to wish for her mother. Mabel would have known what to do. Flo would have had a home and wouldn't have had to pay rent. Mabel might have looked after the baby. Then she remembered that Mabel had taken most of her Saturday earnings as a schoolgirl and had herself been working, so she would have expected Flo to pay rent and wouldn't have been free to look after William.

Flo began to be late for work because she was exhausted, but this didn't please Mr Tressall.

'I'm giving you a week to get into a regular routine. Otherwise, you'll have to go,' he said.

Flo struggled through the week, but she failed to satisfy him. She had not fulfilled her earlier promise. At the end of the week, he called her over to his desk.

'I'm sorry, Miss Haldon. When you first came to work for me, you were efficient and hard-working. That was why I offered you a full-time job when that other wretched woman left. Now, my business is being put at risk by women who are more interested in pursuing their own lives than in doing the job I pay them for. I'm getting an agency girl for Monday, although they cost the earth. You'll have to go. Here's your due.'

He handed over a thin brown envelope. He had sacked Flo. Looking at his stern face, she felt that he had done more than that. He had robbed her of the means of keeping William.

Without the job that had offered her a lifeline, Flo began sadly to think that it was impossible to keep her baby. She felt too tired and low to find another job and yet she couldn't otherwise keep William. And Jessie was right. An illegitimate baby would be looked down on and William would grow up to think he was inferior. Not only that, but he would hamper her chances of marriage and a family. As a young girl, she hadn't been sure that she wanted to be married and have a family, but it was what she wanted more than anything now. After the years of war, she yearned for a peaceful family life.

With the heavy heart which followed the loss of Bill and her mother and daily more conscious of her dwindling savings, Flo inched towards a decision to give William up for adoption. The nurse at the clinic advised her to write to the Church of England Waifs and Strays and gave her an address in central London. Flo wrote a letter that day.

Monday 9th April, 1945

Dear Madam,

I have come to a decision about my baby William, who was born on 12th January and is three months old.

I am writing to ask if you would accept him for adoption as I can't afford to keep him. His father was killed in the war.

Yours sincerely,

Flo Haldon (Miss)

A welfare worker, Mrs Green, wrote back almost by return of post, offering Flo an appointment at home the following week. Flo was taken aback at the speed of the reply and went over to William's cradle, with the letter in her hand. She gazed at his sleeping face, not knowing how she could she bear to let him go. Yet she had made up her mind to do exactly that.

Welcoming Mrs Green to the house a few days later, Flo

saw that she looked too old for the armed forces and guessed she was working for the Waifs and Strays while their regular members of staff were away at war. Flo made two cups of tea and they settled down to talk. Mrs Green began by asking Flo why she was thinking of adoption. Flo listed a string of problems; the death of her mother and illness of her sister; the absence of the rest of her family; the need to move soon as Jessie's husband would be coming home now the war was ending and finally her exhaustion and loss of her job.

'I see. At the same time, you love your baby and don't really want to give him up,' Mrs Green said.

'No, but I owe him the best chance in life. Even if I felt stronger, I would be out working all the time to keep a roof over our heads and I wouldn't see him. He needs a mother at home.'

'Of course, but there is help available, you know, especially as you don't have any family around you at the moment. Adoption is a big step and we feel a baby is best with his mother.'

'What help?'

'Well, we can look after William in one of our homes until you're more settled or we can help with maintenance. There's also the National Council for the Unmarried Mother and her Child. One of their moral welfare workers could visit you.'

'I don't want him going in a home. And I'm not looking for charity.' Flo had her pride.

'All right, if you're sure.' Mrs Green turned her attention to what she needed to know about William. When it came to information about the baby's father, Flo hesitated. Bill's words about secrecy came into her mind, but in the end she spoke.

'His father was a sergeant in the RAF who was killed in action in France last year. I want them to know that.'

Mrs Green, who was taking notes, looked up from her writing. 'I'm sorry to hear that and we'll tell the new family.'

'Will he know that he's adopted?'

'I hope so. We advise parents to be open about an adoption and tell the child as early as possible. Of course, there's no guarantee what they will say.'

Flo nodded. She gave Mrs Green the number of Bill's squadron, the circumstances of his death as far as she could and what she knew about his background.

Mrs Green listened and wrote. Flo was grateful that her manner was sympathetic.

'I do know of a nice young couple nearby,' she said, but stopped as she saw Flo's look of alarm.

'I don't want to run the risk of seeing him around. I couldn't bear it.'

'I don't mean in the next street and I wouldn't tell you where they live. They have a son of their own, who is two now, but they can't have any more children. They're hoping to adopt a baby. They'd give him a comfortable and loving home and you could be sure that he wouldn't want for anything.'

Flo took a deep breath. 'All right. I hate the thought of losing him, but it seems so impossible to keep him and I owe him the best chance in life.'

'Are you really sure? Adoption is for keeps and you wouldn't ever hear from him.'

'I know. When... when will you come for him?'

'As soon as you're ready, but if you're really sure, the sooner the better. There will be some forms to sign.'

'Tomorrow, then,' Flo heard herself say. It would only make it harder to delay now and they arranged a time. Mrs Green explained that there would be a court case three months after William had gone to his new family. Flo would be told the date, but wouldn't have to attend the hearing. After she had gone, Flo couldn't help thinking that, by contrast with her struggle to keep William, giving him up for adoption was proving to be easy, even though it was a dreadful thing to have to do. At least Mrs Green hadn't looked down on her.

Flo had used some of her precious savings to buy new clothes for William when she made her decision. She dressed him carefully on his last morning with her. He wasn't going off to his new life in Jessie's hand-me-downs. She also wanted to send a message with him and she thought hard about how to do that. She didn't know what his new family would think about a letter, pinned to his clothing. Would they save it and keep it for him or destroy it because they wanted him completely for themselves and couldn't bear to think of his real mother? She knew she could give a letter to Mrs Green for the Waifs and Strays to keep for him, but would he ever see it?

In her bedroom, Flo looked at the charm bracelet from which she had taken a heart to give to Bill before he left to join the British Liberation Army. It had been her most precious possession as a child and she had taken it with her when she joined the WAAFs.

Flossie hadn't meant to break the bowl that was hiding the bracelet. Her mother had always said that it was the only nice thing they had. It came from Flossie's grandparents who were richer than they were.

She had been whirling around one day, arms outstretched, when a flying hand had knocked it to the floor, smashing it into several pieces and scattering its contents. She had seized on the charm bracelet that sprang from the bowl as if escaping from a prison and in seconds it was on her wrist. The find meant she had cared less about the caning that followed the breaking of the bowl.

The next day, Flossie had seen her mother hunched over the pieces of bowl, sticking them together and later putting the bowl back with the least cracked side showing. Flossie had been glad because it undid the accident in a way. She had looked at the bowl properly for the first time. On the outside was a woman with a yellow apron, carrying a basket.

A crack crossed her now, but it didn't stop her walking. She must have been from the olden days because she was wearing a long skirt down to the ground. Flossie had wanted to go for a walk with the woman on the bowl, a walk away from being told what to do and caned for what had been only an accident.

Flossie had loved the charm bracelet, noticed the way the links moved and the tiny sounds the charms made as they jostled each other. The other girls at school would be jealous of it and it was worth being caned to have her first ever piece of jewellery. There were twelve charms – three hearts, three boots, three flowers and three tiny rings. She had vowed that she would never lose the bracelet in a bowl full of odds and ends, like her mother. She would be sure to look after it forever, no matter what happened.

Now, fingering the charm bracelet, Flo thought of its missing heart, last seen around Bill's neck and wondered what had happened to it. Had it been buried with him in France or sent back with his possessions to his parents? If only it had been big enough to deflect the bullet that had killed him, what a miracle that would have been.

She settled on giving William a heart from her charm bracelet, just as she had given to Bill. It could say as much as any letter because everyone knew that a heart meant love and it was fitting that she should give a heart to each of the two people who mattered most in her life.

With the aid of a kitchen knife, she detached a second silver heart from her charm bracelet and tied it around William's wrist with a blue ribbon from Jessie's sewing box. She couldn't be sure that the heart would survive and become his only link with her. She could only hope that his new parents would keep it for him and tell him how he came to have it and what it must mean. She wanted him to know that she loved him and had only given him away because she had no choice. He must have the best chance in life.

Only one heart was left on the charm bracelet. Surveying the gap in the charms, Flo thought that there were three people in this story – Bill and William and she herself – and they each had one of the three silver hearts. The hearts should be together and so should the three people, but now they were forever apart.

Flo kissed William goodbye while she was alone with him and let tears escape onto his head as she held him. How difficult it was to do this and yet a hard core of determination told her that there would be no fuss when she handed him over. She had made her decision and she would see it through. She had no choice.

Mrs Green arrived on time to take William. She came in a car which waited outside the house. Her manner was a shade brisker than it had been the day before, as if the decision had been made and there was to be no nonsense. Flo, holding herself under strict control, almost felt as if she wasn't breathing.

'Here are the forms to sign, one for us and one for you,' Mrs Green said, passing them over.

Flo took them wordlessly. William was asleep in his cradle, oblivious to the momentous change in his life. She signed the forms and was given one copy to keep. Business over, Mrs Green moved towards the cradle. Flo picked him up and handed him over to Mrs Green without a further word, grateful he was making it easier for her, even though he couldn't possibly know what was happening. He squirmed a little, but didn't wake.

As she gave her baby away, she told herself that it was for his sake, however hard it was to see another woman holding him and walking out of the door. She didn't let herself think that she would never see him again, that she had exchanged her baby for a mere piece of paper and she went through the motions of giving him up as if she were a clockwork toy. It was Tuesday, 17th April 1945, a date that Flo never forgot. Like the date of William's birth, Friday, 12th January 1945, it was lodged firmly in her mind.

As Mrs Green and William left, Flo stood at the window and watched the car leave. She stood there for a long time, gazing at the empty road, before she turned away and allowed the sobs rising up in her to escape and a storm to tear through her.

Calming down, she picked up the signed form lying on the table in the living room and took it up to her bedroom. She hid it in a clothes drawer, underneath lining paper, in the company of William's birth certificate. She was tearful and lonely that night and grateful for Jessie's company.

The house was unbearably empty, as if a death had occurred. It was a matter of minutes to return the clothes and equipment that she had used for him. Silently, she gave back the baby things to Jessie. The grief that she had felt on hearing of Bill's death and discovering her mother had been killed was joined by fresh grief for the loss of her baby. She dragged herself through the rest of the day and the days afterwards.

She wondered what William's new parents would be like. Would they be strict, like her own parents, who had grown up under the long reign of old Queen Victoria? Yet William's new parents were surely nearer to her own age, in their twenties or early thirties at the most. In her mind, William had gone to the family Mrs Green had mentioned to her. Flo hoped that they would love her son, that they would not be strict, but would allow him to be true to himself, even if he were to turn out to be different from them and that their natural son, two years older than William, would welcome him and be a friend, the way that she and Rosie were friends.

Flo had ideas about bringing children up. She would be different from her parents. She wouldn't make any daughters do as much housework as she had been made to do and nor would she let the sons off scot free. She would allow her children to stay on at school as long as they wanted to, because the only way to get on in life was to have a good education. But it was no good. She might wish for parents of a certain kind for William, but she couldn't influence anything now about what would happen to him. She had given him up completely, as if he had never been born.

She wouldn't return to the WAAF. The war was nearly over and she needed to make a new life for herself. The flying bombs had stopped, their bases silenced by the British Liberation Army. Bill hadn't died in vain. He had given his life to free France and he had helped to bring the war to an end. She had to believe that, or she felt that she would go mad.

Flo didn't think about trying to find William. Although Mrs Green had hinted at a local family, Flo didn't look for her baby on the street. Instead, she set herself to living with her decision. William would be her secret. She didn't want to make her future any harder for herself than the present. No one would be any the wiser if she passed herself off as a slightly older version of the girl that she had once been. She would be a young woman, surely not the only one, who had seen out the war without meeting a suitable young man. She would tell no one what had happened to her, so that only her sister Rosie and Jessie, would know. She swore them both to secrecy.

Keeping her secret meant losing her friend Ellen. Now that William had gone, she stopped replying to her letters. Ellen knew too much about her. It was a shame to have to sacrifice her best friendship since leaving school, especially after losing Bill and William, but she felt that she had no choice.

Yet she didn't have to destroy every scrap of the past that meant so much to her. She kept letters that Bill had written to her from France because she couldn't bear to destroy them. Now that she knew that he was dead and no longer missing, presumed dead, they were almost all she had of him. She also kept the photo that Ellen had given her as she was leaving RAF Burghfield and a photo that Bill had taken of her, in memory of herself when she knew him. She even kept the letter from Bill's mother, unpleasant as it was, because it told her what had happened to him. She couldn't bear to throw away the charm bracelet, even though it was incomplete. She took the signet ring that Bill had given her off her ring finger and put it with the other mementoes.

She wanted to concentrate on her future, but found it hard. At twenty-four, she was still young enough to think of marriage and she wanted to be married and have a family, yet she didn't feel ready to look ahead. She was still immersed in Bill's death and in thinking of William, although she never spoke of William of her own accord, even when people accused her, as they sometimes did, of not giving much away about herself.

To those who asked about her baby, she said simply that he was being adopted, that she couldn't manage to support him on her own. No one queried her decision when she said she was giving him the best chance in life. She pretended, at least to others, that life in future would be better than it had been in the war years and she believed that it would be in some ways. Yet she did not expect ever again to find the happiness she had known with Bill or that she would ever stop missing him and William.

The war in Europe ended on 8th May, scarcely four months after William's birth. Like many streets in Britain, Flo and Jessie's street celebrated with a Victory in Europe party. Everyone who was left at home contributed to the tea laid out on tables covered with old sheeting. An effigy of Hitler with the famous slick of hair and the moustache hung from a lamp post.

On a sunny May afternoon, voices were loud and the party went on for hours. Everyone was relieved that the war was over and the bombing and blackout were at an end. People knew that life wouldn't be easy. There were deaths to live with, bomb sites to clear and build on, the streets were shabby and rationing was to continue. Yet there was no doubting the joy that the war in Europe was over. Flo went to the party and tried hard to join in. A new life awaited her. Bill was gone and she would never see William again.

- Part Two -

Will

1959-1977

Chapter One

Will knew that he was adopted. His parents had told him when he was a small boy, but, as far as he could remember, they had hardly mentioned it since and it wasn't something he thought about much, until the day Aunt Janet came to tea.

His mother, Marion, was a small, plump woman with mousy hair, even-tempered and kindly in her manner. She had a taller, older sister, Janet, who was single and who was having tea with them in their terraced house in Plaistow in East London one Saturday when he was fourteen. It was a wintry afternoon in March and the light had to be on in the dining room. Flower-patterned paper covered the walls, giving way to green lino on the floor. The table had a leaf at each end and what their mother called barley sugar legs, which made Will and his brother Frank laugh because you couldn't eat them. They sat around the table on wooden chairs with circles in the back. A dresser full of crockery lined one wall and a single, curtained, window looked onto the small back garden, where Will's father grew vegetables.

They had been listening to the wireless, but their programme had finished and Will's father had reached over to the dresser, where the wireless sat, and switched it off. The raucous voice of a comedy act died away. It hadn't been funny enough to make them laugh out loud and everyone's attention had wandered. They had been talking through the programme about neighbours who had just had a baby girl.

Will had been called Billy as a little boy, but had changed his name as a teenager. Billy sounded too babyish and he already knew one or two Bills. No one was called William except people in history like William the Conqueror, other kings he was vague about and William Shakespeare, so he had become Will. He had written Will Tyler on his school exercise books; he had refused to answer to Billy and asked his parents if he could change his first name by something he had heard of called deed poll. They had said that he didn't need to, that anyone could shorten their name and he could just use the name Will, if that was what he wanted to do. Soon everyone was calling him Will, his family, the neighbours and people at school.

Will didn't like Aunt Janet. She questioned him about his school work as if she were a teacher, when she was a hairdresser and she didn't know anything about teaching. She was famous in the family for demanding a great deal of attention and exhausting everyone, but the good thing about her was that she did his mother's hair for nothing. She was always well dressed and carefully made up. Her hair was thick and what his mother called beautifully set. Her visits at tea time were rare, but when she was invited for tea, the household tiptoed round her.

Will was refusing to join in the conversation and eating as much as he could cram into his mouth.

'Oh, Will,' his aunt was saying as he demolished a third piece of cake, 'if your parents had only known what a greedy boy you would turn out to be, they would never have given you a home.'

Her pronouncements sounded like truth, when they were only her opinion, but Will was not intimidated.

'Never given me a home?' he said.

'No, you would have gone to someone else,' his aunt said. She muttered something about the wrong side of the blanket. Will was puzzled. The blankets on his bed were the same on both sides.

'No, I wouldn't. This is my home.'

A silence fell. His mother said, 'Hush, now,' to his aunt and looked uncomfortable.

His mother could be in a bad mood, if he or Frank misbehaved, or if his father had one too many down the pub and didn't give her enough housekeeping money, but she was usually all right. She didn't go out to work. She said goodbye to Frank and Will when they left for school in the morning and she was always at home after school. Will knew several boys who wore a key around the neck and went home to an empty house after school and he was glad he wasn't one of them.

His parents exchanged glances. Will finished off his piece of cake, while his father, Joe, a postman, began talking about a vicious dog.

Joe was easy-going by nature, always ready for a laugh and a joke, but, at the same time, punctual and alert at work. He was up and out of the house before the two boys woke up in the morning, but was often at home by the time they came back from school. He was slim and fit. He said it was all the walking that he did, although he had backache sometimes from the heavy bag, slung on one shoulder, which he carried full of letters. He liked his job, though. He told Will that he liked the exercise and the way the bag felt heavy on his shoulder at first, but grew lighter and lighter as he went about his walk, until by the end he hardly noticed it and the job was done for the moment.

The dog of the story was one his father often met and Will laughed because the dog had chased him this time, leaped up at him and torn his trousers. His mother, who was going to have to patch them up, was less pleased. Conversation veered towards the bad behaviour of dogs rather than boys.

His aunt made no further comment on Will's appetite, but after she had gone, he turned to his mother.

'I hate her. What did she mean by saying you'd never have given me a home?'

'Don't say she, Will. It's Aunt Janet to you,' his mother said automatically. 'Oh, Janet forgot or she didn't think before she spoke. She only meant that we might not have adopted you, but it's not true, Will. We loved you as soon as we saw you.'

'Oh that,' Will said, as if it meant nothing, but after a second's pause he asked 'Why did you adopt me?' He couldn't remember if he had ever asked before.

'After Frank, the doctor said I shouldn't have any more children because my blood pressure was too high all the time I was carrying him. But we wanted another child so we thought we would adopt a baby. You came to us when you were three months old, such a perfect baby,' his mother said with a smile.

'But who am I then?' Will was surprised at his question. He had never thought like that before.

'You're our child, Will, except you weren't born to us. We've always loved you just as much as we love Frank, but we don't know where you came from. We do know that your name has always been William. That was the name you were given by your… mother. We think she couldn't afford to keep you, but that's all we know. We never met her, you see. We might have seen her name on the record of your birth when we put the papers together for the court, but I don't remember it. Your birth certificate has our name on. That's what we were given after we went to court to adopt you. You know all this, Will, because we told you, but you've forgotten,' his mother said.

'So you don't know who I am except that I was always William?'

'I do know you were making a terrible racket when you

were handed over to us,' his father said, with a mock grimace.

'Don't you know anything about me?' Will was almost pleading.

'You were born in Charing Cross Hospital,' his mother said.

'Yes, but that's what you've always said.'

'There is the silver heart. I'll fetch it,' his mother said.

She ran upstairs and was back in seconds with a small cardboard box. Opening it, she took out a blue ribbon from which dangled a tiny silver heart.

'This was tied to your wrist when you were given to us. I'm looking after it for you,' she said, handing it to Will.

Will took the silver heart and peered at it closely. It was tarnished, but that didn't matter. His mother could always polish it.

'I'm sure it means she loved you and didn't want to give you away,' his mother said.

'Three months. She must have loved me if she kept me for three months. She didn't just give me away the minute I was born. I want to meet her.' Will handed the heart back to his mother. She looked shocked at what he had said.

'I don't know about that, Will. Oh, you were such a lovely baby with your blue eyes and dark, curly hair, even though you're darker than the rest of the family.'

'And you completed the family for us,' his father said. He had said little so far.

Will looked from one parent to the other. His father was ginger and his mother what she called mousy. They looked so familiar and yet he didn't look at all like them. He had never thought about it before. They were his parents, who were always there and always had been, even though he was adopted.

Will retreated to the room he shared with Frank to think alone. Fortunately, Frank had gone out after tea. At sixteen, he was free to come and go as he pleased. Will felt a mixture of things. He had always taken for granted that he was adopted, but now it seemed strange.

Will was growing up in London in peacetime after the war. People referred to it as the war as if there had never been any other, but no one was confused by that, even though it was the second world war of the 20th century. As a small boy, he had thought that the war was still going on, because his parents talked about it all the time. He hadn't even been sure what it was at first, but he had been afraid it was coming to get him.

He had been four when he finally understood that the war was over and that he was safe. There had still been signs of it everywhere; food on the ration; people with missing arms and legs; bombsites with craters full of broken bricks; the air raid shelter at school and the sound of the all-clear siren. They had never sounded the warning siren for fear of alarming people. He had been glad that the war was over.

Despite his formless early fears and the shadow of the war, Will had had a largely untroubled childhood. He had enjoyed war games with the other boys on his street. He had played in the old air raid shelter at school and listened to his parents talk about their war, although it didn't sound like much compared to the stories in the comics. They hadn't seen any action. They had both been in the armed forces: his father in the army and his mother in something she called the Auxiliary Territorial Service. That was how they had met, although they always said that they might have met anyway because his father came from Plaistow and his mother from not far away in East Ham.

Now that being adopted seemed so strange, would everything be different? He looked around the bedroom from where he sat on the edge of his bed. It was the same bedroom as always. He half expected to find that the curtains had changed colour, the two beds had been moved, the old chest of drawers or the wardrobe had grown or shrunk, but everything was unchanged. His pile of annuals was beside the bed; his pictures of footballers were still pinned to the wall; a coat that was too small for him now hung on the back of the door. Everything was the same, but he felt different.

Frank wasn't adopted. Was Frank really his brother? They got along well most of the time. Frank never said so, but he seemed to like having a brother and they had played together well when younger, Frank taking the lead at first, but Will soon catching up and playing an equal part in games. Their mother had handed down Frank's clothes to Will when they were too small for him. They shared some of their things and they shared their parents. Will could never have said that Frank received more attention or indeed anything more than he did in an unfair way.

Frank had failed the eleven-plus and had gone to the local secondary modern school. He didn't mind because that was where all his friends were and he was going to leave school at the end of the summer term, in a few months' time. He wanted to be a postman like his father and didn't mind Will doing better at school. He called Will a swot, but in a teasing not an angry way and was proud of being bigger and taller and better at football than his younger brother.

Will carried on with life as usual after that teatime with Aunt Janet, but he began to seek out stories about boys who were different in some way. He dismissed words like foundling and changeling. He was adopted, but he hadn't been a foundling or a changeling. He liked to read newspaper articles about lost or abandoned babies and about anyone meeting their parents for the first time or not living with their parents.

That other mother was more real to him than his other father because she had given birth to him; she had kept him until he was three months old; she had named him and given him the silver heart. He began to think of her as his real mother. His real father was a complete mystery.

He wondered who this real mother was and began to daydream about her as his parents didn't seem to know anything. Especially at night before he went to sleep, he would see her as some sort of angel who flew down into his bedroom to take him away. She was beautiful, with dark, curly hair like his hair, only longer, as long as a curtain stretching down to the ground and when she turned round the curtain of hair turned with her, with a swishing sound.

Sometimes the daydream took the form of meeting her on the street. She was equally beautiful then and she claimed him with outstretched arms that became a hug and she said, *William, I've found you at last.* She always called him William in the daydream because that was the name she had given him and she didn't know that he had been Billy and was now Will.

The problem with the daydream, if he took it too far, was that he had to leave his parents and Frank and that was scary, even if he wasn't always sure that he liked his family. He might then embark on a daydream that his real mother had come to live with them all, so that he had both mothers there, but his ordinary mother wouldn't have liked that. As the weeks passed, he noticed that she didn't want to talk about Will being adopted. He could tell by the way her face changed if he mentioned it. It tightened up, the way it did when she was doing something she didn't like.

Supposing that his real mother lived round the corner from him in Plaistow? He began to look at women on the street, to see if he might recognise her. He didn't see anyone who looked enough like him or who he wanted as his real mother. A lot of women were old and cross-looking. Some of them didn't seem to have any teeth and they shut their mouths into a straight line so you couldn't see their lips. Some women had several children in tow and shouted at them. And the young girls going off to work in the morning, when he was going to school, didn't look like mothers, not like his mother, someone who cooked his meals and washed his clothes and used to read to him, even though she said she didn't like reading much, until he said that it was babyish and asked her to stop.

'Why did she give me away?' he asked his parents after tea one evening not long after the teatime with Aunt Janet. He said *she* because he didn't know what to call her. Nothing seemed right, but there was no need to explain what he meant. His parents knew immediately.

'I told you, Will. We don't really know, but we think she wasn't able to keep you,' his mother said.

'I want to find her. I want to see who she is and ask her why she gave me away. She'll want to see me and to know that I'm all right,' he said.

His mother had been about to clear the table, but she stopped gathering plates. He noticed a look of alarm in her eyes.

'What do you want to go doing that for, Will? We're your family. When you're adopted, you don't see your other family again,' she said straightaway.

His father put down the newspaper that he liked to read at the table after they had finished eating.

'I don't think you can, my boy. We don't know her name or where she lives.'

'Doesn't it say on my birth certificate?'

'No. Your birth certificate was given to us when we adopted you. It has our name Tyler on it as your surname,' his mother said.

Will had thought that this might be a problem and he was ready with his answer.

'I'll ask the people who gave me to you, if you give me their name and address,' he said. 'I need to know where I come from and all the things you know about your family already.'

'We've brought you up to be part of our family, Will. You can't go back now.' His mother pursed her lips to suggest that the conversation was ended.

'You're scared of losing me.' Will could see from the glance his mother shot at him that he was right.

He gave up on the idea of finding the people who had arranged his adoption, at least for the present. In his heart of hearts, he didn't want to do anything to hurt his parents, but he promised himself that one day he would still find his real mother.

He wished that he were more like other boys he knew, boys who were not adopted, but the ordinary children of their parents, boys like Frank who had no doubts about where he had come from. Will began to feel conspicuous when he was with his family outside the house. It wasn't often that they went out together, though. Mostly he came and went alone these days, on the second-hand bicycle that he had received one Christmas.

Will was growing in all directions. His voice had changed, there was hair in many new places and he was taller and more solid than he had been. He had wet dreams at night sometimes and was glad his mother didn't say anything about the state of his sheets, but just washed them in the copper in the ordinary way.

It wasn't enough to be growing. He felt that he was odd, some sort of freak. He began to wonder more about his real mother. Why had she given him away? Was it because she hadn't been married and she couldn't bring him up on his own or had she thought there was something wrong with him? Perhaps he reminded her too much of his father and she couldn't bear it because she had lost his father in some way. Perhaps she wanted to marry someone else who didn't want him tagging along, a baby with a different father, a cuckoo in the nest as people said, although he had never seen a cuckoo and had no idea what they looked like.

Who was she, anyway? And who were all her family? Did he look like her? He looked at his parents and Frank again and was aware of what he had never much noticed about them. Frank looked so like their father. Sometimes you could see their mother in him as well. Frank obviously belonged to them. Did he, Will, belong to them in the way that he had felt he did when he was younger? He began to feel that they were all strangers or that he was a stranger, an outsider.

How tall would he be? His father was of average height and Frank was now slightly taller. Will didn't want to be left behind. He had been pleased when he overtook his mother at fourteen and then started to rise to the height of his father. He might not look like them, but at least his height gave him something in common with his family.

He spent anxious moments on several occasions in front of a mirror looking at his dark, curly hair, straight nose and square chin and comparing them with Frank's ginger hair, snub nose and round face. The two boys looked even less alike than when they were younger and no one had ever said to Will, *oh, I guessed Frank is your brother, because you look just like him.*

He had a lot of questions and one day he would find answers to them.

Chapter Two

Will started to argue with his parents, to chafe against silly restrictions. He knew in his most honest moments that he was rippling the smooth surface of family life and even possibly making them regret taking him in, but he excused himself on the grounds that he couldn't help it. And anyway, he had done something for them. He had completed the family when they couldn't do it for themselves. They had said that.

He had a raw deal with his family. If his parents argued, if either of them tried to tell him what to do, if Frank got in his way, he would want to leave and be with his real family. Surely, it would be better? His real mother might give him more than the shilling (5p) a week pocket money that he had now. A shilling didn't go far. He could buy a comic like the *Lion* or the *Wizard* and there would be change for sweets, a gobstopper and perhaps a few penny chews, but nothing more. It was a shame because he loved sweets.

His real mother might let him stay up later in the evening than his nine o'clock bedtime. It wasn't fair to have to go to bed so early in the summer when it was still light and other boys of fourteen were playing on the street until it got dark. She might even let him eat as much as he wanted of things he liked instead of saying *that's enough now, Will,* as his parents did with toast and jam at breakfast. She might say that he didn't have to eat any greens instead of making him finish them. He didn't like greens.

There wasn't much to say about being adopted after all because he knew nothing about those other parents. He would have to imagine them. His real father must have been a hero in the war, perhaps a bomber pilot who shot down German planes.

'My real father was a war hero, a bomber pilot.' he said to his friend Jim. It was much more exciting than the manual work his ordinary father had done in the war.

'No kidding! Was he really?' Jim was impressed.

'Yes, but he was killed in the war. That's why I'm adopted,' Will said. It might have been true.

Will's parents had been proud of him for passing the eleven-plus and he was doing well in the grammar school, but in the fourth year, when he was fifteen, he began to go later and later to school in the mornings, cutting things fine because some of the lessons were boring. Yet he didn't quite dare to play truant.

'Will, come on, you're going to be late for school,' his mother said one morning. He was in a bad mood because he had lost his pocket money that week from what his father called insolence to his mother and he needed to buy a bicycle light.

'Leave me alone! Don't tell me what to do. I don't belong to you and you're not my real mother,' he said. The words flew straight out of his mouth.

His mother's face fell. 'Don't say that, Will! Now, look, it's ten to nine and the bell goes at nine o'clock. You'll be in trouble if you're late.'

'You can't tell me what to do, just because you adopted me. I didn't ask you to and it doesn't mean anything. It's only a… a piece of paper.'

He was thinking of his birth certificate. His parents had shown it to him, with his name on – William Joseph Tyler.

Will raised his voice with each sentence. Then he ran out

of the house, jumped on his bike and pedalled furiously to school. He was a few minutes late. It didn't matter. It was only biology with that boring Mr Johnson who was scared to teach them anything about sex except what rabbits did.

He was in the bad mood all day. He couldn't help it. He brought Jim home from school. Lately, he had been given a key and so he let himself and Jim into the house. Jim lived nearby. They went to and from school and spent break times together, sticking up for each other when necessary.

'Can Jim stay for tea?' he said, entering the kitchen where his mother was taking a cake out of the oven. It was a chocolate cake, one of his favourites and it smelled good. He was hungry enough to eat the whole thing. He didn't say Mum. Lately he had avoided calling his parents by any name.

'Will, I'm sorry, but he can't. Your Aunt Janet is coming and you know how difficult she is,' his mother said.

'I can't stand Aunt Janet. I'm not staying here any longer. I can't bear it. I'm going somewhere else, to Jim's house. I'll live there.'

He ran upstairs and a few minutes later came running down again with a small knapsack that he had been given for Christmas that year. He had crammed some clothes into it.

'I'm off and I'm never coming back,' he said. He couldn't bear his family any longer and he had to do something about it right now, or he would explode.

His mother's face was white. Instead of letting him go, she left the cake and walked to the front door where he stood, barring his way.

'Will, don't be ridiculous. You're making something out of nothing. I don't want you to go. You're our son and this is your home,' she said. He could tell that he had scared her, because her voice was shaky.

'You can't stop me. You're not my parents and the adoption is only a piece of paper.'

He pushed her out of the way. He was so angry that he could have strangled her and wasn't sure why he didn't. He was taller than she was by now and when he was standing close to her, she looked so small that it was easy to push her out of the way, open the door and leave. Jim, who had watched all this in silence, was close on his heels.

Jim lived a few streets away from Will, in a similar house, crammed full of people because he had two sisters as well as parents and a grandmother who lived with them. His father was a motorbike enthusiast. One vehicle, missing a wheel and never likely to be stolen, was parked in the front, outside the house. The house inside was full of motorbike parts for people to trip over. Even the table in the dining room would grow them when it wasn't needed for meals. Jim often had to do his homework sitting in an armchair or on his bed.

No aunts were expected, however, and Will and Jim had an enormous tea. Jim asked his mother if Will could stay the night. He had often done so before.

'Well, yes, if you like, Will, as long as you give your mother a ring to tell her,' Jim's mother said. Both families had a phone.

'She's not my mother,' Will said, still angry with her.

'She's the only mother I've ever known you have, my boy, and you must ring her if you're going to stay the night, or she'll be worried about where you are,' Jim's mother said.

Will made the phone call. He couldn't feel the same kind of anger towards Jim's mother that he felt towards his mother, especially after being so well fed. They had even had chocolate marshmallows, wrapped in silver foil, of the kind that his mother only ever bought for birthdays.

Staying with Jim helped Will to realise that other families weren't perfect either. Jim's parents snapped at each other now and then, Jim's two little sisters whined a lot and Jim's mother told him what to do.

'You think everything's because you're adopted, but it

isn't, you know,' Jim said that night when the two boys were getting ready for bed. Jim, as the only boy, had a bedroom to himself and Will was going to bunk down on cushions on the floor as he had done in the past.

'What do you mean?'

'Your mum and dad aren't so bad, even though you're adopted. They're all right, really. I want to run away sometimes, but I don't.'

'You do?' Will said, surprised because Jim seemed to take everything in his stride and never to be upset about anything. It puzzled Will, when his own moods were so up and down these days.

'Yes, if my sisters are annoying or my dad starts laying about,' Jim said. Will, who had suffered only the occasional smack by his mother as a child and never seen his father hit out at anyone, was silenced by the thought of Jim's father's hands in action.

One night stretched to two and three and then Jim's mother began to say that it was time Will returned home. His parents would be worried about him. Will had calmed down by then and had even decided that he needed some clean clothes and his books and records, all his things. He was also getting fed up with the motorbike parts, after falling over one and scratching a knee.

He arrived home after school one day as if he had never been away. His parents welcomed him without recriminations and he even mumbled an apology unasked.

'I hope you're not going off the rails, Will,' was all that Marion said. He didn't know the answer to that.

Things were easier at home after that. His parents seemed to give him more freedom and he realised that Jim was probably right. Parents were awful anyway and maybe his parents weren't worse than any others and even not as bad as some. At least his father didn't beat him up.

He began to play football, not only at school, but afterwards as well. He became a strong member of the school football team. Playing football made him feel less angry.

At school, Will began to take heart from the fact that some of the other boys he knew were different from his idea of normal, even if they weren't adopted like him. One boy lived with grandparents because his parents had died in a car accident; one or two boys at his school had no father at home, only a mother, or lived with foster parents, but weren't adopted like him. He tried to think that his difference didn't matter so much, especially if he didn't talk about it a lot. It wasn't as if he looked so different from his family. He was the same skin colour, not like the black boy who was living with a white family down the road. Yet he hadn't forgotten what he called the piece of paper and he still wondered about his real mother and whether she ever thought about him.

Not long after the row which had led to those few days at Jim's place, he was reminded of the silver heart tied to his wrist as a baby.

'Can I have the silver heart now?' he asked his mother when they were both in the kitchen one day after school.

She knew immediately what he meant. 'Of course, Will. You should be old enough not to lose it by now. I was only keeping it safe for you.'

She went upstairs straightaway to fetch it from her bedroom and came down again with it in her hand.

'Here you are.'

She looked fearful as she held the silver heart out to him, still attached to its blue ribbon and just as tarnished as when he had first seen it a few weeks previously.

'Don't worry, it's not magical. It's not going to take me away from you.' He felt a mixture of protectiveness towards her and irritated by her love of him.

'Of course not. Don't be silly,' his mother said, but she relaxed at his words.

‘Do you think my father was called William?’ Will asked next, struck by the idea and surprised that he hadn’t thought of it before.

‘I don’t know, but he might have been. It would make sense, wouldn’t it?’

‘He might never have met me or even know about me, though.’

‘No. Now, that’s enough, Will. I’ve got to get on with the tea or we’ll starve.’ His mother turned towards the sink and began to peel potatoes.

Will dug into the broom cupboard, where cleaning materials were kept and brought out some silver polish. Taking a rag from the ragbag and applying the polish, he rubbed the silver heart until it shone. He stared as it lay gleaming in his palm, as if it might open up and reveal something. Nothing happened. Its only message was what he made of its shape. A heart meant love. Everyone knew that.

Apart from the idea about the bomber pilot, he didn’t give much thought to his real father. It was his real mother he thought about, but less often as he grew older. Sometimes he would go for days, or weeks, or even months without thinking of her, perhaps because she didn’t offer much to think about as he knew almost nothing about her. His fantasies about her were dimming, from repetition and lack of material, but he didn’t forget about her altogether.

Girls occupied his daydreams now. It was boring, going to a boys’ school, because there were no girls and he had no sisters whose friends he could have met. There were some girl cousins in the family, but they were too young and he didn’t see them often.

One day he saw a girl in the sweetshop that he visited on the way home from school, if he had any money. He could tell from her uniform that she went to the girls’ grammar school. She was pretty and slim, with brown curls and a laughing face.

He took to going to the sweetshop more often and occasionally he would see her, but he couldn't think what to say to her and after a while he gave up on her.

He had known the girls on his street all his life. He was friendly with Vera in particular, because she was outspoken and funny. She seemed to know what she wanted and she obviously liked him. Notes appeared on his desk at school, which everyone seemed to know came from her, brought in by her brother, who was in Will's class. This coincided with the appearance of spots on his face, which was a disaster, because no girl would want a boyfriend with spots, although Vera didn't seem to mind them.

Vera was talkative and laughed a lot and her voice sounded warm. He liked the way her mouth curled at the corners and her blonde hair framed her face. He wanted to kiss her and one day he found the courage.

The first time was in an alleyway off their street where he had thought they would be safe from prying eyes, but then he heard cries of, *Oh, look at Will kissing Vera,* and he turned round to see a gang of their friends peering at them and laughing. He made a joke of it, to cover his dismay. After that he made sure they were alone before he kissed her, although it wasn't easy with people in the way all the time and not wanting to invite Vera home where he knew Marion wouldn't allow him to take her up to his bedroom. He couldn't bear the thought of sitting downstairs, with his parents embarrassing them.

Will immersed himself in rock and pop music, driving his parents mad when he played the records he had bought with money from a paper round. He liked Pat Boone, Ricky Nelson, Tommy Steele and in particular, Elvis Presley. He played his 78s and 45s over and over again, as well as his one or two 33s. By the early 1960s, the Beatles and the Rolling Stones and many other groups were centre stage in the lives of Will and his friends.

As Will climbed higher at school, he had to work harder.

'I've got too much homework. It's killing me,' he said at home one evening, as he began to work on a history essay. He was in the sitting room, beside the coal fire where the family gathered. It was winter and too cold to be upstairs in his bedroom. His parents both said that it was the coldest winter they could remember since 1947. Will was too young to remember 1947, but he knew that 1963 was cold.

'You want to work hard for your exams, my lad, and give up on all that music you waste your time on. I want you to do better than I did. I never had much time for school. And you can do better than Frank,' his father said in a rare moment of disloyalty to his older son, who was out at that moment.

At just eighteen, he listened to his father with half an ear. His parents wanted him to do well. Since he had passed his exams with flying colours two years previously and was now in the sixth form, they had treated him with a kind of deference that showed their pride in their clever son, although they were careful, he noticed, to praise Frank as well. Frank had left school at fifteen, the school leaving age, and was now a postman like his father. Will didn't want to be a postman and his envy of Frank was confined to money and free time.

Will's favourite subject at school was history. He was fascinated by what life had been like before he was born, how it had changed to become what it was now and how much of the past was in the present. He wondered if his love of history was because of the reminders of war around him as he was growing up or because of what he now thought of, with all his unanswered questions, as the mystery of his birth. He had so many questions about his real family past that seemed unanswerable. Who were his real parents? Had his father been a bomber pilot in the war? Why did his mother give him up? Had she been forced to, when she really wanted to keep him? Studying history as a subject could turn out to be the next best thing. It ought to show how the past came to be the present, except that they only went up to the First World War in history at school, which was a nuisance. Anything since was not considered to be history, merely current affairs and everyone knew that wasn't a proper subject.

With the hope of doing well in his A-levels, Will applied to go to the new University of York, which was opening in the autumn of 1963, just when he would be ready to go to university. It would be no fun to be a student at London University, with the danger of having to live at home, like a big child or like Frank. He liked the idea of being one of the first students in a new university. He liked the York history syllabus which went beyond 1914 to include the Second World War. He went to York on the train for an interview. It wasn't too bad, although he worried afterwards that he had made a mistake in mentioning historical novels by writers like Dennis Wheatley and Georgette Heyer. They might have thought he wasn't serious enough. He was pleased a few weeks later to be offered a place to study history in York as part of the first year's intake.

Will left school with good enough grades at A-level to take up his university place and spent the summer working in a timber yard in order to support himself until his student grant came through. He was going to get about £350 a year in maintenance grant from his local council, an enormous sum of money. His parents wouldn't have to pay anything towards it, because his father didn't earn enough. His local council had also promised to pay his student fees, which was good because they were over £200 a year.

Walking home from school one day, he saw Vera ahead and ran to catch up with her.

'I don't think I'll be coming home at weekends at all, unless I hitchhike. It'll cost too much, so I'm going to be away from the beginning of October until Christmas,' he told Vera when he had given her his news.

'Are you now? Well, that's a long time. Did I tell you that Neil from the grocer's has asked me out? He came round the counter when I was in there with a list for my mum the other day.'

'Did he? And what did you say?'

'I said yes.'

'All the best, Vera!'

Will was relieved. He still liked Vera, but he wanted to go to York free of any entanglements. He would leave his old life behind him and start afresh there. He had the idea, which he kept to himself, that studying history might lead him indirectly to the discovery of his first mother. The training of a historian might be put to other uses than those intended by the university tutors.

Chapter Three

During the summer after leaving school, Will thought again about going to see the adoption society that had given him to his parents, to ask if they would be willing to tell him anything. His mother had told him that it was called the Church of England Waifs and Strays and he had even once looked them up in the phone book and found they still existed somewhere in the centre of London, although they had changed their name. When he thought about contacting them, her worried face rose up before him. He knew she was afraid of losing him. She was losing him in one sense, because he would be leaving home soon, but that was different. Besides, now wasn't the right moment. He was about to leave home and start a new life. He needed to concentrate on that, but he wouldn't forget his promise to himself to find out more about his past.

He wanted to leave home. His parents' and Frank's horizons were limited and he still felt like an outsider in the family. He didn't know how much that was to do with growing up anyway and how much it was to do with being adopted. Wanting to leave home was about more than being adopted because Jim and others in the sixth form were preparing to leave home and they were all impatient for this change in life, a sign of approaching adulthood.

Although younger than Frank, Will was the first to go.

Frank seemed to have dug himself in with their parents and had no plans to leave. Aged twenty when Will left home to go to York, Frank had been a postman for five years. Plenty of girlfriends and his love of football entertained him outside work and he belonged to the working world in a way that Will, with several years as a student ahead, could hardly imagine for himself. They were friendly enough at home, but a gulf seemed to have opened between the two brothers since Frank had left school at fifteen. Will noticed that Frank put him down when he could and seemed jealous of his younger brother at times.

Will said goodbye to his parents at King's Cross Station, as he caught the train to York in October 1963.

'I'll write and tell you I've arrived. I'll write regularly,' he said.

His mother nodded eagerly. 'Of course and I'll write to you every week, Will.'

'I'll post her letters. I know how to do that,' his father said with a grin. He always found it hard to pick up a pen.

Will hardly thought about the family that he had left behind him. He was too excited about his new life and fell easily into conversation with other undergraduates he met on the train. On arrival in York, he had the impression that most of those he met among the new students shared the intoxicating feeling of being on the threshold of a new life, a feeling amplified by attending a new university.

Will settled easily into life as a student. The newness and smallness of the university lent an experimental air to student life that he liked to think made it more of an adventure than going to an old university. The students, taught in lectures, small seminar groups and given individual attention through tutorials, felt themselves to be special. Many had been privately educated, but quite a few came from grammar schools and the new comprehensive schools. Once he got to know people, their background mattered less and what counted was how much he liked the individual.

He lived with a York family in digs in his first year. Although he liked the family, he spent as little time as possible with them, heading for the university straight after breakfast every morning, except Sunday when he stayed around long enough for a good lunch.

History was taught at King's Manor, a beautiful stone building in the centre of York. In his first year, Will's visits to the main university campus at Heslington were few. When teaching was over, he spent his time at King's Manor, in the library, the student reading room, the refectory, the junior common room and the bar. Students who had tried for Oxford or Cambridge said that King's Manor was not unlike one of the colleges there and Will felt privileged to be a student in such a distinguished place.

He concentrated as much as possible on the later periods of the history syllabus, which stretched into the twentieth century, although not far enough to encompass the murder of the President of the United States only a few weeks into Will's first term at York. He never forgot the conversation he was having with a politics student who was dismissing the relevance of history on the evening that he heard the news and he cast envious eyes towards the politics course in the ensuing weeks.

Will's own mystery made the Second World War seem more fascinating than it might otherwise have been, but he guessed that discovering his past would not be an acceptable reason for studying history and so he didn't tell his tutors about his wish to do so.

With Vera firmly behind him, Will was free to go out with a number of girls during his first year at York, but he didn't meet anyone he felt he could be serious about. He wanted a girlfriend, but had the idea that it might be better to find out who he was before getting seriously involved with anyone.

After his first year at university, three months of summer vacation yawned ahead. For six weeks, he worked in the timber yard, hauling wood about, saving every penny that he could. Then he took off on his own. He wanted to go somewhere completely different, to satisfy a reckless feeling that he felt building up inside him. He hitch-hiked through France and Spain. Arriving in Algeciras, he boarded a boat for Tangiers and avoiding cities, hitch-hiked on into the Atlas Mountains, where he moved from village to village, learning a few words of Arabic here and there and resorting to school French where necessary.

No one in his life knew where he was. Anything could happen to him and he might never be seen again, but he wanted to pit himself against the world he knew. The village people lived without any advantages of modern, western life. They used donkeys for transport, took their water from a river and cooked in clay ovens with coals for fuel. They were hospitable to the stranger on their doorstep and in return he gave them as much money as he could spare wherever he stayed the night. Will didn't mind what could have seemed like privation. He didn't even mind the complete absence of alcohol, although he had been drinking as heavily as he could afford at York. He arrived back home at the end of September and horrified his parents not only with his adventures, but his plans.

'I've made a decision. I'm not going back to York,' he told them on his first night home.

'Will, what do you mean?' Both parents turned towards him.

'It's irrelevant. I'm going back to Morocco, to help with aid programmes,' Will said. 'There was a school in a village where I was staying. It was empty. The building had been constructed with aid money but there was no equipment, no books and no staff. I might be able to get it going again.'

'But do you have a job there?' his father said.

Will hesitated. 'Not exactly, but I'll find one. Don't worry about me. I'll be all right.'

'Will, this won't do. You're going off the rails,' his mother said.

He looked at them almost pityingly. Nothing they said would persuade him to change his mind, but he did arrange for the university to keep his place open for a year. He was lucky to have a tutor who spoke up for him.

A month later, Will returned to Morocco, supported by a small loan from his parents, once they had recovered from their astonishment at his change of heart. He stayed in Fez for a year, renting a room and teaching English where he found people willing to pay for lessons. He spent some time volunteering in a school where he taught English to boys eager to learn a foreign language. He returned to the abandoned village school he had discovered, taking books and spending time with some of the children, but he was the wrong person to help them because he didn't speak enough Arabic.

He returned to York after a year, ready to tackle the history course again, his wish for relevance satisfied, at least for the present, by his year of work. The death of Winston Churchill in 1965 largely passed him by, but he noticed a sentence in a letter from his mother, who found it hard to believe that the man who had saved Britain from invasion during the war was gone.

One evening, at the beginning of his second year as a student in York, he was in the college bar in Heslington with a friend. He lived in the college now and the bar was an easy distance from his room. The university was being constructed around an artificial lake, with buildings made of reinforced concrete and the presence of water added character to the setting.

A girl he didn't know was sitting near him, talking in a small group. It was a warm evening, although October, and she was wearing a summer dress and lacy green cardigan. Long brown hair fell below her shoulders. Her bright smile appealed to him.

He seized a suitable moment to introduce himself when his friend was caught up with someone else and the small group that included the girl was breaking up. He was sure she must be as new to the university as she was to him.

'Hello, I'm Will. I haven't seen you around before, but I'm sort of new here,' he said. It wasn't an inspired opening, but it was the best he could think of at the time.

'Hello, Will. I'm Anna. Second year English, but I haven't been around much until now,' she said.

Will didn't ask why, thinking that she would explain if she wanted to.

'I'm in the second year as well, doing history. I took a year out last year, but I'm living in Derwent College now.' Will introduced his friend, who had turned inquiringly towards him.

A general discussion sprang up around them, with everyone giving their views about student demonstrations against the university administration and any chance for a personal conversation was lost. During the course of the evening, Will found out that the mysterious Anna was with two other students, girls who were sitting nearby.

Anna was almost his height, he noticed, as they stood up at the end of the evening, and distractingly pretty. He could hardly stop looking at her. He waited to see if she would leave the bar with anyone apart from her two girlfriends and was relieved when he saw them walking away together.

He wanted to meet Anna again, but didn't know how to contact her apart from asking around among people she might know. He preferred not to do that. He was still wondering about it the next day when, by the purest chance, he ran into her in a second hand bookshop near Micklegate Bar, in York.

'Oh, hello, it's you!' he said, noticing her as he entered the shop.

She looked up from the book she was holding and smiled in a conspiratorial manner that Will found irresistible.

'Look at these novels by George Eliot, with green leather spines and marbled covers. They're beautiful, apart from anything else and the complete set is only £5,' she said, pointing at a row of books on a shelf in front of her and showing him the one in her hand.

Will wanted to say that he thought Anna was beautiful, but it would have been a clumsy comparison. He didn't want to disconcert her.

'I've read *Silas Marner*, about a foster child,' he said instead, not quite able to believe his luck in meeting her by chance.

'If I don't eat much this week, I could just about afford them.'

'They'll feed your mind, anyway,' Will said.

She smiled at that and decided to buy the books. They were just what she needed for her special subject. While the shop assistant was parcelling them up, Will suggested a walk around the city walls, offering, as an incentive, to carry the books for her. She accepted.

'So why haven't you been around much? Have you been in hiding?' he asked, giving into his curiosity and stashing the books under one arm as they set out from the bookshop. It was a Saturday afternoon and there were no classes. Despite the pressure of second year exams in the near future, they were enjoying a moment of relative freedom. Will was heady with a sense of excitement in having Anna to himself, especially on the city walls where they would encounter few people. He had no trouble banishing his weekly essay from his mind.

'Oh, yes, of course. I've been in hiding for a year,' she said, laughing. 'No, I had a boyfriend for a long time and we spent most of our time together. I've hardly had a chance to get to know other students. It's a great relief to be free again, especially as he's left York and I don't have to see him around. He's decided to take a year out and come back to finish his degree later.

'Oh, dropping out, like me,' Will said, noticing with relief that Anna wasn't hankering after the boyfriend.

'He's going to do VSO (Voluntary Service Overseas). He should have done it before coming here, but he couldn't go because his mother was ill. Anyway, he's free now.'

She didn't sound at all distressed by the breakup and Will was reassured by her words. He liked her too much to think of losing her now that they had met. He wanted to kiss her more than anything, although the city walls, where other people were out walking as well, were too public, even had the moment been right.

'I've just made the link between you and *Silas Marner*, because one of the girls I was with last night told me that you're adopted,' Anna said. 'Sorry for being slow on the uptake.' She turned to him, smiling again.

'Oh, that's all right. Yes, I suppose that's what drew me to the novel.' He was gratified by her interest and yet tried to sound casual, whilst his mind was spinning. Had she asked her friend about him and did it show she was interested or had the friend merely mentioned what many people in the small university of only a few hundred students knew about him? She didn't change the subject, Will noticed, but asked him what it was like to be adopted.

'It seems normal to me in a way, because it's all I've ever known. Yet it's not normal because it's rare, at least in my experience. I was given to my parents when I was about three months old,' he said.

'It must have been difficult for the mother who gave you away. It sounds as if she loved you, though, or surely she would have given you up straightaway,' Anna said.

'True. It's frustrating not knowing so many of the things that people take for granted, like who my original parents were, for example. I'm going to find out more about it all when I leave here. I can't seem to get on with everything properly as it is,' Will said.

'You mean you can't plan the future if you don't know the past? I don't think all adopted people feel like that. A girl in my class at school was adopted, but I've heard her say she's happy with the family she's got and doesn't want to know where she came from.'

'That's fine, if that's what she wants. It's just that I feel differently. I've got a brother, but he's my parents' natural child, so I'm the odd one out at home,' Will said.

'Don't you feel part of the family then? I'm curious because I come from an ordinary family. Not so ordinary, because my parents are divorced now, but you know what I mean.'

'My parents have always treated my brother Frank and me equally, but in some ways I do feel different from them. It's hard to know whether that's because I'm adopted or whether it might have happened anyway.'

'So did you have a normal childhood, apart from being adopted?'

'Yes, I suppose I did. I used to wish my real mother would come and rescue me if anything went wrong, but that was just a fantasy. I didn't want to leave my family. Frank and I get along well, although we don't have a lot in common, now. He's following in my dad's footsteps and he's become a postman, and I'm here, studying history. Frank and I are going to lead different lives and I'm going to lead a different life from my parents.'

'Yes, but you could be leading the different life from your family if you hadn't been adopted, simply through the chance to go to university,' Anna said.

'True. What sort of family do you have, then?' Will asked.

'My father is an engineer and my mother is a primary school teacher and I have two sisters who are still at school. I grew up with my mother and I live with her in the vacations, but I see my father quite regularly.'

'So you're the eldest?' Will said.

'That's right.'

'Tell me more,' Will said and spent the next half an hour listening to Anna's tales of her family and her schooldays. Her parents had divorced after her mother had discovered that her father was having an affair with a much younger woman, whom he had refused to give up. Then there was Anna's student year in York, a year that she had apparently spent so wrapped up in the now vanished boyfriend that she had been invisible to others around her. It was something to do with her parents separating when she was fourteen. That had made her feel that the world was falling apart and she had clung to the boyfriend on meeting him when she first came to York. She had grown up a bit since then and was enjoying her newfound freedom.

In exchange, Will told her about his year in Morocco. By the time that they finally clambered down from the walls, having walked almost the whole way around the city, he began to think that he might have a chance with Anna. Afterwards, he couldn't stop thinking about her and he dared to ask her out, seeking her out on the following Monday after lectures to do so. It was fortunate that, although he had first seen her at Heslington, her subject, English, was also taught at King's Manor. It made it easier to run into her. He was joyful when she accepted and found it hard to concentrate on his work for the next few days until their date at the weekend.

They went to a restaurant where Will knew his student grant would stretch to a meal, although it was saved from stretching too far by Anna offering to pay her share. Will was relaxed about that. They had chicken in a basket with chips, followed by fruit salad and ice cream and then a drink in a nearby pub. The evening passed in a blur of jokes and laughter laced with serious conversation. Will dared to take Anna's hand as he walked her back to the digs where she was living, before returning to his room in college at Heslington, and she didn't refuse. He kissed her out of sight of her landlady's house to avoid any twitching curtains. The kiss was brief and gentle and she nodded when he suggested meeting the next day at King's Manor.

On the bus going back to the college, he was so excited about Anna that he told himself he was falling in love and any idea of finding out about his past before becoming seriously involved with someone was quite forgotten.

Chapter Four

After their first date, it was understood by Will and Anna and then by others that they were going out together. They both needed to concentrate on exams that year. Will was studying the growth of the British Empire in the nineteenth century and facing formal exams. Anna was reading 19th century fiction, with a special emphasis on George Eliot and had exams in view as well. They set themselves strict hours for working which allowed plenty of time for long conversations about each other and for making love on Will's narrow college bed. Anna grew used to arriving home late, but knew without asking that the family she was living with would not welcome a boyfriend. Will always accompanied Anna back to her digs at night before catching the last bus back to Heslington.

Their conversation on the city walls of York was the first of many that Will and Anna had about his past. Adoption was final, like a locked door. It seemed wrong to Will that he shouldn't be able to answer the ordinary questions about his past that everyone else could answer and his conversations with Anna took the form of rebelling against a key idea in adoption – that he should have no contact with or knowledge of his natural family. Anna suggested that he find out more about adoption in Britain by reading up on it, so that he could see if ideas and practices were changing.

Will burrowed in the social science section of the university library and found out that thousands of babies were adopted every year as he had been, with the expectation that they were starting life afresh. He also learned that the only way he could learn his surname at birth, if he didn't already know it, would be to obtain a copy of his original birth certificate and the only way to do that would be through a court order. He had never had anything to do with courts or lawyers and it all sounded insuperably difficult.

The Church of England Children's Society, as it was now called, which had arranged his adoption, seemed far away when he was living in York. He was busy in London during vacations because he was always working to supplement his grant. He was also absorbed in getting to know Anna better and in studying. It was never the right time to seek out his past.

Will didn't say so to Anna at this early stage, but he wanted to get married and have a family. He longed to be as ordinary as possible, to have children in the normal way, to bring them up; his own children, not adopted, not different in any way from others. Away from his parents, he was beginning to appreciate them, but he wanted to give his children what he had not been able to have for himself, an upbringing by their natural parents.

Anna was a Londoner like Will, but she was better off. Her mother had kept the family home in Islington when her parents separated and Anna, her grant boosted by a generous allowance from her parents, sometimes went home for weekends during term time. Will couldn't afford to do that unless he hitch-hiked, which he found took up too much time to allow for a weekend at home. His parents expected him to manage on his grant and holiday earnings and couldn't afford to give him any extra. Will noticed that Anna was better off than he was, but they both said they didn't care about it. They were in love, which was all that mattered.

When Will thought of asking Anna to marry him, towards the end of their second year at the university, he wondered if she might hesitate to accept. He was adopted and came from nowhere, or nowhere that he knew of. There might be all sorts of traits and diseases in his family background that would give Anna pause for thought and that he knew nothing about. It was one thing to accept him as a boyfriend, but marriage was meant to be for life, even if it hadn't worked out like that for her parents.

Should he wait until he knew more about his past? But what if he never found out? And surely she loved him for himself? She had never suggested that there was anything lacking in him.

A walk around the city walls one day reminded them both of that first walk when they had met by chance in the bookshop. They began to talk about their relationship and then it was easy.

'Anna, I love you so much. Will you marry me?' He took her hand.

'I love you too. Yes, I'll marry you,' she said, with a huge smile and a firm grasp of his hand. 'I want to be with you always.'

Will kissed her then, with growing passion, even though they were so visible on the city walls. Fortunately, it was a blustery June day. Will hoped people were more occupied with hanging on to their hats and scarves than in gazing around them.

Will and Anna's first home together was a tiny flat in York which they rented boldly before their wedding, even though it was generally frowned on for an unmarried couple to live together. They were glad to shrug off the parenting of the university in their undergraduate years. They graduated in 1967 and married the following year, during all the student unrest of May 1968, while staying on for an extra year to train,

Will as a history teacher and Anna an English teacher. The student unrest seemed far away, in London and Paris, although there were echoes in York.

Anna chose to teach English as a second language. People would always want to improve their English and it would be possible to work part-time and fit her work around the family that they both wanted. Will considered teaching history in a secondary school, but was besieged by doubts about it, doubts that, when he examined them, were not particularly about teaching, but more a wish to do something else first. That something else was to find out about his origins. He felt frustrated by the way he was prevented from doing so and unwilling to throw himself into a career until he knew how he had come to be adopted.

Will and Anna wanted to live in London. Both had grown up there and Anna was keen to be near her mother in Islington. Scouring the papers and traipsing the streets looking at flats led them eventually to one in Hackney that they could afford. Will's parents were pleased to see their younger son living not far from their home in Plaistow. They gave Anna a warm welcome as a new member of the family. Her friendly manner immediately put them at their ease.

After the birth of their first baby, Susie, named after Anna's mother, Susan, Will and Anna were propelled out of their flat by a landlady who didn't want children on her premises. With help from Anna's parents, they bought a small terraced house in Hackney. All their meagre savings went into the purchase and all their earnings were swallowed up by the mortgage and everyday expenses.

Part of the reason for the tightness of their budget was that Will wasn't earning much. His doubts about teaching as a career had grown, despite his training, and he was now working in a second-hand bookshop, selling books and learning about the business. He earned less than Anna did.

'Do you think you'll ever get a teaching job, Will?' Anna said one day after the birth of their second daughter, Lizzie, in 1972. It was clear that ends wouldn't meet that month and that they would either have to borrow from her mother or try to extend their overdraft.

Will looked across at her from the newspaper he had escaped to when Anna started looking at their bank statement. 'I don't know. I'm not ready for teaching. If it comes to it, I'll get a second job, working in the evenings.'

'Oh no! You'd never be at home. You'd earn more as a teacher and only need one job.'

'Everyone expects me to behave in a certain way, even though I'm not allowed to know the truth about my past,' he said. In the last few years, he had decided that he wasn't prepared to follow the expected career path if he couldn't find out about his origins. He felt as if he were arguing all the time with the people in government who had decided that he shouldn't know. He felt a kind of sulkiness about it and was taking a stand. He dismissed any thought of contacting the Church of England Children's Society because his reading about adoption had made it clear that the records of adoption societies were confidential.

Anna sighed. Will and Anna had both wanted children and had both been euphoric about the birth of Susie and Lizzie. Will didn't know if this feeling for his daughters was anything to do with being adopted. His children gave him blood relatives for the first time in his life, but Anna had been just as pleased as Will by their birth.

Blood relatives were special. His desire to seek out his original parents was the stronger since he had become a father. Will had found himself looking first at Susie and later at Lizzie for any resemblance to himself. He had to admit that it was hard to compare his large face, its biggish nose, firm black eyebrows and wide mouth with the smooth, chubby faces of his little daughters. Anna laughed when his only finding lay in Susie's brown eyes, while Lizzie shared her green.

He didn't know whether either of his daughters would later on bear any further resemblance to him or not; in one way, he hoped not, for their sakes, as he joked to Anna, because he wanted them to inherit her looks. Before long, he stopped wondering about it. Each little girl was herself.

Approaching thirty, Will was a tall young man with dark curly hair and a kindly face rescued from plainness by a rueful smile which suggested life was not quite as he wanted it to be. His parents had told him not to look over his shoulder, because there was nothing to see. He belonged to them and that was all that mattered. Will had accepted their advice because there was no choice, but when he discovered that adopted people in Scotland were allowed to have information about their origins, he had begun to wish that England would follow suit.

Anna's long, brown hair still framed the lively face that had attracted Will the first time he had met her and ever since, with its clear skin, straight nose and scarcely crooked smile. Will was happier with Anna than he had ever been in his life. Like their children, she made him feel that he belonged to the world in which they lived; that he had a future, if not the past that most people took for granted. In a way, the past troubled him less after meeting Anna than it had done before. What did his family of origin, his ancestors or his heritage matter if he could be with her? She made everything seem all right, so that even difficulties melted away or became manageable. Her presence in his life had subdued the streak of recklessness that he thought might be related to being adopted. He had never felt such passion and such love, never felt so complete, so special and so normal. Yet, despite all that, he couldn't let go of the wish to know about the past. It nagged at him, as it had done since he had been a teenager.

The dining room where Anna and Will were sitting over

their meal one evening was sparsely furnished and the walls had received no more than a hurried coat of white paint to cover florid wallpaper and make the room seem bigger and lighter. Theirs was a quiet street and the sound of traffic didn't often penetrate the house, but now they could hear a squeal of brakes from the main road nearby.

Anna, skilled in the swift production of tasty suppers, had made a pasta dish with bacon and tomatoes. Will, a new man and a supporter of the feminism enlivening 1970s London, had added a green salad. He waited for the mealtime, when the girls were in bed, so that he and Anna could talk uninterruptedly, before he told her about a discovery he had made that day. The sound of Keith Jarrett's piano, Will's latest musical find, floated through their conversation.

They were looking glum because they were yet again in difficulties over money, difficulties which Anna was sure they could avoid if Will would take a job that matched his talents and qualifications. The economic squeeze which began in 1974 wasn't directly the cause of their troubles, but Anna liked to say that there was a squeeze going on with their own finances.

'It's not working,' Anna was saying with mounting frustration. 'We're only in the second week of the month and we're already overdrawn. We can't live like this, Will. I'm thinking of taking the girls to stay with my mother for a while until you sort something out.'

'You're not leaving me?' He laughed, because she must have been joking.

'No, of course not. I'm just trying to think of ways of saving money. Something's got to give. We can't carry on as we are because we can't afford it. I wish you would get a teaching job. You could earn so much more and life would be easier for us. Or perhaps you should give up work altogether and look after the girls so I could work full-time, although I don't think that would bring in enough.'

Will ignored Anna's plea about earning more. He would deal with that later because there was something else he wanted to talk about.

'I saw a newspaper article today. There's going to be a change in adoption law. It's been on the cards for some time, but the government have now agreed it. It will mean I can find out my original name and even perhaps meet the family. At last I can find out why I was adopted and who I am!' He ended on a teasing note. Both of them were perfectly aware that, in most if not all senses, he knew who he was.

'You're just changing the subject, Will.' Anna relented and added, 'Well, perhaps it will help you to find out, because you certainly want to know.'

'It's partly because of Susie and Lizzie. Imagine their questions, as they grow up, just as I questioned my parents. I don't want to have to say what Mum and Dad said to me, that they knew almost nothing.'

'I suppose not.' Anna had finished eating and was looking at Will, one elbow on the table and her chin propped on her hand.

Always alert to Anna's tone as well as her words, Will detected a reservation. He ploughed on in the hope of persuading her to agree with him.

'I wasn't unhappy as a child…'

'I know, but I don't think Susie and Lizzie will be that curious. Their grandparents are the people they know – my parents and yours. That's what will matter to them. Of course, you want to know more about your background, but now it's a real possibility, I'm not so sure,' she said.

'What do you mean?'

'Aren't you just complicating things? Do you really need another family? I know you've been wondering whether your original mother might be afraid of hearing from you, but look at it from the other point of view. Suppose she makes demands on you that you don't want or doesn't want anything to do with you? You don't know what you might be getting into.'

Will laughed. 'Well, I hope I didn't come from a den of monsters. I'm not looking for another family in the same way – they'd never replace my parents. It's about satisfying my curiosity more than anything. I don't think there's anything to be afraid of. If I don't like them, then I'll keep my distance, I promise you, Anna.'

Will assumed that his original mother had kept him for three months before giving him away because she had wanted to keep him. Circumstances must have forced her to give him up. It was that knowledge as much as anything that lay behind his wish to search for her.

'Some bits of the jigsaw puzzle are missing. I want to see if I resemble that original mother and I want to know who my father was. I don't think it means I love my family any the less.'

'I can see you might wonder about some kind of illness or condition, but apart from that, I'm not sure it's necessary. After all, you already have a perfectly good family, better than many and you don't want to upset them,' Anna said.

Will was silent for a moment and she continued.

'Blood isn't everything. It's almost as if you think your original mother made a mistake in having you adopted, but maybe she didn't. Maybe she couldn't keep you. Besides, the person you are now is partly a product of your upbringing. If you'd grown up with your birth family, you'd be different. You can't turn the clock back, you know.'

Will caught her hand and squeezed it and was about to follow that up with a kiss when they heard a cry from upstairs. Anna moved towards the door which they had left ajar in order to hear any sound from above.

'I'll go. It's Lizzie,' she said.

'Thanks for the meal. I'll clear up,' Will said, collecting plates and making for the kitchen.

Will knew from their many conversations about it that, on the whole, Anna supported his wish to seek out his original family. The people he had to move carefully with were his parents.

Chapter Five

Will's parents had never encouraged his questions about where he came from, partly because they had little to say, but also, he had long since recognised, because they feared losing him, or at least, his mother feared that. They had told him he was adopted and had been sensitive enough to realise that he needed to talk about it at different ages, but he knew that they wouldn't welcome his plan. They had lost him in a sense already, because he had long since left home, but the loss his mother feared was different. It was the loss to another woman of her place in his life as his mother.

He was determined to search for his original family and he didn't want to do it in secret. The best approach was to talk to his parents about it from the beginning and give them time to get used to the idea. He visited them with Anna and the girls one weekend afternoon after his discussion with Anna about the new law. His mother saw the children regularly, because she looked after them while Anna was at work, but his father had been complaining he hadn't seen his granddaughters lately and the visit was to make up for that. Frank, who still lived with their parents, was there as well.

The sitting room of the house where Will had grown up, with its battered but comfortable furniture, looked much as it had always done. An old sofa leaned against one wall, flanked by easy chairs. A fire in the grate was intended to combat a chilly afternoon. Will's parents had been talking about central heating, but they had not yet been able to afford it.

Will told his parents about the proposed change in the law and showed them a copy of a newspaper article while his father gave horseback rides to the girls.

Will's mother put down her knitting to take the article and wrinkled her brow.

'Yes, I know about this. I read an article in my magazine. So you want to find your… mother, I suppose you'd call her, but she's not your mother, is she? That's all wrong. Adoption is for life, Will. You're not meant to go around undoing it.'

His mother's face was disapproving and she handed the article on to his father, after a brief glance which showed Will yet again what he had known for years. She was reluctant to talk about the subject at all. He occasionally wondered if his parents were hiding something from him. Was there a secret about his background which they had always kept from him? Supposing his real mother had been a convicted murderer or his real father a traitor during the war? His father, never much of a reader, did little more than scan the headline of the article that Will was showing them before handing the newspaper back.

'I'm not undoing it. You're my mother and you always will be. You brought me up and I couldn't have wished for better parents,' Will said patiently.

'I could,' Frank said. He was reading a newspaper in a corner of the sitting room, half-listening to the conversation. His smile gave him away and Joe, releasing Lizzie from the horseride, threw a cushion at him. Frank wasn't interested in the conversation and returned to the football pages of the paper he was reading.

'Well, then, why do you want to go turning things over like that and upsetting everyone?' his mother said. She had picked up her knitting, but was dropping stitches and Will, although he knew nothing about knitting, thought the needles looked more agitated than usual.

'Because I want to know why she gave me away, oh, and little things that everyone else knows, like what time I was born and how much I weighed. And then there's what she's like and what sort of family she comes from. And I would like to meet her.'

Will didn't identify *her*. He couldn't use a name when he didn't know it and the word *mother* was, he knew from his mother's hesitation in using it of someone else, fraught with danger. He may have left home, but he was still one of her boys.

'Well, I can see it's got under your skin and you're going to keep worrying away at it, but you'd better be careful. You don't know what you're taking on,' his mother said. The needles were clacking away again and she seemed to have accepted that she wouldn't deter her son.

'You sound just like Anna. Are you two in league with each other? Anyway, it isn't going to happen tomorrow, Mum. The law hasn't gone through Parliament yet, but it looks as if it will get support,' Will said.

The conversation moved on to more immediate things – Susie's nursery school and Lizzie's first steps – but for all Will's declarations about how good his parents had been, he could see that his mother in particular was uneasy. He wasn't sorry about that because it showed she cared.

He knew his father cared too, but Joe was more easy-going about it. He was a naturally home-loving man, although fond of a pint at his local, who had never ceased to be glad of the peace that had followed the war of his youth. He disliked conflict and was always the first to make a joke to ease any tension. He wouldn't stand in the way of Will's enquiries or make things difficult for him.

Will could only hope that his mother would be able to

quash her reservations. He wasn't about to give in to her reluctance. After years of being kept in the dark, he wasn't going to turn away now that it was becoming possible to find out more.

Will was alert to the changes in adoption law. Adopted adults would be allowed to obtain a copy of their original birth certificate and possibly make contact with their birth families. He followed the debate in Parliament as well as he could by reading newspapers and magazines. He noticed dramatic newspaper headlines. The *News of the World* thundered *Mums in fear of knock at the door.* The *Daily Mirror* ran with *Haunted by the past* and *the Daily Telegraph* came up with *Fears of emotional upsets over 'reveal all' Adoption Law*.

'There's some fear that adopted people will be vindictive or harass their original parents. It seems unlikely to me. All I want to know is why I was adopted and to meet the family.' Will was telling Anna about the newspaper headlines, one evening after work. He had arrived home to find his family in the kitchen making peanut butter biscuits.

Anna had not gone to stay with her mother because Will was applying for teaching jobs. Her threat to leave had impressed him with the seriousness of her worry about whether they could manage on their income, but that wasn't all. Something had shifted in him with the news of the change in adoption law and he felt more willing to tackle challenges now that he would be able to find out about his past.

'Do you think your original mother fears a knock at the door or is haunted by her past?' Anna was showing Susie how to press down plastic shapes into the dough to cut the biscuits out and her voice tailed off as she concentrated on her task.

'I don't know. It's possible, I suppose. I don't really know anything about her, so I'm working in the dark here. I just can't imagine how she could have given me up. I could never give up the girls.' Will was gazing fondly at his daughters and hoping after he spoke that neither of them had understood what he said. Fortunately there was no competition. The peanut butter biscuits were about to go into the oven and all eyes were on them.

Will had to wait for the new adoption law to come into force. He took far less notice of the referendum on EEC membership in June 1975 or even of the end of the Vietnam War that same year. He was impatient to get on with the search for his original mother, but there was no way of doing so straightaway. Weeks and then months passed, giving Will and Anna plenty of time for further conversations about his quest and about his new job, beginning in September 1975, as a history teacher in a comprehensive school nearby.

Will had already been teaching for over a year when the new law came into effect. At home, one evening in November 1976, he told Anna that he would now be able to apply to see his original birth certificate. He had been reading the girls a story, which Susie had been pleading for ever since his arrival from work.

'Oh, so it's happening at last,' Anna said. 'Are you sure you want to go ahead?'

'Yes, why not?'

Anna was chopping onions for their evening meal and she gave him a glance which he could only think was uncertain.

'I don't know. I mean, I'm sure it'll be all right. In a way, I'm as curious as you are, but at the same time, I have a sort of... I don't know what to call it... a foreboding.'

'Oh, Anna! That's not like you. I thought I was the cautious one. And foreboding is an old-fashioned word. You've been reading too many Victorian novels,' Will said. He was feeling cheerful, because things were going his way at last. The door to the past was going to open and his curiosity would be satisfied. He wanted Anna to share his optimism.

'No, it's not that. It's just that I hope I'm not about to

lose the Will I know and find another one has taken his place,' Anna said.

Will didn't share Anna's doubts. 'I shall always be the Will you know,' he said. 'Don't worry about it. We'll go into this together and we'll talk about it as it goes along.' His tone was breezy. He put down the story book that he had been holding. Susie had been happy with the story and hadn't yet asked for it to be read again, but was now absorbed in playing with a favourite doll. He took Lizzie onto his lap, where she snuggled up against him.

Anna didn't push her point. Will knew she didn't want to quash his curiosity and that neither of them were sure of what they might encounter as he made his enquiries, so there wasn't a great deal more to say.

He mulled over Anna's words that evening. Would the search for his past change him in some irrevocable way? But why not? Life changed people all the time, surely all the way through. And any change might be to his benefit; if not, as he remembered once saying to Anna, he would keep his distance. No harm would be done. Surely his new knowledge could only add a dimension to what he already was? It couldn't change his character, which had been formed by his upbringing with his parents and Frank. If he discovered that his original mother was a convicted criminal and his father an alcoholic, for example, it wouldn't be welcome news, but he wouldn't be diminished in any way.

In his childhood, he had absorbed a narrative from his parents about their families. As well as his parents, he had been given grandparents, aunts and uncles, cousins and his brother Frank to provide the forest of which he was a single tree. There were stories associated with everyone, characteristics, a reputation for being like this or doing that. All the trees in that forest formed his family. He knew now that he wasn't an outsider. He belonged to the family of his childhood and there was now his own immediate family of Anna and their daughters. He wasn't looking for another family. He simply wanted to know what the other trees, the main ones, were like in that other forest, the forest of his original mother and father.

Yet he was glad that Anna had questioned the wisdom of searching for his original parents. It had made him think and helped to prepare him for what he might learn. His original mother would not be the angel of his teenage dreams, but a middle-aged, even elderly woman. He might or might not like her.

Will applied to the Office of the Registrar General in Hampshire in search of his original birth certificate. He knew that the new law required him to see a counsellor first and he chose to go to their central London office. He had to wait a few weeks for the interview, but was given an appointment after school one day, with a Mrs Bradstreet. Will telephoned to confirm the appointment and went along to the interview, rehearsing on the way what he was going to say. He took his adoption birth certificate and some exam certificates with him as proof of his identity.

It was a wet December day, but Will was not deterred by the weather. He was too bent on the job of tracking down his past. A thin drizzle dampened his coat as he walked along to the appointment and he was glad of his scarf.

He found the office without difficulty and sat down in the reception area, after giving his name. He was not kept waiting long before Mrs Bradstreet came into the reception area and introduced herself. She was a middle-aged woman, with neat, brown curls and a comfortable manner.

The office where the interview took place was small, its walls lined with books and files. A desk stood in front of a window, but Mrs Bradstreet sat next to Will, against one wall of the room.

'Let me say, first of all, that you're entitled to the

information I'm about to give you and so this interview is not a test,' she said.

Will relaxed, shrugged off a certain tension. He had not been sure whether Mrs Bradstreet might be able to decide he wasn't a suitable candidate for the information he was seeking. His search was taking its toll of him.

'What do you know about your adoption, Will?' she said.

Will told her that his birth mother had named him William, that he had lived with her until he was three months old and then gone to his adoptive family. All he had from his birth mother was a tiny silver heart on a blue ribbon, but he assumed it was a token of her love. He knew nothing else about her. His parents had told him about the adoption when he was old enough to understand it, but they had scarcely talked about it since. He produced the evidence of his identity.

'Thank you, Will,' Mrs Bradstreet said as he finished. She looked briefly at his papers, satisfied that he was who he claimed to be. 'You were a war baby and I'm sure you understand that records of Second World War adoptions are patchy. I can tell you that your birth was registered in the name of William Haldon and your mother was Florence Haldon. Here is the information we have obtained.'

She picked up a sheet of paper from her desk and handed it to Will. His hand trembled as he took it from her. Had he made a mistake? Was it better to allow a mystery in his life, with all its cherished possibilities for fantasy and daydreaming than exchange it for the cold certainty of what might be unwelcome knowledge? Yet it was too late for second thoughts. Even as he hesitated, he began to read.

Then he glanced up at Mrs Bradstreet, puzzled. 'There's nothing about my birth father.'

'If your parents were married, your father will be on your original birth certificate.'

Will stared at the sheet of information again. His parents

had told him that the name William had been chosen by the woman he could now call Florence. They had liked it and let him keep it, adding his second name of Joseph after his father. Even so, seeing the name William made Will feel an odd closeness to the mother he had only known as a new born baby, closeness that he had never felt as a teenager when he had dreamed of an angel who would come and sweep him up in her arms to bear him away.

'I've always wanted to meet her, to meet… Florence,' he said, pronouncing her name for the first time. 'I hope it will be possible.'

'I hope so, too,' she said. 'First of all, you might want to apply for a copy of your original birth certificate. You can then search the public records. Florence may have married and be living under another name, so it will be important to check that.'

'Yes, of course.'

'You'll need to find where she's living now, either from a phone book or electoral records because it's unlikely that she'll still be where she was at the time of your birth. Once you know her address, you may want to ask an intermediary to contact her, rather than doing it yourself directly. I could help, or the agency which placed you for adoption. You see, she will have been told that she would never hear from you and although she may know about the change in the law, it may be easier for her.'

'Oh, yes. I wouldn't want to upset her.'

Will thanked Mrs Bradstreet and left her office, the sheet of information placed securely in his briefcase with his certificates, but his mind in a whirl. He had taken a big step forward, but there was still much to do and he had the strange feeling that Florence receded into the distance as he reached out for her. Knowing her name allowed him to start on the next stage of his quest and it was obvious that finding her might be difficult.

Chapter Six

'At last I know her name,' Will said to Anna that evening, after greeting her and the girls. Anna didn't need to ask who he was talking about.

'It matters more than learning my original surname,' he said after he had given Anna his news. 'I've got a surname already and don't need another one, but what I haven't had until now is a name for my birth mother and now I know she's called Florence.'

'It's a pretty name. It means flowering. It's the name of a city and of course there was Florence Nightingale, which is why it was popular as a girl's name,' Anna said. Her sense of foreboding had given way to curiosity now that Will was discovering his past.

'I'll think of her as Florence now, especially as the word mother means Marion to me,' he said.

He sent off to the Registrar General's Office for a copy of his birth certificate straightaway and received it just before the end of the autumn term. Unfolding the form in the kitchen after work one day, he saw at once that his birth had been registered in Plaistow where he had grown up. There was an address in Plaistow, where Florence had been living at the time of his birth. He recognised the name of a street about a quarter of a mile away from his parents' home.

'Look at this,' he said, showing his birth certificate to Anna. 'Florence might even have been living nearby when I was growing up. I might have seen her often on the street.'

'Or did she see you and wonder if here was the baby boy she had given away?' Anna said, joining in the fantasy.

Knowing her name and that she had once lived near him brought her closer, but it wasn't enough. He felt a great thirst for more than just her name and the other information on the birth certificate. A name on its own didn't mean a great deal. He wanted to meet her, to give the name meaning and to find out why he had been adopted.

There was nothing on his birth certificate about his father. He thought back to the interview with Mrs Bradstreet. It meant that his parents hadn't been married. It wasn't surprising because it was more likely that an unmarried mother would have given up a baby for adoption.

In the days that followed and despite all the bustle and excitement of Christmas, he couldn't stop thinking about the address on the birth certificate. He was too busy to do anything about it immediately, but one icy afternoon between Christmas and New Year, he stood outside Plaistow Station. He was on his way to see his parents, while Anna had taken the girls to a birthday party. He had read Florence's address so many times that he knew it by heart and felt that he would never forget it. It would be easy to make a detour of half a mile on his way to his parents' house. He had roamed the streets of Plaistow extensively as a boy and he was pretty certain that he knew the way to the street where Florence had been living then.

He also remembered Mrs Bradstreet's suggestion about an intermediary to pave the way to Florence and knew that he shouldn't try to find her by dropping in at her home. She had a right to refuse to see him and a right to live without being pestered. On the other hand, she was most unlikely to be still living there after such a long time. This address must have been where she used to live and where he would have spent those first months of his life with her, the three months before she gave him up. It wouldn't be pestering just to go and look at the house.

His feet turned in that direction, even as he was debating the idea. Ten minutes of brisk walking took him to a street which had obviously been bombed in the war, judging by gaps filled with more recent housing. He found the street number, twenty-six, and looked at the house from the other side of the street in order to see it as a whole. As a typical Victorian terraced house, it could have been attractive, but it was down at heel, with peeling paint. One small window pane was missing and someone had blocked the gap with an ill-fitting piece of hardboard. He crossed the road to stand directly in front of the house and told himself that he wouldn't knock at the door.

Instead, he moved a few paces to stand in front of the newer house next door. It was a postwar house and there had clearly been a bomb on the street. He moved back to number twenty-six and saw a curtain in one of the windows twitch. Someone was in and watching him. Will's right hand had found the door knocker and given a double knock before he remembered his decision not to do so. He waited and then heard footsteps in the hall. His heart was beating faster. Despite his assumption that she would have moved years ago, was he about to meet his birth mother?

A woman opened the door. She was in her fifties, he thought, so she could have been Florence. Immediately he began to hope that she wasn't, because her face looked hard and dissatisfied and her eyes were unfriendly. Straggly hair had escaped from an attempt to tie it back. She was wearing a print dress with stains down the front. Her shoes were battered. She looked poor and unhappy.

'Excuse me,' Will said. He found it hard to speak, but he had to say something. 'I'm looking for Florence Haldon. I know she lived here during the war...'

His voice tailed off as the woman spoke.

'You've got the wrong address. There's no one of that name here.'

'Oh, so you've never heard of the Haldons?' Will said.

'No. I've lived here for ten years and the people before us were called Craig or something like that.'

Her manner was cold and matter of fact and she was clearly not interested in his inquiry. She brought a hand out from behind her back and Will saw she was smoking. She closed her eyes as she dragged on her cigarette, dismissing him and his questions.

'Sorry to have bothered you,' he said, backing away. The door had closed almost before he had turned to walk back down the street.

So he had been right. Florence had moved away years ago. She hadn't been called Craig, but that could have been the name of later residents. After all, over thirty years had passed since Florence had given number twenty-six on that street as her address on his birth certificate. Walking back down the street, Will was relieved that the woman who had answered the door of number twenty-six to him wasn't Florence. He wanted his birth mother to be likeable and he would have struggled to like that woman.

Will was unable to pursue his quest any further until the new year. Fortunately a day remained before the start of term when he was free to search the public records. It was not long before he found that a Florence Haldon, of an address in Plaistow different from the one that he knew, but not far from it, had married a George Cruise, also of an address in Plaistow. He thought it likely that she was his Florence and now that he knew her married name, he was in a position to try and find her.

The easiest place to begin was the London telephone

directory. Florence may have left London, but he would start by assuming she had stayed, because she had married a local man. Coming home from the Public Record Office, he sat down in the sitting room with the fat volume that covered the whole of London and looked up the surname Cruise. There was a daunting number of them, but only one Cruise G, who lived not in Plaistow, but on the other side of London, in Putney.

'People move around London all the time. It could be Florence's address, but I'm not sure,' Will said to Anna. 'I'm going to check the electoral roll for that street in Putney, because it may give first names.'

He wrote straightaway to the Electoral Registration Office that covered Putney and then there was nothing further he could do about his search for the moment. He plunged into the start of the spring term at school. It was two weeks before he received a reply to his letter, but it told him what he wanted to know. The entry for the address in the phone book he was enquiring about was for George and Florence Cruise.

Rather than ask Mrs Bradstreet to act as an intermediary, Will decided to write to the Church of England Children's Society, which had arranged his adoption. Contacting them could serve two purposes. They could act as an intermediary with Florence and might well have other information about him, dating from the time of his adoption. He found the current address in the telephone directory and took time over writing the letter because he knew enough about the emphasis on secrecy in adoption to fear they would refuse to help an adopted person seeking information about his past.

1st March 1978

Dear Sir/Madam,

I was adopted through your agency on 24th July 1945 and grew up with Marion and Joe Tyler, whom I regard as my parents. I was placed with them on 17th April 1945 at the age of three months.

Under the new adoption legislation, I have obtained a copy of my original birth certificate and wish to contact my original mother, Florence Haldon. I am hoping you will be able to help me contact her.

I should like to come and see someone in your agency, preferably late one afternoon.

I look forward to hearing from you.

Yours sincerely,

Will Tyler

He was pleased to receive a reply giving him an appointment after school one day and asking him to bring his birth certificate as proof of his identity.

'Another interview with a social worker,' he said to Anna, with his rueful grin, on the morning of the appointment, although he wasn't complaining.

Later that day, reaching the offices of the Church of England Children's Society, armed with both his original and his adoption birth certificates, Will was shown into a waiting room. The walls were covered with posters about adoption and fostering. A few moments later, a brisk young social worker introduced herself as Paula Heron and took him to an interview room. Her short hair and glasses conveyed a sense of purpose, but she listened calmly and without interruption to what Will had to say.

Will went over the contents of his letter – which said that the agency had placed him for adoption over thirty years previously and that he wished to see his birth mother, under the new provisions. He explained that his parents had given him a good upbringing and that all he was trying to do was satisfy his curiosity about his past.

After examining Will's birth certificate, Paula Heron nodded. 'Our policy used to be never to tell adopted people about their birth family, but since adoption law has changed, we've decided that we can be more helpful than that. I've dug out your records, but I don't think we can tell you anything more about your birth mother that you don't already know. I can tell you that your birth weight was 7 lbs and that you were a healthy baby, placed with your adoptive parents at the age of three months.'

'Can you help me contact my birth mother?' Will gave Paula Heron the address that he had found and explained how he had come to it. She agreed that the Florence Cruise in Putney could be the one he was seeking and that it was worth a letter.

'I don't want her to be upset, though,' he said.

'It will be a careful letter, as she may not have told her husband about you. It will simply say that someone who may be connected to her family has contacted me and invite her to write to me or telephone. If she wants to see you, she'll get in touch.'

'Thank you. That would be helpful. Now, I've been wondering about my father. I know nothing about him at all, not even a name.'

'We do have some information. He was Sergeant William Martin of 743 Squadron in the RAF and was from Epsom, in Surrey. Your birth mother told us at the time that he was killed in France in September 1944. It says here that she wanted that information passed on to your adoptive family.'

'Killed in France!' William repeated her words, even as he felt that a gate had slammed shut across his path. 'So he died during the war. I used to think of him as a war hero and I remember even telling my friends that he was killed in the war, so I wasn't far wrong. And I had no idea about it, so either your people didn't tell my parents, or… or my parents didn't tell me. But why wouldn't they?'

He was silent for a moment, thinking of the father he had

never known. It was a loss of a kind, because he had been hoping that he might be able to meet him. Even though he couldn't feel grief for someone he had never met, Florence's refusal to see him had increased his wish to meet his father, a wish that could now never be granted.

'I don't know what happened there,' Paula Heron said. 'Either your parents didn't want you to know, or our social worker at the time didn't pass the information on.'

'I'll ask my parents about it. So I was called William after him. I've often wondered about that. You see, my adoptive parents kept the name I was given at birth,' Will said, brushing aside his reaction to the news of the death of his father. He would deal with it later.

He relayed this conversation to Anna when he arrived home later that evening.

'At last I'm getting there. Of course Florence will have had problems and I don't expect her to be any kind of angel, but I'm pretty sure she'll want to see me.'

'She might *want* to see you, because what mother wouldn't want to see a son, but whether she will *agree* to see you is a different matter. Think of it from her point of view. She might have had a family who knows nothing about you,' Anna said.

'True. And I can't help wondering if there might be something extraordinary in my background, some terrible conflict or deeply buried secret behind the adoption, so I suppose you could be right,' Will said, his spirits dampened by Anna's warning. 'It's strange, isn't it, how *mother* is the person nearly everyone else, you, for example, knows so well and yet is the person I know least, in fact, not at all.'

'You know Marion. She's your real mother,' Anna said.

'You're right, Anna.' Will scratched his head. 'Oh dear. Sometimes I wish I could be free of all this, but I can't seem to leave it alone. I wonder if I haven't quite grown up or whether some vital element is missing in my make-up.'

'All that's missing is some knowledge about your past, but you're working on that, silly man,' Anna said, pulling Will towards her to hug him, while Susie and Lizzie fought to be included.

He found it hard to concentrate at school and each day he came home hoping to see a letter from Paula Heron lying on the kitchen table. The post always came after he left for work in the morning. Yet, day after day, nothing but bills, or the occasional personal letter unconnected with adoption, was waiting for him. Anna often had to repeat what she said to Will because he was miles away. Only Susie and Lizzie seemed able to command Will's full attention at home while he was waiting for Florence's reply.

- Part Three -

Flo

1945-1977

Chapter One

On a Saturday morning in late June 1945, Flo ran into her old school friend, Carol, on Plaistow High Street. Carol, now married, but with no children, invited Flo to come to her mother's teashop one evening the following week after work.

A few days later, pushing open the door to the teashop where she had worked as a schoolgirl, Flo saw that little had changed in the ten years since then, except that it was all more worn. Her eyes took in green lino, the wooden chairs and tables, the long counter stacked with cakes and buns. Carol's mother stood behind the counter, older, but still the same woman who had welcomed Flossie in plaster after she had broken her wrist. People were talking and laughing, and Flo came in to the scream of a boiling kettle.

After giving William away, Flo had gone back to Selfridges, the department store where she had worked before the war. She was shocked at the destruction of Oxford Street, but Selfridges had survived the bombing and it was heartening to see the efforts being made by the shops to return to a state of normality. With the help of her old boss, Mr Meakins, she had found a job as a secretary to a senior executive.

In the tea shop, Carol brought Flo over to the counter to say hello to her mother, who remembered the schoolgirl doing a Saturday job before the war. She poured Flo and Carol a cup of tea each from a big enamel pot sitting by the gas stove and put two iced buns on a plate, on the house, to welcome Flo back. Flo was always hungry after work and her eyes lit up to see the buns.

There was no queue, so no need for Carol to help serve the customers. Instead the young women sat at a table in the window, moving a full ashtray aside, enjoying the tea and buns and talking about their families. Carol's elder brother Joey, an air crew gunner, had been killed in a dog fight over Germany during the war. Flo had lost her mother and her sister was ill.

'Mum had time to spare, once the three of us were at school. She went out to work to help make ends meet, but there's more to it than that. She enjoys the company and now we've lost Joey, it helps to take her mind off him,' Carol said.

'Yes, going out to work takes my mind off Mum and Rosie,' Flo said.

'No young man then, Flo?' Carol was curious. 'You didn't meet anyone during the war?'

Flo hesitated. 'Not to write home about,' she said. It was literally true. She had always kept their wedding plans secret, as Bill had asked her to, and this had extended to not writing to her parents about Bill. She feared for a moment that Carol might have heard about her pregnancy. However, nothing in Carol's manner suggested that Flo was keeping anything from her.

While they were talking, Flo saw a smart young man come in, like a businessman, she thought, looking idly at him. He stood out from the other customers because he was neat, with shining glasses and hair kept in place by what looked like Brylcreem.

'It's my other brother, George,' Carol said, seeing Flo's gaze. The young man came over to their table and Carol introduced Flo as an old school friend.

'I remember you,' Flo said, looking at the thin, regular features of his pale face not greatly changed by the war years and thinking that he, as an older boy then, might not remember her as Carol's friend. She was wrong.

'You're the girl with the broken arm,' George said, his face lighting up. 'I signed your plaster. You used to come here sometimes after school and then you had a Saturday job here.' He smiled at her.

'It's nice to be remembered.' Flo returned the smile.

George disappeared to fetch more tea. In a few minutes, he came back with a loaded tray. He offered more buns round and then they were busy eating. He swallowed his last mouthful before he spoke. Flo thought he looked nervous, but then she saw that, in Carol's company, he smiled easily.

'I was starving! Do you know what happened today? I lost a sandwich to a goose in St James's Park.'

'Were you in a daydream or what?' Carol said.

'No. Well maybe I was looking at some girls walking past. I was sitting on the grass with a friend from the office, about to take a bite, and the goose came up and took the sandwich out of my hand and ran off.'

George acted out the story and made Carol and Flo laugh.

'Serves you right for looking at girls.' Carol gave him a playful punch on the arm.

Flo felt at ease with George. His nervous manner gave her confidence, although he was a couple of years older than she was. Without asking, she learned that he was a government clerk in the War Office. He had matriculated at sixteen like Flo and gone into the Civil Service straight from school. At eighteen, he had spent a year doing National Service. He had been in the army during the war, but poor eyesight had meant that he had not seen much action. He had recently been demobbed.

'I work in Westminster, only a short bus ride from where

you are in Oxford Street,' he said in answer to a question from Flo.

'It's another world to me. I've never been there.' Flo was aware of how little she knew her own city, an ignorance not helped by her years away during the war.

George was dressed like a civil servant, in a pin-striped suit, stiff collar, tie and polished shoes. He had thrown an umbrella and briefcase on an empty chair beside him before he sat down. His government job gave him an air of importance, but his manner was modest.

'I'm just a junior in the office, near the bottom of the heap,' he said.

Flo was impressed nonetheless and glad that he didn't talk about the war.

'So what do you do?' she asked.

'I work in an office which deals with food for the troops. It means choosing the best company to supply each kind of food, say biscuits or bully beef, usually the company that offers the lowest price, under contract. Even though the war is over, there's still plenty for those left in uniform to do, especially in Germany, and the troops always need feeding.'

On her way home from the teashop and in the days to follow, Flo found herself wanting to see George again. It was a calm, determined wish, lacking the excitement she had felt about Bill. It was over a year since she had last seen Bill and six months since she had learned of his death. She felt ready to leave him to the past. She wasn't quite sure what to do next, though, because she sensed that George wouldn't welcome a first move from her.

Just when Flo was about to send a postcard to Carol to suggest meeting again, she saw her on the street. Flo couldn't resist bringing the conversation round to George.

'Your brother's quite a tease, but he seems fond of you,' she said to Carol.

'Oh, yes, he's good fun. A bit shy of girls, though. You seemed to bring him out of himself. Come to the teashop again – why not Tuesday?'

It became a habit to visit the teashop once a week after work when Carol was there and Flo grew used to running into George. When she missed a week because she was off sick from work with flu, George asked Carol where she was and enquired solicitously after her health the next time he saw her. Flo was quite recovered and said so, charmed by his concern. When he asked if she was well enough to go to the cinema at the weekend, she found that she was indeed.

In the cinema, halfway through a showing of *Casablanca*, starring Humphrey Bogart and Ingrid Bergman, George reached for Flo's hand and she let him hold it. Later, he leaned towards her and they kissed. It was gentle, lacking the passion of kisses with Bill, but Flo was not deterred.

Rosie didn't come home. She died in the summer of 1945, when she was twenty-one. Flo visited her every week and then more often until the end, telling her about the world outside, trying to entertain her favourite sister even though her own life seemed quite the opposite of entertaining. She and her family were grief-stricken by Rosie's death. Alf had lost a daughter as well as his wife and Flo and her brothers and sisters had lost a sister as well as their mother. A gap yawned, that would not be filled, even though the family was changing all the time. Yet, Rosie's illness and death made it easier for Flo to keep her secret from her family, as the attention was on Rosie. Flo kept the teddy bear that Rosie had made for William and it became a treasured possession.

Growing closer to George, Flo experienced a strong wish to unburden herself of her secret. She wondered how to introduce such a tricky subject, but a chance arose one day when George was flicking through a local newspaper in the tearoom after work. It was drizzling outside and clouds of steam from boiling kettles made it seem as damp inside. The wet clothing of customers added a fusty smell. Droplets of moisture trickled down the wall near where they were sitting, facing each other over their cups of tea. It was noisy and crowded and Flo didn't think anyone would overhear them. She was reading over George's shoulder about a girl who had been turned out of her home by her parents for becoming pregnant and had drowned herself in the Thames.

'What a sad story,' Flo said. She was edging towards telling George her story, testing a different kind of water from that which had drowned the girl, before she plunged in. George glanced to where she was pointing with a finger and read the few short paragraphs.

'Yes, very sad, but it needn't have happened. If only she'd waited to be married, she would have been all right,' he said. 'I suppose she knew that no one would have her now, so she was done for.'

Flo changed the subject, not daring now to tell George the truth. He wasn't an unkind man, quite the opposite. He was conventional and gave the impression of little experience of women. He might have possessed the largeness of heart to accept her as she was, a woman who had had a child and not the childless young woman she appeared to be, yet he might not. Flo didn't want to risk losing George, because she was beginning to wonder if she would meet anyone else if he threw her over. She didn't want to be left on the shelf.

Yet there was a penalty to pay for silence. She explained it to Jessie one summer evening at home, when they were sitting over empty plates after a meal of tripe and onion stew.

'I'm afraid that one day my secret will just fall out of my mouth. Keeping it is hard work. Remember when I told you how I ran into my old enemy from school, Betsy, in the butcher's shop late last year and she saw I was pregnant?

That's what I'm afraid of. I'm always looking over my shoulder, expecting someone to mention my baby, someone round here, if not Betsy, who knows about William and will ask me about him in front of George. After all, everyone on this street knows everyone else's business and some of the neighbours knew about the baby. I just hope that the war has taken people's minds off what their neighbours are doing, so they won't be thinking about what's happened to me.'

'No one's said anything to me. People are too busy with their own lives,' Jessie said. 'Your George is a nice young man. You're well set up with him.'

George was not particularly curious about Flo's past life. As his sister's friend from school, someone who had grown up in the same area, Flo knew she must seem so familiar to him that he didn't need to question her much about her past. When he asked about her experiences in the WAAF, she was able to say a lot about learning to type at RAF Debden and being a secretary at RAF Burghfield to Wing Commander Grant, without mentioning Bill.

When Bertie was demobbed in the late summer of 1945 and came home to Jessie, it was time for Flo to leave. Fortunately, Alf arrived home at about the same time and rented a house in Plaistow for her two younger sisters, Joan and Annie. Flo joined them. The boys, Bobby and Jeff, trained as plasterers and took lodgings near their work.

George's hands didn't stray far before he asked Flo to marry him. One day in the teashop, after Carol had left, when only a few regulars were sitting over cold cups and it was almost closing time, he took Flo's hand.

'I want you to be my Flo. I want us to get married,' he said quite simply.

Flo's mind went straight to the summer's day in 1943 when Bill had proposed to her on Burghfield Common, in the sunshine, with a posy of meadow flowers. She caught her breath, squeezed George's hand, smiled at him over the empty teacups and said yes.

She would learn to love him and she hoped that telling him she loved him meant that it would come true. She was taking less of a risk than she would have done by revealing her secret and she would have to live with the consequence, the feeling of anxiety that he might find out. She would find ways of lessening the risk and time would surely help.

Flo and George were married in the summer of 1946, in Plaistow, with Alf to give Flo away and her sisters and brothers trying to make up for the absence of Mabel and Rosie.

Their first baby, a girl, was born two years later, in King's College Hospital, not far from where Flo and George were living in a rented flat in Camberwell. Flo would have preferred to be at home, so that the birth could be as different as possible from the birth of William, but she accepted that first babies, as hers was thought to be, were born in hospital these days. At least it was a different hospital. It was an easier, quicker birth and Flo wasn't so tired afterwards.

There was a difficult moment when the midwife who attended her spoke quietly to her. 'It says on your notes that this is your first, but that's not right, is it?'

'No, I had a baby before, but please don't give me away,' Flo was almost whispering.

'Mum's the word,' the midwife said and Flo relaxed.

Flo didn't love this baby immediately. She could have been holding back because she expected to lose her as well, or wanted her to be William and not someone else. She didn't say anything in answer to George's excitement when he first saw his daughter and held her in his arms, only nodded and took the baby from him to feed her in a kind of acceptance.

Only gradually did Flo begin to feel affection and then love for her new baby. Far from allowing her to forget William, this baby, named Valerie and who quickly became Val, caused her to miss him even more. At times when she was alone with Val, she fell to daydreaming about William, imagining him at home, playing and running about. If she closed her eyes and blocked out the real world, she could almost see, hear and touch him.

When the National Assistance Act was passed in 1948, Flo, always alert to the news, noticed that she would have been able to claim money for William and herself had she kept him. She had missed out, by only about three years, on being able to support herself and her baby without half-killing herself by working full-time.

Flo and George had three children, Val, Evelyn and Steve. One day, in front of two-year-old Val, William's name slipped from Flo's lips. She was taken aback at her carelessness at letting a wall in her mind give way. Supposing George had been there? She became afraid that one day she would mention William in George's presence and then the truth would be out.

In her mind, William was growing to look like Bill, whereas Val looked more like George's side of the family. Tears threatened sometimes when she thought of William. She would never know him as a child and instead it would be Val always in his place. Yet at the same time, she was upset because she didn't yet love Val as she had loved William.

Flo often thought of William and was always aware of his age. Every year on his birthday, her daydreams about him were more compelling, but other daydreams were powerful too. If ever a quiet moment beckoned at home, she would lose herself in a daydream about William and then find Val demanding her attention. Reluctantly she would rouse herself, leaving the past in order to deal with the present.

Flo saw William more easily as a tiny baby than she did her other children on reflection, because there were no later memories of him to obscure the early ones. She continued to daydream about him, adjusting the dream all the time to suit his age. How long would she need to keep her secret? Would she ever feel that it was safe to tell George? Would her worst nightmare come true if someone else were to tell him and cause him to leave her?

Steve, a year younger than Evelyn, was Flo and George's last child. He was born six years after William, when Val was four and Evelyn not yet two. When she knew the baby was a boy, Flo wondered if he would remind her of William and was relieved that, like the girls, he seemed to take after George's side of the family rather than hers. She was able to love Steve for himself, free of thoughts about William.

When Steve was old enough to realise that he was the younger brother of two sisters, he started to ask for a brother. Flo couldn't tell him that he already had one, if he but knew it, even though she wanted to say that.

Evelyn and Steve were easy children, but things were always difficult with Val. She liked to claim that she wasn't loved like the other two and always bullied the younger, quieter Evelyn, so that Flo never had the pleasure of being able to think that her daughters were friends and would sometimes wonder whether she had been too preoccupied over William when Val was a baby.

Flo learned to love George for his love of her, for his kindness and reliability, his steady common sense. There was never the excitement that she had felt with Bill, but he was long gone now. The pain of losing William remained and she continued to daydream about him. Occasionally she would dream about him at night and these dreams always had a terrifying edge – he was accusing her of abandoning him or he was dead.

Flo's father, Alf, died ten years after the war and Jessie some years later. There was no one in her life after that who knew about William. That was a relief and a loss at one and the same time.

George wasn't ambitious. He was a kindly, easy-going man, who liked things to tick over. He was a family man at heart. He moved from one job to another in the War Office and then in the Ministry of Defence, when it was created from the ministries of the three armed forces. Occasionally he was promoted, until he settled at a level beyond which he doubted he would climb further.

Some years later, when it was clear that they were growing out of the Camberwell flat, George was keen to move further west. The family moved to Putney in the summer of 1959, at the end of Val's last term at primary school, a move that money left to George by his parents made possible. Flo felt safe in Putney, further from Plaistow than Camberwell. These days she only wondered if her daydreams and dreams about William would fade and whether she would ever have the courage to tell George her secret.

Their new home was a Victorian terraced house which was solid and well-proportioned. Two storeys high, with a bay window, it stood in the middle of a long terrace of yellow brick with slate roofs, giving a first impression of cheerful solidity.

The new house had a tiny front garden, overflowing with hydrangeas. Flo was in the front garden one day, soon after moving to Putney, cutting flowers to display indoors, when a passer-by stopped to talk to her.

'Ooh, what lovely hydrangeas. Mine always turn pink even if they begin life blue.'

'Oh, thanks.' Flo looked up from her weeding at the figure in front of her, a woman a few years younger, whose colourful make-up and clothes easily put the hydrangeas in the shade. 'I can't take any credit for the blue, because we've only just moved in, and we inherited them.'

'I'm Doris. I'm a few doors down from you. I think the blue is to do with the level of acidity in the soil.'

'Flo. It's nice to meet you, but I won't shake hands as mine are dirty from gardening,' Flo said, keeping hers firmly behind her back.

Doris told Flo about her new neighbourhood and the weeding was forgotten as they talked. After that, they bumped into each other frequently on the street or when they were out shopping. Doris's love of colour made her visible, even from a distance. She had a daughter of a similar age to Val, attending the same school. Flo and Doris, both mothers at home during the day, became friends, despite Doris being some years younger. She was a mine of local gossip and helped Flo to feel at home on the new street. Surely nothing to do with William could pursue her here.

Chapter Two

Flo and George's children grew up with no further mention of William's name, even though she thought of him often. Val trained as a teacher and married Dennis, who owned a perfume factory in Croydon. He and Val bought a house near the factory. Evelyn moved out, to share a flat with a friend. Steve began studying engineering at university in Sheffield.

By 1975, Flo noticed the change to her family life in many ways, not least in the ironing basket. For years, it was piled high, like a yacht with sails billowing on the ocean of the scullery floor. Their cat would climb to the top and settle in until Flo pushed him off. George had to have a clean shirt for work every day, as London was so dirty, and many of the children's clothes needed ironing. When all the children finally left home, the ironing pile shrank, at least during term time. It rose again when Steve came home for the holidays, but it was during term time, with the cat dispossessed, that Flo would now easily finish the ironing. Staring at the bottom of the empty basket one day set her thinking about finding more to do.

She may have been in her fifties, but she didn't want to sit around doing nothing for the rest of her life. She wanted distraction. Her dreams and daydreams about William had a life of their own and she didn't want to fall prey to them. With more time to herself, she had lately formed the idea that they were gaining a grip on her. William was older than Bill had been when he died and for her lover and her son to resemble each other in her mind wasn't an entirely comfortable thought.

George had never wanted her to work and had persuaded her to give up her job on marriage. She had been younger and more malleable then, but now she insisted that she wanted a job and he gave in, even though he didn't like the idea of working wives.

Would he have also changed in his views about unmarried mothers? All those years ago, when they had been discussing the pregnant girl who had drowned herself after her parents threw her out, George had said she should have waited until she was married before becoming pregnant because nobody would want her. Would he still say that?

The secret was deeply buried now, but it gnawed away at her and she would so much have preferred to tell George all about it, to have the air clear between them, and for him to accept her as she was, not as he thought she was. It would bring comfort to her and create such ease between them.

Yet she drew back from saying anything, because she still didn't dare take the risk. Supposing he was so upset about William that he left her, or, worse, stayed with her for the sake of appearances, while despising her in his heart? The time for telling was never right. One day she would have the courage to tell him the truth, but she had no idea when that day might come. First of all, she would find a job.

Opposite the tube station, a few minutes' walk from their home, Flo began to notice an antique shop. She peered in the windows one day. It wasn't a junk shop with all the goods jumbled together. There was space around each object, displaying it to best advantage. She saw silver spoons, willow pattern plates, china dogs, glass and pottery vases and behind them some prints. In one corner of the window was a framed notice indicating that the shop was interested in buying from customers as well as selling to them.

Flo was surprised that the shop front made her feel at home. She and George had no antiques at home. She thought of the chipped white plates that had done service year after year when she was a child and a bone-handled carving knife so well used and so often sharpened by her parents that most of the blade had worn away. Almost every Sunday of her later childhood the family had speculated on whether this week's joint would snap the blade. Then she remembered that her grandparents on Mabel's side had been better off than her parents and at their home, which she had visited frequently as a child, she had seen ornaments like those in the shop window. The goods in the shop window took her back to her childhood between the wars and a world she had lost.

Flo wondered what the shop was like inside. The window was inviting without being intimidating. Plates, spoons and vases were objects that everyone was familiar with. She had no business going in, especially when they couldn't afford to buy antiques, but her curiosity won, combined with the odd sense of familiarity. She went to the shop door and pushed it open. A bell jangled above her head.

Stepping into the shop, Flo saw that it was narrow inside, but not gloomy, even though it went back a long way. A window halfway along on one side let in some natural light, the advantage of being on the end of the terrace. She breathed in a musty smell that she liked, not the sharpness of dirt, but a softer smell of oldness. Shelves on both sides were full of objects of different kinds and small pieces of furniture were fitted in to corners, leaving space for customers to wander around. She felt as if everything were waiting quietly to be discovered, to come to life in her hands and explain its purpose and the way of life of which it had once formed a part.

She began to explore. The shop was crammed from floor

to ceiling with paintings, pottery and porcelain, unblemished glassware, wooden mantelpiece clocks with calm faces and a hole for inserting the key to wind them, other clocks and watches, a locked jewellery cabinet, silver cutlery, old toys, a selection of books with fine bindings and marbled endpapers and old prints and postcards of Putney.

A woman of about her age was sitting at a counter halfway down the shop, taking some ornaments out of a cardboard box. She was examining them as if she had bought them and was pleased with her purchase. She was well dressed with neatly waved hair and she looked stylish and even slightly foreign. She smiled and said hello as Flo approached, but otherwise left her to her own devices.

Flo stopped in front of a pair of silver candlesticks, such as she wanted for the mantelpiece at home, but she knew they would be too expensive. She picked up a stubby little silver candlestick instead.

'That's a chamber stick, and look, it has a little snuffer to go with it,' the woman said, seeing Flo toy with it. 'It's early 19th century and someone would have used it to light their way to bed.'

Finding that the chamber stick was not expensive, Flo bought it in an impulsive moment, took it home and polished it. On the mantelpiece in the sitting room it gleamed so brightly that it attracted George's attention when he arrived home from work. He didn't say it was a waste of money.

After that, Flo often found herself looking in the antique shop window, and going in. The shop was as close to the underground line as her home, only a few corners further along, and the same light rumble could be heard in the shop as in their house. Flo couldn't buy something on every visit, or George would have had a reason to complain, but she made a small purchase now and again and she became friendly with Monica, the shop owner.

Monica was English, but had grown up in France. She had come to live in England on her marriage and she and her husband ran their antique business together, living in a flat above the shop. She looked after the shop, while he spent most of his time going to auctions and antique fairs or to see private sellers to buy stock. They even went antique-hunting in France during holidays there and shipped their findings back to London. These purchases gave the shop what Monica called *cachet*.

Monica was glad of someone to talk to as she was on her own much of the time. Getting to know her, Flo felt as if her life were opening up. A new friend and a new interest might bring some sense of fulfilment, even solace.

When Monica's husband became ill with cancer in 1976 and died some months afterwards, the shop closed. Flo missed her friend. Seeing a new notice in the shop window one morning, she feared that Monica was selling up and moving away. She was surprised at how sorry she felt, and only too pleased when she was close enough to read that Monica was advertising for a part-time assistant.

Flo went into the shop, breathing in the familiar musty smell. She and Monica talked about the death and the funeral, and then Flo changed the subject.

'I see you're advertising for an assistant,' she said. Monica's eyes lit up.

'Well, yes I am. Why, are you interested? I need someone to help run the shop with me and hold the fort when I'm away. I can't manage it on my own and I dread having to sell it. What would I do all day alone at home at my age after losing my husband and my job?'

'I'd love to do it, but I don't know anything about antiques.'

'Oh, I can teach you the business and you would be working with me.'

'I'll have to let you know,' Flo said, wanting to talk to George before deciding. She left to do her shopping. Outside, on the street, she desperately wanted the job. For the rest of that day, she felt excited at the prospect. George had already agreed to her working, so he could hardly object to a part-time job in an antique shop. The next day, after securing his agreement, she accepted the offer.

She changed her name to Florence as she started her new job. Only George was allowed to call her Flo. The shop was her salvation. Here she was the woman with a place in the working world that she had always wanted to have. Monica taught her about the business. Here, too, Florence could keep her secret at bay. She still thought about it, but it was nothing to do with her job or with Monica and so it seemed less powerful.

When Monica explained the difference between solid silver and electro-plated nickel silver, Florence thought of the silver charm bracelet, safely stored in her jewellery box at home, from which she had taken hearts to give to Bill and to William. She always knew how old William was and didn't have to do a quick calculation to tell herself that in 1977 he was thirty-two. His birthday on 12th January had been only the previous week. Did he have the silver heart and if so, had he ever thought about what it might mean? Was he even looking for her? She had heard nothing from William and was beginning to think that she might never do so because it was some time now since the new law had been passed.

Florence had taken a quiet interest in any news about adoption over the years and she knew that it was now possible for adopted people to trace the parents who had given them up. She had wondered, when she heard about the new law, if William might contact her, but she didn't expect him to. Adoption had meant the end of any connection between mother and baby in the days when she had given William up. None of her memories of William or her longing to see him had ever included a possibility that they might meet.

Not long after Florence started her new job, she came across a bowl that reminded her of the one she had broken as a child, the one that had hidden the charm bracelet. She picked up the similar bowl. A man was painted on the side, wearing a costume. He was carrying a spade and he looked like the husband of the woman on her bowl.

'Do you like that?' Monica asked, coming up to her. 'It's French *faience*. That piece was made in Quimper in Brittany. See the mark underneath?' She turned the bowl upside down to point out the pottery mark and added, 'The man is a *Breton* wearing traditional costume. It's not a particularly valuable piece, but even this sort of *faience* is popular because of the colourful design and of course it's from *la France!*'

She rolled the 'r' in France and they laughed. Monica had a grace and elegance that Florence admired.

'I do like it. It reminds me of one at home.' Florence put the bowl back. She recounted her story about breaking her bowl and finding a charm bracelet amongst its contents, but she didn't mention the two missing hearts.

Florence was at home one morning when she heard the post arrive and went to the front door to find a single letter on the mat. In the kitchen, where she was making a cake, she opened the letter. The plain brown envelope with only her typewritten name and address gave nothing away. Inside was a single sheet of paper.

Tuesday 25th January 1977

Dear Mrs Cruise

I wonder if you can help me with an enquiry I have received from a young man born in January 1945 in London. He thinks he is connected to the Haldon family. This is, of course, quite a common name, but if you think this may be your branch of the family, please send me a note and I will be happy to pursue it.

Yours sincerely,
Paula Heron,
Social worker

Florence knew immediately that the letter was about William. She hadn't had such a shock since she had been told that Bill was dead. She didn't faint, but she grabbed the edge of the table for support and sat down. Even though she had imagined William growing up, and thought about what he might be doing at different ages all through his childhood and since then, she had never allowed herself to think with any real intention that he would get in touch with her. He was living in a different world from hers, a parallel world with no connection.

She sat at the kitchen table, lost in thought, the cake forgotten, hardly conscious of the day continuing around her. The sound of the radio, the twittering of the budgie, the rumble of the District line trains passing nearby, the groan of planes on their way to Heathrow and the noise of traffic on the road all seemed far away.

What was William like now? If she were to pass him on the street, would she know him, this blend of herself and Bill? He was thirty-two, older than his father was when he died. Perhaps he had children himself and that was why he wanted to meet her. He must be taking advantage of the new law she had read about in the paper, but what a shock! That someone might casually reveal her secret had been much more on her mind than the possibility that one day William would want to see her.

Goodness knows how this woman had found her. Of course, she and George had always been in the phone book and hadn't moved around that much, but how did she know she was a Cruise and no longer a Haldon? She must have looked up the marriage records. Busybody. What an intrusion on her peace of mind! All her careful work of keeping the secret could be blown apart and she would be exposed for what she was: an unmarried mother and a deceiver. She wasn't a liar, though. She had never told an outright lie. She hadn't needed to deny her relationship with a man she wasn't married to or the birth of a baby outside wedlock. George had never asked her questions of that kind because, as far as she knew, he had never suspected the truth.

Her heart was racing and she clutched the letter so hard in one hand that the paper creased. The mad thought danced into her mind that she might meet William in secret. She dearly wanted to see what kind of man he had become, to know that she hadn't harmed him in any way, to tell him about his father. But it was too risky. George might find out, even if she were to meet William only once. She had betrayed William, by depriving him of his real mother, and she had deceived George, who for all these years had believed that he married an innocent, young woman whose only children were the three they had together, but she would not add to her deception of George by meeting William in secret. Nor could she stand the strain of it.

No, it was impossible. She was as certain now as ever, more certain in fact, that George must never know about William. She had kept the secret all these years and the chance event she had always feared that would tell George the truth, that in her mind always took the form of Betsy spreading stories about the pregnant Flo she had seen in the butcher's queue in late 1944, had never happened. She dared not risk anything now. The longer she kept the secret, the more she deceived George and their children, but she had no choice.

Had she made a mistake, giving William away? It wouldn't be necessary nowadays. There were so many unmarried girls with babies. She was glad they could keep their babies and didn't have to go through the misery she had endured of missing her baby, her little boy, her young son. Her other children hadn't made up for the loss of William. Of course she loved them dearly, although things were always difficult with Val, but she had always wanted William as well.

It was lucky that George was still working and hadn't yet

retired. He was due to retire at sixty, in a couple of years' time. If he'd been at home, he might have picked up the post from the mat, handing the letter to her and probably asking what it was about. She had to get rid of it before he came back from work. At least she had all day to think about it.

No, she wanted to be rid of the letter straightaway. What was she doing, sitting here dreaming about William? She felt panicky, and thought of putting the letter in the kitchen bin. No, George might discover it. Burn it, then. No, she had to reply or they might write again. Oh, that was the answer. She would send their letter back to them with a note.

She found a pen and wrote hastily on the bottom of the single sheet: *I don't want any contact and you are not to write again.* Then, thinking that wasn't quite enough, she added, *Leave me in peace.*

It wasn't peace that she lived in, though. Real peace would have let her reveal her secret without a penalty or not have a secret at all. Real peace would have let her see William.

She signed her note, readdressed the envelope, stuffed in the letter, sealed it, stuck on a stamp, snatched up her keys and walked quickly to the pillar box around the corner, without even putting on her coat, despite the chilly day. She was holding a burning coal. She thrust the letter deep inside the pillar box, as far as her hand would go. It was gone. It was the only thing to do. It would be as if the letter had never been sent to her.

Don't think about the madness of meeting William, only about the need for George not to know, for life to remain calm and ordinary. How was it that those joyous times in a poppy field and on the RAF station with Bill all those years ago could be affecting her now, thirty years later, when she was in her fifties? When she gave William up, she had never expected to see him again and, hurtful though it would be to him, she couldn't face seeing him now. It would upset everything.

Coming back into the house and closing the front door

against the outside world, the world that could bring mention of William into her home without so much as a by-your-leave, she leaned against the door and spread her hands against its solidity. She felt as if she couldn't quite stand up unaided. Her eyes filled with tears.

Now that she had so hastily refused the invitation to meet William, she was overwhelmed by a desire to see him, to talk to him, to know that he was all right, despite what she had done to him in the past and what she was doing now by refusing to see him. She was saying *no* to him now, on top of giving him away. She wouldn't even see him, when she had given him up, refused to be the mother that every child needed. It seemed so cruel of her, yet how could she see him? How could she deceive George even more than she had done? She wouldn't be able to stand the anxiety of a secret meeting with William even if it were possible to see him without George knowing. George would be bound to notice her agitation and then what would happen? She was trembling, but she wouldn't give in to herself. She had to let the day become ordinary again. She had to be his Flo again by the time George came home from work.

Florence stood away from the door and went into the kitchen. The cake mixture lay in the bowl as she had left it, the handle of the wooden spoon she had been using to stir it pointing towards her, as if urging her to finish the job. She slowly finished mixing the cake, turned the mixture into a baking tin and placed it in the hot oven.

It took her ages to calm down, far longer than it took the cake to cook. She was surprised to see it come out nicely risen and golden brown, when she was still in turmoil. She had expected that at least a gash would form in the smooth surface, like a grimace. Yet, within the turmoil was a thread of pride. She had given birth to this young man. She knew now that he had grown up and was making his way in life. She had never known that before. It was slender news, but a comfort nonetheless.

For the first time in many years, she remembered the form she had signed, giving William up for adoption. She had left it in the bedroom drawer in Jessie's house, with his birth certificate and never retrieved them. The documents might have been discovered or might still be where she had put them. They didn't matter now. It was all too long ago and far away. What mattered was that William wanted to see her. Would they ever meet?

- Part Four -

Will

1977-1978

Chapter One

Anna was at home with the girls when Will came in from work one February afternoon. She was trying to hang wet washing on a dryer at the same time as preventing Susie and Lizzie from squabbling over a doll that one of Anna's sisters had given to them to share.

'I wish my sister had given the girls a doll each or nothing,' Anna said, after greeting Will with a kiss as he came into the kitchen. 'Oh, by the way, there's a letter for you. It came this morning,'

She handed over an envelope which had clearly been too near to the wet washing and looked limp and soggy.

Will flung his briefcase onto an empty chair in the kitchen. 'Oh, thanks. Do you know, I've had enough of 3C,' he said. 'Half of them hadn't done the homework I set them the other day. They had all sorts of excuses. One boy had to spend too much time on football practice, one girl said her mother put it out with the rubbish by accident and another girl claimed to have lost it. I've given them two more days and threatened dire consequences if they don't do it. If they were half as creative with their homework as with their excuses, they would walk the exams.'

It had been an exhausting day at school, one of those days when everything conspired to be frustrating. Will was opening the soggy envelope as he spoke. Inside was a brief note from Paula Heron asking him to telephone her. He glanced at his watch. It was only 4.30 pm as he had left school earlier than usual that afternoon. Paula might still be in her office.

On the phone, he listened in silence as she explained to him that Florence had refused to see him.

'It could well be because she has married and not told her husband about you,' she said.

Will agreed, but he was taken aback. He hadn't expected a refusal.

'What am I going to do now?'

'Well, nothing, as far as Florence is concerned. She is entitled to her privacy, but you could try to track down your father's side of the family.'

'I don't know much more than his name which you gave me last time,' Will said. I'm not sure… I'll have to think about it. I need to take this in first. I didn't expect it.'

He felt stumped. There was nothing else he could do. He would have to stop thinking about Florence, forget about any condition or tendency he might have inherited from her, any interests or traits that they might share, squash his curiosity and be prepared to tell his children he knew little about his original mother. It was frustrating to be at the mercy of her wishes, but he had no choice. He wouldn't go against them.

'Of course. Let me know if you need any further help,' Paula Heron said and once again Will thanked her. He put the phone down and turned to Anna.

'Florence doesn't want to see me! I never thought that would be the answer. You know, I imagined not being able to find her or that perhaps that she had died, but even though you warned me, I never thought she would refuse to see me. She was so easy to find and now this has happened. I can't believe it.' His voice rose with astonishment.

'I'm sorry, after all your efforts,' Anna said and he nodded, feeling suddenly exhausted from more than the day at school. He was the young man Florence had given away as a baby, but who had wanted to meet her from the moment he had begun to think properly about being adopted. Yet she was refusing to see him. It was almost as if she had abandoned him twice.

'So it might be because she is now married,' Anna said, when he had relayed the discussion with Paula Heron.

'Well, either she's hard-hearted and thinks that the past is the past, or else it's because she's married and the husband doesn't know about me.'

William stood up. They were in the kitchen as the girls were having their tea and it was all at once stiflingly hot, even though it was a cold day.

'Yes, and she's afraid to meet you in case he finds out.' Anna picked up Lizzie, who wanted a cuddle and was pulling at Anna's jeans.

'So I don't have to take it personally, to think that she doesn't want to see me, only that she can't because it would upset the apple cart?'

'She might always have been afraid he would find her out. Maybe she passed herself off as an innocent young girl when she met him. After all, you know you were adopted just as the war was ending. Things were different then. It was frowned on for unmarried girls to have a baby. It's much easier than it was to admit that sort of thing now,' Anna said. 'She's probably too frightened to meet you in secret and equally frightened to tell her husband the truth.'

'I suppose the husband could be a bit of an ogre. In that case, the letter from the agency probably gave her quite a nasty shock,' Will said, sighing. A newspaper headline from a couple of years ago, when the legislation was being debated, something about mothers fearing a knock on the door, flashed into his mind.

Thinking about it over the days that followed, it was

obvious that he shouldn't take the rejection personally. Florence had never met him. Paula Heron and Anna must be right in saying that the refusal was connected with Florence's circumstances. She had probably not told her husband about the baby she'd given away before she knew him. She might have been afraid that he wouldn't marry her if she'd had a child, even though she had given the child away.

It still hurt though. It was still a kind of rejection and he didn't like it. Since adolescence and before he even knew her name, he had wanted to meet Florence. His parents had always said that it wouldn't be possible, that nobody knew where she was and in any case adoption meant a complete break with the past. Now that it was possible, now that the nature of adoption had changed, he had come up against a simple refusal from the one person he wanted to see. All his efforts to find his real mother had come to nothing, except that he now knew her name. But what was the point of a name when its owner didn't want to see him?

He had no choice but to accept Florence's refusal, as much as it hurt. He tried to put it all out of his mind, but he talked to his parents first. He remembered his mother's dislike of the idea of searching for his birth mother, even though he was an adult now and not a child who could be taken away from her.

He told his parents about Florence's refusal during a weekend visit. Will was careful to keep them informed about his search for his birth family, because he wanted them to accept his need to satisfy his curiosity. They listened in silence until he had finished speaking.

'It doesn't surprise me,' his mother said. She had been sitting awkwardly on the edge of her seat while Will was talking, but now she relaxed. 'The old idea of adoption has been turned upside down with this new law. When we adopted you, it was for good. There wasn't to be any going back on it. I expect you're right about her husband, but perhaps she also thinks it's all in the past. Can't you see that we're your family, Will? You don't need to do all this chasing around after someone who doesn't want to see you.'

'I didn't know when I began searching that she didn't want to see me,' Will said mildly. He had learned to make allowances for his mother's dislike of his search.

His father seemed more nonchalant, but then he had less to fear. No one had been trying to contact Will's birth father and nothing was known about him.

'Of course you're my family. I've always known that, Mum. It's just that I'm curious about where I came from and why I was adopted and the best way to find out is to talk to Florence,' Will added. 'It's such a shame she won't see me. I don't know what to do next, but I've been thinking that I need a break from this. I might try and find out about my father instead.'

'Oh, my goodness, Will! When you said a break, I thought you meant stop doing this. You don't give up, do you?' his mother said, but with an amused laugh. Will knew that the idea of finding his original father was more bearable than his search for Florence.

Will deliberately turned his mind elsewhere after Florence's refusal to see him. He talked it over with Anna and later with his old schoolfriend Jim. He and Jim had remained friends, even though they had gone to different universities and Jim had studied science and was now working in a medical laboratory. Jim listened, but said little. Will wasn't looking for advice, because Florence's decision seemed so final. There was nothing that he could do about it. No one could force her to see him and he wasn't in a position to try and persuade her.

Fortunately, life was busy with his family and his job and time seemed to fly by. There was always preparation to do on a school night and Susie and Lizzie would surround him, full of excitement, as he came home from school, so they could tell him about their day. He loved listening to their chatter.

'I'm trying not to let Florence's refusal get me down. It's all about what's important to her. It doesn't reflect on me. I'm a complete person without her, without knowing everything that she could tell me. I'm different from other people, people who are not adopted, even people who are adopted and know about their past,' he said to Anna one evening at home, after the girls were in bed.

'Well, as you know, I think she wants to meet you, but doesn't dare to. Feel sorry for her, Will. She has a secret she can't talk about.'

'That's right, but I can't forget about her. Something is still missing from my life.'

Anna nodded. 'Maybe one day she'll change her mind, but for the moment, there's nothing more you can do.'

Will had noticed some time ago just how close Anna was to her mother, Susan. Will, Anna and the girls alternated Sunday visits between her mother in Islington and his parents in Plaistow, driving a battered car they owned. Anna's father lived in Surrey with a new wife and visits to them occurred less often.

Anna's two younger sisters had left home by then and Susan lived alone, or she would have done, had she not filled the house with tenants when her youngest daughter left. The tenants were all women because Anna's mother wouldn't have men living in the house. She said it was for safety reasons. Such was her generous nature that sharing the house with tenants meant that Sunday lunch was extended to whoever was in that day.

One Sunday, Susan was carving second helpings from a large joint of beef. The blade of the knife flashed in the light which filtered into the dining room from the garden. The exchange of news at the beginning of the meal had given way to a discussion of parental responsibilities, in the light of the debate about women's rights. One of the tenants, a feminist, had been telling them about the consciousness-raising group she belonged to and encouraging Anna to join it. Anna's mother was arguing that men didn't play their part in bringing up children.

'Anna and I share the childcare and the domestics and we're both working. We're trying to be equal, but it's not always easy,' Will was saying.

'I hope it lasts,' Susan said, as if she doubted Will. 'Men have a lot more freedom and don't feel as responsible for children as women do. But my girls have turned out well despite an absent father much of the time. You could argue that men aren't really necessary as parents.'

Will wasn't going to let her get away with that last remark.

'I don't agree with that. My father was as necessary as my mother and I'm necessary to our girls.' Lizzie was sitting next to him and he ruffled her hair as he spoke.

Then he was struck by a further thought. All his effort at tracing his natural parents so far had been about Florence. He had done nothing about finding his original father, despite suggesting to Marion that he would do so.

'Susan is bitter about your father. That's what the conversation at lunch was about,' Will said to Anna later. They were in their sitting room at home, after the girls had gone to bed.

'I can't blame her in a way. She built her life around her family and Dad just destroyed it by walking out.'

'I feel some sympathy for her. The thought of losing you is unbearable, my love, but I hope the girls aren't listening to her.'

'No, they won't take any notice. What they notice is how we treat them and they see you're trying to be a good father.'

'Only trying, eh? Not succeeding?'

Will put down the Sunday paper he had been reading and Anna laughed at his mock outrage.

Anna was unperturbed by her mother's pronouncements, but Will wasn't too sorry when work meant he had to miss Sunday lunch with Susan now and then, even though it also meant losing out on his family for a large part of the day. Anna was adamant that she needed to see her mother regularly and that meant one Sunday a fortnight. He would then spend the Sunday at the dining room table at home, not enjoying a Sunday roast, which was what the table had been meant for, but marking or preparing work in the company of a sandwich and a beer.

Still thinking of the girls' questions in the future and still at the mercy of his own curiosity, Will delayed finding out more about his original father. After all, he was dead, so there was no prospect of meeting him. He let a year elapse, let Florence's refusal sink into the past, before turning his mind to that unknown father.

'There isn't really anything else in our records about your father, but you might be able to find out more from the Commonwealth War Graves Commission,' Paula Heron said, when Will went to see her again. 'They should be able to tell you where Sergeant Martin is buried and give you details of his service record. If it would help, I'll write you a letter giving you the information we have, so you can use it in your search.'

Back at home, William talked over the question of his father with Anna.

'I wonder if my birth parents would have married after the war and brought me up if my father had survived the war. I like to think that, anyway,' he said.

'Then you would have been a different Will and I might never have met you, so I'm glad that didn't happen,' Anna said.

After Paula Heron's letter arrived, containing the information that the Church of England's Children's Society held on his backbround, Will wrote to the Commonwealth War Graves Commission.

22nd March 1978

Dear Sir

I am seeking information about my natural father, Sergeant William Martin of 743 Squadron in the RAF, who was killed in France in September 1944. I was adopted as a baby and grew up knowing nothing about him, but I am now trying to find out about my original family.

I have a letter from the adoption agency which shows the connection and I should like an appointment – in the late afternoon, if possible – with one of your staff who might be able to help me find out more.

Yours sincerely,

Will Tyler

On receiving a letter giving him an appointment two weeks later, Will visited the offices of the Commonwealth War Graves Commission in London, taking the letter from Paula Heron with him. He saw a Major Penfold, an elderly man with a military demeanour softened by desk work. Will told his story.

'The Church of England Children's Society has a record of his death, that is, they were told by my birth mother,' Will said, passing Paula Heron's letter across to Major Penfold.

'Then there must be some mistake. Either your mother was wrong or the agency's records are wrong,' Major Penfold said, reading the letter and passing it back to Will. 'I have already checked our records, on reading your letter. There is no record of the burial of Sergeant William Martin of 743 Squadron of the RAF in one of our cemeteries.'

'Do you mean that he could still be alive?' William was incredulous.

'Not necessarily. What I'm saying is that he is not buried in a war grave. You need to check the deaths' register at Somerset House.'

'I will. Thank you for your help.'

It was too late to go straight from the offices of the Commonwealth War Graves Commission to Somerset House, much as Will wanted to do so. He had to wait for the next day, after school and he only managed to get there with half an hour to spare before it closed. He didn't find anything in that half an hour. He would need to come back on another occasion, when he had more time. It would be a difficult search because the death could have occurred at any time from September 1944 and over thirty years had passed since then.

He decided to wait until the end of term. The first day of the Easter holiday found him at Somerset House, early in the morning. A lengthy search produced nothing conclusive. Men called William Martin had died since September 1944, not surprisingly because it was a common name. With no middle name or date by which to narrow the search, what he discovered wasn't helpful. However, he came away thinking that there could have been a mistake. It wasn't clear that the Sergeant William Martin he was looking for was dead.

Chapter Two

Will and his family rented a country cottage in Wiltshire for the remainder of the Easter holiday and Will gave himself over to relaxing with Anna, playing with the girls and preparing for the summer term. Back at home, when he thought about it again, he was frustrated by how to go about the next stage of his search.

'I've got no leads. No home address or any other names. I'm not sure what to do next,' he said to Anna one evening after their return home. The summer term had started and the girls were in bed.

'Well, you have got leads of a sort because you now know your father's name and that he came from Epsom. Why don't you place an advert in the local papers?' Anna said.

'Great idea! Why didn't I think of that?'

Consulting the Yellow Pages, Will found the names of one or two Epsom newspapers. Rather than advertising in them straightaway, he decided to go to Epsom himself, to see what it was like and buy the local papers in order to decide which would be the best for his advert. It wasn't necessary to do that, but he wanted to take some action connected with his search for his father. The idea of a journey, even an ordinary journey to a London suburb, appealed to his restless mood. He went by train on the Saturday morning after Anna's suggestion, leaving her to take the girls shopping and then to a nearby park with another family.

Will didn't know west London well and had never been to Epsom before. Coming out of the station there, he saw a wide main street flanked by a variety of shops, all of which seemed to be doing well. None of them was boarded up and the windows were full of neat displays. There was no litter on the pavements. People on the whole looked comfortable, even prosperous. The cafés and restaurants were full. Will peered into the windows of an estate agent and was astonished by the high prices of property for sale. Epsom certainly lived up to its reputation of being a comfortable suburb.

It was different from his part of London, from Plaistow where he had grown up or Hackney where he lived now. There were hardly any people from an ethnic minority on the streets of Epsom and there wasn't the street life that he was used to, with market stalls or pavements covered with goods for sale. To Will, whose life in London was spent mainly between home and work with occasional outings elsewhere, Epsom seemed comfortably off, but less varied and lively than the streets he was used to.

He bought copies of three local papers in a newsagent's shop and strolled around the town centre for some time, the newspapers under his arm, before diving into a café to read them.

He returned home thinking that his father William Martin and his mother Florence Haldon had come from strikingly different backgrounds. They must have met in the war, probably in the RAF, where life in uniform would have helped to obscure social differences and being away from home could have increased the thrill of meeting each other. Whatever had happened to his parents in the war was no doubt responsible for his adoption. Had their different backgrounds driven them apart after the war or was William Martin's death in the war responsible? There was a mystery here. Florence had clearly believed that William Martin was dead at the time of arranging for Will's adoption and yet there was some doubt about that.

Back at home, Will composed an advert, in discussion with Anna. Later, he put the same advert in each of the three newspapers he had bought, arranging for it to come out on consecutive weeks during May 1978. He booked a post office box for receipt of replies.

I am seeking news of my father, Sergeant William Martin, a member of 743 Squadron in the RAF during the Second World War.

He came from Epsom and I should like to hear from him or any relatives.

Please contact me, Will Tyler, at POB 85, Plaistow E 13.

There were few words, because there was nothing more to say now that there was a possibility that his father was still alive. He put in the phrase *or any relatives* in case he was dead after all.

In reply, Will received one or two letters from opportunists. One sad letter in green ink was from someone who claimed to have seen his message from beyond the grave. Another was brisk and business-like. A fortune was waiting for him if only he would send a cheque for £100 within three weeks to a certain address in Epsom.

Discarding these letters, Will felt disappointed, but he waited patiently for all the adverts to come out before thinking that he had failed. A week after the publication of the third advert, just as he was about to give up hope, one letter caught his attention as he read it.

30th May '78

Dear Will Tyler,

I saw your advert in the Epsom Gazette. In fact, being an avid reader, I saw it in all three local rags.

I am the younger brother of Bill Martin. I knew he had a son, but it certainly is a surprise to hear from you. Please telephone me at home on 434 7842 as it appears we both want to know more.

Yours sincerely,

Gerry Martin

'Look at this!' Will said to Anna, after opening the letter in the kitchen after school. Here at last was a path ahead, instead of an obstacle in his way.

'It looks as if Bill Martin is dead or why would his brother write to you? Why hasn't he written himself?' Anna was peering at the letter over Will's shoulder, her hair brushing against his neck.

'Well, I don't know. He says I *am* the younger brother of Bill Martin, not I *was*. But we'll soon find out.'

That evening, Will waited for Gerry Martin to arrive home from work, assuming normal working hours, and at 7 pm he telephoned the number on the letter. Someone picked up on the fourth ring.

'Hello, is that Gerry Martin? It's Will Tyler here... Yes, the advertisement... Thanks for your letter. I'm trying to find out about my father... Yes, I was adopted as a baby and when I spoke to someone at the agency which placed me for adoption I was given the name of William Martin for my father. Then I was told he was killed in France, although the Commonwealth War Graves Commission has no record of him and I don't know enough to be sure if his death is recorded at Somerset House.'

'My brother Bill Martin isn't dead. He was badly wounded in the war, but he's living in Epsom,' the voice said at the other end of the line.

Will nearly dropped the phone. 'He's alive!' It was almost too good to be true, after the ups and downs concerning the fate of William Martin.

'He's not fully recovered, so I help him out now and then.

He lost a lung in the war. When I told him about your advert, he asked me to contact you and find out…' He hesitated.

'If I'm genuine,' Will said.

'Well, yes. I suppose so, but you seem to be. He wants to see you, if I'm happy. Can you meet us in Epsom?'

Gerry Martin suggested Will come to the Rose Café in Epsom High Street, near the clock, to meet him and his brother on the following Saturday afternoon at 3 pm.

'How will we know each other?' Will asked.

'Well, it's only a small café, but let's avoid any confusion. Why don't you and I both wear a red scarf? It's a bit cloak and dagger, but more original than a flower in a buttonhole, don't you think?' Gerry Martin ended with a chuckle.

'All right. I'll find something. You're on.' Will thought that he was going to like Gerry.

'It is incredible that your natural father is alive when you were told he was dead. I expect the café is a safety precaution,' Anna said, when Will had put the phone down and relayed the conversation to her.

'You mean, in case I turn out to be a liability and pester him at home?' Will said.

'Something like that.'

'Can you lend me a red scarf, please, Anna? I haven't got one,' Will said. His taste in clothes ran to more sober colours.

'Yes, I've got a plain one.'

He didn't ask Anna to come with him. It wouldn't have been practical unless they had found a babysitter, but in addition, he wanted to meet his father and uncle on his own. For the first time in his life, apart from his girls, he was going to meet blood relatives, something that nearly everyone was accustomed to from birth and didn't have to think about. It was momentous, even though they were not the blood relative he wished for most of all, the mother who was refusing to see him. But a father and an uncle were almost as good, would have been as good, had it not been for the three months and the silver heart. At last he was getting somewhere.

Just as he was leaving on the Saturday afternoon. Will slung his camera on to his shoulder. The occasion was worth a photograph.

It was a long journey from Hackney and the train he took from Victoria was delayed, so he had plenty of time to think about what this new family was going to be like. All the imaginary conversations vanished from his mind as he reached Epsom Station. He hurried along the wide main street, reaching the café a few minutes late, but not so late that his father and uncle would have been wondering if he was coming at all.

As he entered, his eyes fell on a man in a red scarf, sitting next to another man of similar appearance. Seeing Will's red scarf, the man smiled and raised an arm in greeting, explaining that he was Gerry. Both men stood up to shake hands with Will, but the handshake with Bill turned into a hug, with Gerry standing back. As they all sat down, Will was surprised at the feeling that rose up in him as he looked at a natural parent for the first time in his life. He hadn't known in advance how it would affect him, but now he felt shaken.

Bill and Gerry were both heavy set men in their late fifties, with greying, curly hair and regular features, but the similarity between them faded as Will took in the robust appearance of Gerry, the younger brother and became aware of the frailty of the older-looking Bill.

Gerry took command of the conversation, as well as ordering coffee for all of them. Will was grateful, because he wanted time to look at Bill. His immediate thought was that he wasn't meeting his older self, as he had wondered if he might be, but that there was a physical resemblance and Bill might once have had dark hair like his.

'I always knew about you, Will. Flo wrote and told me she

was pregnant. I'm really pleased you've got in touch,' Bill said. He spoke slowly and seemed short of breath.

'I'm so pleased you responded,' Will said, with a glance that included them both.

'I'm an estate agent here. I read the local papers as a way of keeping an eye on the property market. That's why I saw your advert. I told Bill and said I would contact you, but it was a busy couple of weeks. Then I saw the second and the third advert. Being asked three times about it made me get on and write to you,' Gerry said.

Will had given some thought to how to present himself to Bill and Gerry.

'Advertising was a bit of a shot in the dark, but I couldn't think of what else to do,' he said. 'All I had was your name and the word Epsom. In case you need convincing that I'm genuine, have a look at this.' He handed the letter from Paula Heron to Bill, who scanned it briefly and handed it back.

'You look like the genuine article to me. For one thing, you have a look of Flo,' Bill said, adding, 'I've brought something for you.'

He slipped a hand into a jacket pocket and produced a brown envelope. 'It's a letter from Flo, which talks about you. By the way, call me Bill.'

'And call me Gerry,' Gerry said.

Will opened the letter from Florence. It was written on flimsy wartime notepaper in dark blue ink with a fountain pen and it was addressed to Bill's parents. He had never seen Florence's handwriting before and he noticed how upright and square it was.

When Will read that Florence had referred to him as *a lovely baby* but that she was *afraid I won't be able to keep him*, he felt close to tears. Here at last, quite unexpectedly, was clear evidence of how Florence had felt about him. She had loved him, as the silver heart suggested, and she hadn't wanted to give him away, as the three months suggested. It was only that life had dictated otherwise.

On the back of the envelope in which Florence had sent the letter and on the letter itself was written her address at the time, the address he knew. He wondered whether he and Florence had ever passed each other in the street without knowing it. Could she have watched him grow up?

'It's amazing to see Florence's handwriting and to read about what she thought of me as a baby,' he said, dragging his eyes from the letter to look at Bill. 'Thank you so much for agreeing to meet me. I can't tell you how much it all means to me.' He felt he was going to choke and sipped at his coffee before he spoke again.

'There's one thing I don't understand. Why did Florence think you were dead?'

'I was missing, presumed dead, and it was some months before I came back to England. I was shot in the chest and collapsed unconscious. The men I was with couldn't find me and left the village where we were without me. That's why I was reported missing. I never knew how I came to be discovered, but I woke up in a French hospital in late September '44 with only one lung. It was a long time before I was well enough to be moved back to England, but I was home in time for Christmas. I was in hospital there for a while and then I was sent home, to my parents' house,' Bill said. He looked tired as he finished and Gerry touched his arm as if to say he had said enough, but after catching his breath, he continued.

'Even then, I was a bit of an invalid. I had Flo's address. She gave it to me before I left for France and I carried it with me all the time. I wrote to her several times after I came home, but there was never any answer. By the time I was well enough to get up and go to Plaistow, it was all too late. I could see the house I had been writing to had been bombed to pieces, so I suppose Flo never received my letters. I spoke to a woman neighbour, but I can't remember her name. I was standing there, feeling dazed, when she came out and asked if she could help. She told me that Flo's baby had been adopted and that she was serious about a young man she was going out with. So of course I decided not to pursue Flo and asked the woman not to say anything about me to her. I didn't want to cause her any distress, as she had obviously given up on me. I didn't know about this letter at the time. I found it among my mother's things after she died. It's written from the house next door to the address Flo gave me. It could have been the house of the woman I spoke to when I went there, but I'm not certain.'

Bill paused, now clearly exhausted by his long speech.

'So your mother kept it from you?' Will asked, not wishing to press Bill, but unable to resist the question.

'Yes. It was a terrible thing to do. I suppose she thought she was protecting me, because she was snobbish and Flo was... well, from a less well-off family than ours. But I loved Flo and we were going to be married. My mother knew that, because I told her about Flo when I came back home. Thinking about her had kept me alive when I was wounded in France. I was furious when I discovered what my mother had done, but that was years later, long after Flo would have married, long after I had made that visit to Plaistow. I was married to Rowena and our daughter Christine was in secondary school by then. It's all water under the bridge now,' Bill said, with a sigh.

'I tried to see Florence under the new law, but she won't see me. My guess is that her husband doesn't know about me and she's afraid he would find out,' Will said.

'Very likely. I told Rowena about Flo and about you being adopted before we were married,' Bill said. 'Christine is a bit younger than you, of course. You've always been my only son!'

'So Florence doesn't know you are alive,' Will said.

'No, she doesn't,' Bill said. 'Now, that's enough about

me. Tell us something about your life.' He sat back, sounding breathless and clearly glad to stop talking.

Will told Bill and Gerry about his childhood with his parents and Frank and then about Anna and the girls. Then he came back to Florence.

'All I ever had was a tiny silver heart that she tied to my wrist when she gave me away,' he explained.

Bill put a hand to his neck, as if fingering a chain.

'It sounds just like the one she gave me all those years ago, before I left for France. I've still got it at home somewhere. It was a tiny silver heart. She'd taken it from a bracelet, I think. It was a present to me when I went to France with the D-day landings.'

'So you had one too. I assumed it meant she loved me,' Will said. He felt like choking again and steered the conversation into more neutral territory by asking Bill and Gerry about their lives since the war. Bill's shattered lung had left him with poor health and he worked part-time for Gerry's business, helping out with the administration on good days. His wife, Rowena, was their main financial support.

Before he left, Will passed his camera to a young woman sitting across from them, with a request to take a picture. The three relatives posed for a photo at their table, with Will on one side and his father and uncle on the other. Will promised to send Bill and Gerry a copy of the photograph and wrote down Bill's address. Bill invited him to bring Anna and the girls to Epsom to meet Rowena and Christine and promised to ring with a date. He assured Will that Rowena wouldn't mind this introduction of his son into her life and was curious to meet him.

It was obvious that the two brothers were close and Will found himself wondering, on the way home, if he and Frank would have been closer had they been biological brothers. They were friendly, but had little in common. Frank always seemed far too comfortable at home with their parents to move out and set up home for himself, much to the frustration of a string of girlfriends and Will was used to seeing him at his parents' home. He didn't have to make any extra effort to keep up with Frank and wondered how much they would see of each other if Frank were to leave home. Yet brothers related by blood didn't always get along.

Reaching home at the end of a long afternoon, Will told Anna all about Bill and Gerry and showed her the letter from Florence. He read the letter many times and became familiar with her handwriting. Once the film was developed, he placed the photo of himself with his father and uncle in an album which he bought for pictures of his family of origin, hoping that one day he might add a picture of Florence. He sent copies to Bill and Gerry as he had promised. In meeting Bill, he had taken an important step towards understanding the past and the letter from Florence brought him unexpectedly closer to her.

Chapter Three

When Will next saw his parents, he told them about his discovery of Bill and Gerry and their meeting in Epsom. His father was pleased for him, but his mother looked sharply at Will.

'I hope we're not losing you, with all this fishing about for your blood family,' she said. Will thought that *blood family* was an odd expression. It made him think of *blood feud* but he let it pass. His mother was looking tired and seemed dispirited.

'No, of course not, Mum. I'm simply finding things out. Talking of which, I've just remembered something. When I went to see the adoption agency, they told me that Bill Martin was killed in the war. They said that Florence had wanted that information passed on to you. Did you know that she thought he had been killed in the war?'

'No, Will. We knew nothing about him, just as we have always told you,' his mother said and his father nodded.

Will persisted. 'Are you sure?'

'Yes, absolutely sure. Why, do you think we're lying to you? Why can't you accept what we say? We've always done our best by you, always been honest with you and this is how you repay us!' His mother was crying as she finished speaking. She jumped up and ran from the room.

Will was astonished. He had hardly ever seen her cry before.

'Now look what you've done, boy,' his father said, perturbed.

'Honestly, Dad, I didn't mean I thought you were lying. I was just checking you hadn't forgotten something.'

'All right, son. She's not well, you see. She found a lump the other week and she's having some tests. She wasn't going to tell you because she's hoping it won't be anything, but it's preying on her nerves. I'm sure she doesn't think what she said just now. You just need to tread a bit carefully with her at the moment.'

His mother came back into the sitting room and sat down, looking pale and twisting a handkerchief in her hands.

'I'm sorry, Mum,' Will said, turning towards her. 'I didn't know you were having tests or I wouldn't have bothered you. It must be worrying.'

No one mentioned cancer, but the word was hanging in the air. His mother sniffed.

'Sorry to burst out at you, like that, Will. It's the waiting for the results that I can't stand,' she said.

'Let's hope for good news, Mum and sorry I questioned you just now. Only there's a bit of a mystery. Florence seems to have thought mistakenly that Bill was dead. He told me that at one point he was missing, presumed killed. I daresay that after a while, when she didn't hear from him, she assumed he was dead and so that was why she wrote to his parents in Epsom rather than to him.'

'That must be it, son,' his father said as his mother agreed.

'All I can remember is taking you from the social worker and thinking here is our baby. I was so happy, even though you were crying at the time and it was all I could do to calm you down, Will,' his mother said.

'So I was. You've mentioned that before. Maybe that explains it,' Will said. 'I was kicking up a fuss, so everyone was bothered by that and forgot about anything else. So it was all my fault!'

His parents both laughed at that and peace was restored.

Back at home that evening, Will told Anna about the conversation with his parents. She sympathised with his mother.

'I hope Marion's all right. Where was the lump?' Anna said.

Will looked horrified. 'Oh, she didn't say and I didn't ask.'

'I suppose you weren't to know she might be ill if she hadn't told you, but you are a bit inclined to think that your search comes before everything,' Anna said. 'You know how sensitive she is about the whole adoption thing, anyway.'

Anna was more inclined to be critical of him these days. He wondered if she was tired of his quest. It had been going on for three or four years now, since he had first heard about the plan to change the law, but he couldn't seem to stop himself.

'I do, but it's for no good reason. I left home years ago so surely she doesn't think she's losing me to someone else, when she's already lost me to you, my love! Anyway, Florence won't see me, so Mum has nothing to worry about. I suppose she thought I was accusing them of keeping vital information from me.'

'Do you think that?'

'No. The most likely thing is that, as I said to them, the adoption agency forgot to pass on Florence's message at the time. Mum and Dad have always been absolutely straight with me about all this. Anyway, I've met Bill Martin now, so it doesn't really matter what I knew or didn't know about him beforehand. I just hope that Mum hasn't got cancer.'

Not long after his visit to Epsom, Will answered the phone at home one evening. It was Bill, his breathing laboured on the phone, but his voice clear.

'I'm inviting you and your family to lunch on Sunday week, if possible. I'd like you to meet my wife Rowena and our daughter Christine and her family. I'm going to invite Gerry and his wife too.'

‘That would be fine – we’re free then,’ Will said, after conferring briefly with Anna. He was pleased that Bill was living up to his promise without too much delay. Since meeting Bill and Gerry and hearing about other members of the family, he was keen to meet them as well.

‘It’ll be a bit of a madhouse,’ Bill said. ‘I don’t think we’ll manage a sit down meal with so many people. What about your parents? Would they like to come? Or your brother? It would be nice to meet them all.’

‘Thank you… that’s very kind,’ Will said, stalling. He was uncertain that his parents and Frank would want to meet his new family. He didn’t like to mention his mother’s reservations about his new relatives. ‘I’ll ask them and let you know,’ That would buy him some time to think up a good excuse for their absence if, as he suspected, they didn’t want to come.

‘No, I don’t want to meet your blood father,’ his mother said, when he visited Plaistow to see his parents and ask them if they would like to attend the family party that Bill was organising. ‘Try and understand how I feel, Will. You’re our son and I don’t feel easy about what you’re doing. Adoption is adoption. I know you said it’s just your curiosity, but I wish you wouldn’t go unpicking it all. It makes me feel that you think we’re not good enough for you.’

‘I think the boy just wants to find out where he came from,’ his father said easily, but his mother wasn’t about to change her mind.

‘It’s almost as if you wish you hadn’t come to us,’ she said. Will sighed. He had tried to explain that it was a question of satisfying curiosity, but his mother had been unimpressed. He wasn’t about to deny her place in life as his mother and a grandmother of his children. His father understood him, but he hadn’t managed to convince his mother.

‘No I don’t think that, you know I don’t, Mum,’ he said,

giving her a hug. She seemed frail and small these days.

Frank didn't share their mother's reservations, but nor was he particularly interested in Will's discoveries. He would much rather talk about football than families and there was now a new woman in his life. Frank had been slow to find someone of lasting importance to him and had always said he was perfectly comfortable at home, but it seemed that his latest girlfriend might last longer than the others and even that they might set up home together.

In the end, Will and Anna and their daughters made the journey to Bill's house in Epsom on their own. Bill and Rowena lived in a detached 1930s house with a large front garden full of summer flowers. The garden looked so pretty that Anna said she would like to live on a greener London street. Once indoors, Will and Anna, with Susie and Lizzie close behind them, entered a crowded sitting room. Apart from Bill, there was Rowena, their daughter Christine, her husband Tony and their two children and Gerry and his wife Jane. Everyone, it seemed, wanted to meet Will and his family. Even the children were curious about their new uncle. Several minutes were taken up with introductions and explanations of who belonged to whom.

Susie and Lizzie, now aged eight and six, were pleased to see other children there. Christine and Tony had a boy and a girl, slightly younger than they were.

'They're our cousins,' Susie said, working the relationship out for herself.

It was fortunately a warm enough day for the children to be in the large garden for most of the time, making good use of a trampoline and a climbing frame there. Rowena had made a buffet lunch and Will was pleased about that. It meant that he could move around the room and talk to everyone in turn.

Christine came up to him immediately and Will found himself struck by a family resemblance between her and

Bill, with his handsome face translated in her into a startling prettiness that owed a certain amount to Rowena, an attractive woman. Christine had Bill's curly hair, except that, where his was greying, hers was a vibrant black, like Will's own hair. Her skin was pale and creamy and two almost black eyes were focused on him now, two cheeks were pale pink, two nostrils slightly flared, two lips parted, curling, in a smile.

'What a surprise, to find a brother after all these years. I was an only child you know and I always wanted a brother or sister. We don't look very alike, though do we?' Her voice was soft and Will had to bend a little closer to her to hear it properly.

'Not very,' Will said, unable to think of anything except how pretty his new sister was.

Christine turned to her husband Tony and introduced him to her new brother. Tony was a slightly built man, with a reserved manner, who looked as if he had been persuaded against his will to come along. Will was relieved when Christine began to talk.

'Well, this is wonderful. What about your family... I mean the family who adopted you?'

'I have a brother, a couple of years older than me, but no sisters until now,' Will said. 'It's a real surprise to have a sister of my age. When I was a teenager, I used to dream about my original mother. I didn't know her name then, of course. I called her my real mother. I don't know why, but I never imagined brothers and sisters. I persuaded myself she would have looked like an angel, given me more pocket money, let me stay up later in the evening, you know, a boy's idea of the perfect mother!' He laughed. 'It was a lot for my everyday mother to compete with, but I think she did pretty well, when I look back.'

'So the parents who adopted you were good to you, then?'

'They were. It took me a long time to appreciate it, perhaps because I was conscious as a teenager that my life could have been different, but they were good parents. They live nearby and my mother is a great help with the girls. I see them regularly. My brother, Frank, so far hasn't married and still lives with them.'

'It was a success then. That's lucky, because it might be so much more difficult to meet you if things hadn't worked out,' Christine said, her voice a little louder now.

'Yes, it was a success,' Will said. He was increasingly thinking so. It was as if he had been waiting to meet his birth family before he could finally admit that being adopted was all right. Yet, at the same time, he knew that some adopted people felt no need to find their birth families and that, if anything, he was unusual in seeking them out after a secure and happy childhood. He put it down to his restless curiosity.

On that occasion, he talked to Christine more than to anyone else and thought that he liked her the most of all of the rest of the family, even including Bill. Christine took it upon herself to act as the link between Will and the rest of the family, telling him past histories, letting him know gossip and making sure he didn't feel left out, whereas Bill, having made the introductions, seemed to sit back and let the occasion swirl around him. Will was grateful to her, because there were a lot of people to meet at once and conversations were broken up all the time.

'So you haven't got a sister,' Christine said at one point. 'You'll have to let me fill this gap in your life, Will.'

'My sister, Christine. I like the sound if it. My sister. I've never been able to say that before. Just as you've never been able to say my brother. How nice it is to be able to do that now.' Will smiled at her warmly.

In bed that night he found himself thinking about Christine. She was an attractive woman all right. She was too powerful for Tony, who was a slight, quiet man, a bit of a shrimp, with not much to say for himself. What on earth did Christine see in him? Christine was someone he felt he could talk to and she seemed to like him. He hoped that there would be an opportunity to meet her again soon – if not, he would make one.

Will had been looking for a mother and had been sure she would want to see him until he found out that she didn't want anything to do with him. He had been told that his father was dead and then discovered that he was still alive. Everything was the opposite of what he had expected.

Now that he had met one side of his original family and achieved a sort of lifetime ambition, he expected to feel a sense of satisfaction and was surprised not to do so. The odd thing about this quest was that there was always more to find out. Would he ever feel that he had found out enough? He assumed his current urge to discover more was either because he had failed with Florence or because everything seemed so unsettled.

He wasn't sure what was going to happen. He had been concentrating so hard on finding Florence and Bill that, when it came to the next stage, he didn't know what he wanted. How well would he get to know Bill and his family? How much would they matter to him? Who among them would matter the most? In what way? What effect would knowing his original family have on his parents who, after all, weren't so young anymore? He didn't want to call them his adoptive parents. That was social worker language. They were his parents, damn it. And his brother was Frank, although he felt he had room for a sister. One thing he was certain of, more certain even than he was of getting to know Bill, was that he wanted to get to know Christine better.

An influx of relatives shouldn't be so difficult to handle. After all, some people came from large families where they had four or five brothers and sisters or even more. The difference was that they grew up with the thought. They didn't have to take on a father, his wife and a sister and her family, not to mention an uncle and his wife in the middle of their lives and start with them from scratch. It was exciting, but it was also demanding and he had Anna and the girls to think about as well as his job. His new family was a bonus, but would have to fit in with the rest of his life.

In the remainder of that summer term, Will was particularly busy at school, dealing with exams. When term ended, he and Anna took the girls away camping in France. Camping on a site with a swimming pool and plenty of other children to play with was the highlight of the holiday for the girls, but there was also time to visit the war cemeteries where he had expected to find his father's grave, until his fortunate discovery that Bill had survived the war.

When the autumn term began, the family went back to ordinary life, including the routine of weekday family time in the late afternoon and supper together in the evening. Will spent most weekday evenings at home preparing lessons or marking, rewarding himself with a television programme later on, if there was time. He was quite unprepared for what happened next.

Chapter Four

When the phone rang at home early one autumn evening, with Anna out and the girls in bed, Will looked up impatiently from the dining room table where he always worked. He frowned, unwilling to be interrupted. Who could that be? He answered the phone and the frown cleared when he recognised the soft, almost silky voice at the other end.

'Hello, Will. I was thinking about you and how amazing it is that you are getting to know us, so I thought I'd just give you a ring for a sisterly chat.'

It was Christine. Will was surprised at how pleased he was to hear from her. Three months had passed since he had met her and yet he had recognised her voice immediately.

'Hello, Christine. Nice of you to ring. It gives me a break from eternal marking.'

'Oh, so it's true that teachers do long hours!' She gave a little laugh. 'I hope I haven't rung at a bad moment. The kids are in bed now and Tony is working late, so I thought I would see how you are, now that your term has begun. You must find getting to know your new family, or is it your old family, is a bit of a whirlwind now that you've discovered Dad!'

'It's not a bad moment at all. And I wouldn't say a whirlwind. You in particular have been so welcoming to me that it makes it so much easier.'

'I'm glad to have found out about Dad's lurid past. He had mentioned an adopted son, but of course he didn't know anything about you and I never thought that we'd meet. He was excited to see your newspaper adverts, but then he began to think it was all too good to be true, which was why he asked Gerry to contact you.'

Will had straightaway forgotten his work. The essays he was marking might never have been written. He sat down next to the phone and gave himself up to the friendly warmth of Christine's interest in him.

'Of course we want to hear about your life, just as much as you want to know about ours. What was it like growing up with another family? Did you feel you belonged to them?' Christine clearly wanted to go over the ground again, even though she had asked Will similar questions when they had met in the summer.

'Oh yes, I certainly felt I belonged, because I'd never known anything else. Once I knew I was adopted, my parents told me everything they knew about my circumstances. That was precious little, so I used to have fantasies about my mother, Florence, long before I knew her name. I would daydream that she was an angel who would come and rescue me from any kind of trouble, or if anything had gone wrong at home. Of course she never did and I suppose I grew out of the fantasies.'

'How fascinating. And did you rebel against being adopted?'

'Yes. I crushed my poor mother by telling her on more than one occasion that she wasn't my real mum. I've never forgotten saying that as a rebellious teenager and I wish I'd never said it.'

'Oh, teenagers will say anything to be cruel – at least I did. Dad was quite a disciplinarian. I used to tell him it was his military background showing. I wanted to run away from home.'

'Well, I did run away from home, but not for long. No doubt I wanted to punish my parents for adopting me, but they merely wanted to complete their family and did so in the only way they could.'

Will went on to tell Anna about his years in York and his futile hope that studying history would help him find out about his origins. Christine was sympathetic and understanding, anxious to be assured that he welcomed her call and keen to know that she might ring again. She wasn't unlike Anna in her interest in him, he thought later, after putting the phone down. He quashed the disloyal thought. No one compared with Anna. No one ever had or ever would compare with her. He glanced at the pile of exercise books sitting on the dining room table, waiting to be marked and was surprised at how little he had done that evening. How long had he been on the phone? It must have been forty minutes. When Anna returned, he was hard at work again.

'Oh, are you still at it? Any callers?' she said on coming into the dining room and giving Will a kiss before sitting down opposite him.

'I've got quite a bit more marking to do. Yes, Christine called.'

'Your new sister? She's not planning something else, is she? It doesn't seem long since we went there for lunch, although I suppose it was last term.'

'No, she just rang for a chat. She asked me about being adopted. Did you have a good time?'

'Yes, we sat in a pub and talked about our families, mostly. Don't worry. I didn't say anything much about you! They wanted to know about you and Florence, but there's not much to say as she won't meet you, so I told them about your discovery of your father, after you thought he was dead. They were all fascinated and asked lots of questions about how it all happened. I did my best to answer them… I thought you'd already told Christine about being adopted?'

'Yes, well… there was more to say. Nothing I haven't told you many times, though.'

Will was aware of an edge in Anna's voice, but he was too pleased about the phone call from Christine to mind about it. Although Anna supported his exploration of his birth family, there were times, he knew, when it threatened to go too far for her. He hoped that Christine wasn't going to become a symbol of going too far in Anna's eyes. He didn't regret having to work later than he had intended, even though Anna was asleep by the time he tumbled into bed late that night and he felt less alert than normal in the morning.

Somewhat to Will's surprise, Christine called again the following week. They didn't talk for so long this time as Anna was at home and he felt less free to indulge himself in a long, cosy chat. Then Christine began to make a habit of ringing Will at home in the evenings, once every week or so and sometimes he would ring her. He enjoyed those conversations more and more. There was so much to catch up on, his childhood, her childhood, the life of their shared father, Bill, what they had done since childhood, what they believed in and hoped for.

Anna went out alone at least one evening a week. She belonged to what she called a girls' night out, a group of mothers with children of similar ages to Susie and Lizzie. The mothers had all met originally at the primary school gates and they would go out together for an evening once a month or so. Anna always looked forward to the girls' night out and Will always enjoyed her account of it afterwards. She also went out babysitting. She and her group had formed a babysitting circle, which enabled all its members to go out for the evening without having to pay a babysitter.

After a few such calls from Christine, Anna began to express surprise at their number and frequency. She didn't try to talk much to Christine if she answered the phone, but passed it over quickly to Will.

'This bill is quite a bit higher than usual,' she said to Will one afternoon after school, flourishing the phone bill, which had arrived that morning. 'Local calls aren't itemised, but you must have been calling Christine as well as receiving calls from her. I can't think that anything else would be responsible for the rise. I hope we can afford it.'

With all the expense of a family and a mortgage, Will and Anna found it hard to make ends meet, even though he was earning more as a teacher than he had in the bookshop. The latter part of each month always involved anxious calculations about what they could afford before pay day.

'Oh, it's possible I've been making extra calls.' Will's manner was offhand. He couldn't deny that Anna was right, but he didn't like his new friendship with Christine being made quite so clear and nor did he like the thought that it was upsetting the family finances. He couldn't believe that a few phone calls made such a difference, but he didn't want an argument about it.

Made aware of Anna's unease at Christine's attentions, Will took to ringing her on the nights that Anna was out. That didn't help with the phone bill, but it did make the calls less obvious. Christine was normally alone, because Tony seemed to work late on a regular basis. Her children were in bed by eight o'clock, so mid-evening was a good time to call. If it wasn't convenient, she said so. Will did the same if Anna was in when Christine called. He was getting to know his sister well. He was conscientious about marking homework and always made sure to finish it before he went to bed on the nights of Christine's phone calls.

During that autumn term, he became aware that the phone calls were taking him away from time with Anna. It was not in any serious way, but there were nights when he tumbled late into bed, finding Anna already asleep. Their normal routine was always to go to bed at the same time and often to make love. He put the change down to marking, but he knew in his heart of hearts that it was because of a phone call that had meant he hadn't finished the marking until later than usual. It was then harder to get up on time the following morning.

There was also something else. He hardly liked to admit it to himself at first, but as the term wore on, he was conscious of a growing attraction to Christine. He began to think about her when she wasn't there and some of his thoughts shocked him. He was stirred by the experience of the phone calls, not wishing to put an end to it and yet not entirely comfortable with his sexual feelings for a woman who was related to him and who was not Anna and whom, rather unbelievably, he had met only once. Christine was alluring and there was something about her voice on the phone that was almost more powerful than her physical presence. Her voice, his main contact with her, was still soft, but also lively and amused by life. It was true that she didn't look much like him, but there was a resemblance and he was definitely drawn to her, intrigued by any similarity in behaviour or circumstances that came up in their conversations.

She was pretty, with a generous figure and she dressed well, or she had done on the one occasion that they had met, despite her references to financial constraints arising from problems that Tony, an accountant, was suffering at work. She had a powerful presence and gave an impression of wanting more from life. Perhaps that was why she was turning towards him or maybe it was more basic than that, simply a sexual attraction between two people that was behind the phone calls.

Although he had only met her once, he found himself imagining her naked, imagining kissing her, making love. The fantasies disturbed him, even though he knew he had always been prone to fantasies of one kind or another, right from the time that he had fantasies about the angel mother who had given birth to him. He had had fantasies about Anna, in the early days before they knew each other well, but not these days, no doubt because she was always there and available. There was no need. The fantasies about Christine were unexpected at first. He had begun by thinking of her as a sister, but it was turning into something more. He wasn't quite in control of himself.

He had always been faithful to Anna in thought, word and deed. Some men and women strayed after marriage, perhaps in mid-life, caught up in one or another irresistible temptation, but he had never been one of those people. He had never thought that it was in his nature to stray.

Casting about for an explanation of his feelings, he even wondered absurdly if it was the fault of the phone, whether talking to someone you couldn't see created a sense of closeness that might not exist face to face. Then he chastised himself. He was nothing if not honest. The phone simply provided the opportunity. The truth was that he fancied Christine. In earlier centuries, those he taught about at school, such a relationship would have occurred through letters, which were at once more dangerous because they could be discovered and less intimate because they were less direct than a conversation on the phone.

Something was happening that he didn't want to discuss with Anna, something that he was concealing from her. She knew about the phone calls, but he sensed from one or two comments, from her behaviour if she was there when Christine rang, that she wasn't happy about them and he, for his part, didn't discuss them with her in any detail, didn't relay the jokes and laughter, the growing intimacy.

He felt odd, having sexual fantasies about a sister, of all people, even if she was a half-sister and he had only met her for the first time recently. Yet here he was, tempted by thoughts of Christine, ringing her up whenever he could, having conversations with her that were ostensibly about family history in the main, but that he was increasingly aware were fuelled by his attraction to her. Their conversations became more and more intimate. There was much laughter and joking, there were more stories about their lives when younger, their likes and dislikes, family relationships. There was so much to say and Christine was clearly as attracted to him as he was to her.

They're just phone calls, Will said to himself, attempting to make light of it all. They can't be doing anyone much harm. Just innocent phone calls. Nothing has been said or done that shouldn't be. Yet he knew that he and Christine were talking almost like lovers and that perhaps the only reason that things were not going further was lack of opportunity.

One evening, Anna came home unexpectedly early from a girls' night out and found him in the hall on the phone to Christine. The phone call finished twenty minutes later.

'You've been on the phone for a long time. Who was that?' Anna said, looking up from a newspaper as Will came into the sitting room.

'Christine. How was your evening? You're home early.'

'Yes, I am. No one liked the film, *Straw Dogs*. It was so violent. So we left half way through and everyone decided to go home because we had already been to one pub. You seem to be on the phone a lot to Christine these days, Will.'

'Do I? Just getting to know my sister,' he said lightly.

'I think there's more to it than that. I couldn't help listening to your conversation. It wasn't what you said, more your tone of voice. You like her a lot, don't you?'

'Yes, I do. She's friendly and she knows how I feel about finding my family after all these years.'

'And I don't?' Anna's voice was dangerously quiet.

'No, Anna. That's not what I'm saying at all!'

'I think you're getting too close to her.' Anna's face was set and she looked serious, even troubled, in a manner quite unlike her normal self.

‘Well, I’ve never had a sister before. We have a lot of catching up to do.’

‘It looks like more than that to me.’

Anna didn’t say anything further on that occasion. Will wasn’t sure if she had been warning him, but if she had, the warning wasn’t effective. The long conversations with Christine continued. Will was too flattered by her interest in him to want to stop them. Anna was being unreasonable. She had no idea what it was like to have a father, uncle and sister, not to mention their families, to get to know at his age. She had grown up with her family and her relatives were all well-known to her now, part of the furniture of her life. He was having to acquire in months the knowledge that she had had a lifetime to absorb. Yet Anna’s reservations were only about Christine and did not extend to anyone else in his birth family.

As Christmas drew closer, a silence grew between Will and Anna on the subject of Christine. Will contrived to avoid talking at length to her if Anna was there and soon he was telling Christine when Anna would next be out, letting her know without being explicit when he would be free to talk to her.

Chapter Five

Whenever Will was alone at home, with the girls asleep in bed, he would think of ringing Christine. He would go through a performance of trying not to, busying himself with some task and realise that he had failed when he found himself on the phone to her. That didn't always work out well. Once or twice Christine was busy and couldn't talk to him. When Tony answered the phone and Christine was out, Will found himself having an inane conversation, which he ended as quickly as possible, not always leaving a message for Christine to ring back.

One evening at home, Anna was expecting Will to watch a favourite television programme with her, when the phone rang. It was Christine. She had chosen an inconvenient moment, because it was clear from the expression on her face that Anna didn't want to watch the programme without him. The girls were in bed.

'I'm sorry, but I can't talk now,' Will said to Christine. From the hallway where the phone was situated, he watched Anna switching on the television and turning towards him with an expectant look.

'All right. Come and see me tomorrow evening. Tony will be out and the children in bed. It's ages since we've met and we can have a quiet chat on our own. What do you think?' Christine said.

With Anna standing nearby and Christine on the end of the phone, a quick decision was needed. With no hesitation, Will accepted the invitation, ignoring Anna's frown when he told her where he was going. She didn't try to prevent him, which he took to mean that she didn't object strongly to his going. They watched the television programme together. It was about wildlife in Africa, the kind of programme that they both loved, especially as they had both grown up largely without television. They discussed the programme after it had finished and no further mention was made that night of Will's plan to visit his new sister.

The following evening, they all had supper together as usual. While they were clearing the table afterwards, Anna said, 'Have you got much work to do tonight, Will?'

'No, fortunately, because I'm going out.'

Anna looked at him blankly.

'I'm going to see Christine. Have you forgotten?'

'I suppose so.' Anna sounded discontented, but didn't plead with him not to go.

She was putting the girls to bed when Will left a few minutes later. Susie and Lizzie clamoured to know where he was going, but Anna didn't seem interested. She didn't even ask what time he might be back and was immersed in reading a story to the girls as he said goodbye.

Will shut the front door and made his way to the car, which was fortunately parked outside the house. He placed the map on the front seat beside him. It was only a short drive from Hackney to Islington where Christine lived, although in the dark of an autumn evening, he wasn't quite sure of the way, as he had never been to her part of Islington before. Susan lived in an early Victorian house in the south of the borough, but Christine's address was in the north. At least he didn't have any preparation to do that evening for lessons the next day and, for once, no marking, so he was able to take up

Christine's invitation without having to work afterwards.

He had plenty of time to reflect, as he drove. He felt torn. He wanted to see Christine and yet he wasn't entirely comfortable with what he was doing. Anna's goodbye as he left had certainly been frosty and even the girls had looked puzzled on learning that he was going on his own to Christine's house. He sighed at the impossibility of having a private life in a family.

On his arrival, his discomfort was swept away by the warmth of Christine's welcome. She ushered him into the sitting room, explaining that her children were upstairs in bed and that Tony was working late as usual. Will sat down on a sofa and Christine swirled around him, providing drinks and nibbles.

'Tony is busy at work and rarely at home in the evenings until late these days,' Christine said, handing Will a glass of red wine.

She sat down on the sofa, not at the opposite end from Will, but next to him. Close up, she was even prettier than he remembered. She was quick on the uptake, her manner was warm and friendly and she was definitely interested in Will. He didn't normally take much notice of women's clothes, but he saw that she was wearing something silky, not the usual garb of a young mother at home with children and her make-up looked fresh. Will was flattered to think that she had dressed up for him, although he hadn't paid her the same compliment and was wearing the old jeans and shapeless sweater that he had put on after work.

'That must be a bit lonely for you, at least once the children are in bed,' he said, thinking of how he and Anna enjoyed the later hours of the evening, almost the only time that they ever had alone together.

'Well, I read a lot, watch TV and catch up on things. Tony and I have plenty of time to talk as it is,' Christine said. Will found himself wondering if she was bored by Tony and whether their problems extended beyond his workload to their marriage. He didn't want to know the answer, so he didn't say anything. Christine's manner brightened as she started talking to Will about himself.

'I'm still curious about what it was like finding out you were adopted when you were a teenager. Did you feel you belonged to your family?'

'Well, yes, because I'd never known anything else and my parents treated me well. I'm not sure I was always good to them. I didn't worry about being adopted until one day when we had a tactless aunt to tea. She said my parents would never have given me a home if they'd known how greedy I was. It was unkind, without being a terrible thing to say and it sparked a kind of awareness of being adopted in me that I'd never felt before. My parents had told me I was adopted, but I'd never thought much about it until that day. After that, I made them suffer! I would make it obvious I didn't belong and I ran away from home once, despite my mother trying to stop me. I didn't get any further than a friend's house for a few days, but I must have been a trial.'

Christine laughed. 'So you didn't put yourself beyond home comforts at any stage? No sleeping rough, no starving, no hitch-hiking to the other end of the country or begging strangers for money,' she said.

Will gave a rueful grin. 'It wasn't really until I left home at eighteen that I began to appreciate what they'd done for me,' he said.

'It sounds like a pretty normal family life to me. After all, it wasn't as if you had been taken in by them as a teenager with a history of being abused.'

Christine explained that she knew a local family of foster parents who had recently taken in a disturbed teenager who was turning their lives upside down. She was interested in childcare herself and was thinking of becoming a social worker when her children were older.

They had talked about Will's childhood before, but there were always new depths to reach and a sofa talk allowed greater intimacy even than the phone. Christine's interest in Will was more intense than that of anyone since he had first met Anna and he bathed in the warmth of her attention. He found himself talking about his years in York, his wish to contact his original family, his delight when the first news came about legislation which would make it possible.

Christine's glass was soon empty and Will poured her another one, topping up his own at the same time. The conversation continued, to include his later search for Florence, with all the disappointment of her refusal to see him and his attempts to understand that from her point of view. Finally he told Christine about his wish to find his father, his further disappointment at hearing that his father was dead and the pleasure of discovering that he was still alive.

Will didn't mention Anna much in the course of the conversation because he didn't want to talk to Christine about her. He was enjoying talking about himself at the different stages of his life and anything to do with Anna was private. There was no sign of life from the children upstairs and no key in the door announcing Tony's return. Will and Christine sat on the sofa talking more and more freely until he glanced at his watch and realised how late it was.

'Oh, God, look at the time! I must get back. It's school tomorrow and it's going to be a long day, what with a staff meeting as well.'

He didn't say that Anna would be wondering why he was so late, but he was aware of that.

'Why not call Anna and say you've been delayed? There's no need to go now. Tony's probably gone to the pub and it isn't closing time yet. There's a phone just here.' Christine pointed to a small table at the side of the sofa.

Will made a quick phone call to reassure Anna, saying he

was leaving then, but he lingered for a few more minutes, laughing and joking with Christine.

When they finally stood up, Will put his coat on. He was about to give Christine a quick peck on the cheek, when she put her hands on his shoulders and kissed him unmistakably on the lips. These days, Will never kissed anyone but Anna on the lips and he was taken aback, but also tempted. For a fraction of a second it could have become more than a quick kiss between friends, but Will resisted the offering. He stepped back, thanked Christine for the evening and merely nodded when she said that they should meet up again soon.

It was a short journey home and he drove slowly because he knew that he had had too much to drink and shouldn't be driving. He arrived home much later than he had intended. Anna, puzzled and displeased, was waiting up for him.

'I thought you'd had an accident,' she said, looking up from the newspaper, as he came in.

'No, I was just driving carefully.'

'Hm, not carefully enough, perhaps. I can tell you've had a drink.'

'Yes, we did, but…'

Anna put the newspaper aside with a loud rustle and interrupted him. 'I know Christine is your sister, well, your half-sister, but I hadn't thought that getting to know her would take up quite so much of your time,' she said.

'Well, I didn't plan it, but it was nice of her to ask me round and take an interest in me,' Will said. He was tired and wanted to go to bed and think about his conversation with Christine, but Anna hadn't finished.

'You didn't grow up with her, so the normal incest taboo doesn't apply.'

'What do you mean?' Will now knew that look of displeasure on Anna's face. It was a look that he hadn't seen often over the years, but one that had been more evident recently.

'I mean you're attracted to her, just as if she were another woman, not your sister at all. I know you are. Don't think I'm not aware that you're always on the phone to her and now you've started going to see her. Where is it going to end? You don't ring Bill or Gerry. As for Marion and Joe, you seem to have forgotten about them lately. I don't know what's happening, Will, but I don't like it. Christmas is coming up and it's meant to be a family time, but you seem so distant from us now! You aren't joining in on Christmas plans the way you normally do.'

Will was ready for this because he had noticed, during the past few weeks, Anna's disquiet about Christine. He had thought about what to say.

'I don't know where it's going to end, Anna. I only know that it's important to me to have this chance of getting to know my family after waiting all these years. As for Christmas, Marion, Joe and Frank are coming to lunch, so it will be a family time and then on Boxing Day…' His voice trailed off as he tried to remember what was happening then.

'My mother is coming on Boxing Day. You agreed to that, but you seem to have forgotten all about it!

'No, it's just that I've got a lot on at this end of the autumn term. You know that, Anna.'

'Don't change the subject. We're talking about Christine, not Bill and the rest of the tribe. And they are not your family in the usual sense!' Anna was shouting now. 'Florence gave you away. For over thirty years she's pretended you don't exist. Marion and Joe are your parents and Frank is your brother. Just because you think you've risen above them in life with your degree and your teaching, doesn't mean they're not your family. You're neglecting them. You've hardly been to see them since you first met Bill and I know they think they're losing you. Marion practically said so on the phone the other day. And then there's me and the girls. You're forgetting us with your obsession with Christine and that silly smile on your face whenever you mention her. You're just being selfish, Will.'

Will let Anna speak, but by the time she finished he was stony-faced and limited himself to an elaborate sigh. He and Anna went to bed that night almost in silence, with no signs of affection, let alone intimacy. In the morning, the atmosphere was strained over breakfast. Will and Anna argued sometimes, like any couple, but he couldn't remember another time when the argument had stretched into the next day. He was grateful for the lively and oblivious spirits of Susie and Lizzie as they were getting ready for school. They appeared not to notice that their parents were unusually quiet and that Will left the house with hardly a word to Anna.

Away from Anna, Will acknowledged in his heart of hearts that she was right. He had crossed a boundary, possibly more than one, with Christine. He wasn't able to concentrate at school properly that day. His mind was elsewhere when it should have been on his classes. One sixth-former even dared to say to him in class, 'Sir, you're not listening. I didn't say that'. He had to apologise and ask the boy to repeat his answer to a question.

Coming home that evening, Will was surprised to see the house was in darkness. He always arrived to find the lights on because Anna arrived first, picking up the girls from school on her way home from work. He pulled out his key and unlocked the front door. Inside it was silent. He was surprised, as he had expected Anna and the girls to be there, in the kitchen as usual, late in the afternoon of an ordinary weekday. He was tired after the day at school and looking forward to relaxing with his family. He had been so preoccupied that his first thought was that he must have forgotten an arrangement that they had made. He shut the front door behind him, hung up his coat and took his briefcase into the kitchen, always his first port of call after coming home. He switched on the light and put his briefcase on a chair. They were not a particularly tidy family, but everything looked unusually neat. There was a folded piece of paper on the kitchen table with his name on it. He sat down, picked up the piece of paper and opened it.

Will

I've taken the girls to my mother for a few days. They can go to school from there. It will give you a chance to do some thinking. The number is in the address book if you need it.

Anna

That was all. There was no loving or even affectionate signing-off, no kisses after her name. Will knew immediately what Anna's departure was about, coming on top of their argument over Christine. Anna had clearly been even more upset than she had admitted to. She obviously wasn't prepared to allow Will to become better acquainted with his sister because she saw danger in it.

Anger rose inside Will as he read the note again. How dare Anna take the girls away without any discussion! And how selfish she was being in taking this stance instead of allowing him the space to get to know the sister he had only recently met. So much for all her sympathy over his predicament in their years together. She was only thinking of herself and how she wanted his exclusive attention, rather than being prepared to let him get to know his own family. Will looked around at the lifeless kitchen. He had to admit that Anna didn't want his attention at this precise moment. She seemed to have left him.

He remembered a conversation years before, when he had been working in the bookshop and they hadn't had enough money to get through every month. Anna had threatened then to take the girls to live with her mother, as a way of saving money. She had never done it because Will had begun to apply for teaching jobs and to earn more, but she had done it now, for a different reason.

He stood up from the kitchen table, where he had been brooding over Anna's note. The empty house felt odd at this time of day and he missed the girls' chatter after school and the way that he and Anna would catch up with each other after the separation of work. He looked in the fridge. It was about as cold and empty as he felt, with nothing obviously left for him. Anna usually cooked, but this evening he would have to make his own supper.

First things first. He would ring Anna and see what she had to say. He found the number in their joint address book and telephoned. Susan answered and passed the phone over quickly, her normally friendly manner telescoped into a brief hello. Will hoped that Anna hadn't let Susan in on their... not exactly quarrel, but misunderstanding. He didn't want to discuss it on the phone with Anna, either, not with Susan and perhaps the girls listening in. How he felt about Christine was his business, he decided. It wasn't even anything to do with Anna and it was a pity that her jealousy – because that's what it was – was beginning to spoil how he felt about his sister.

'Hello, Anna. It's quiet here. A bit surprising, I must say, to find you all gone. I found your note, though. What's going on?' Will had decided that curiosity would be a better approach over the phone than the annoyance that he was feeling.

Anna's voice was cool and distant.

'You have some thinking to do, Will, as I said in my note. I can't discuss it now.'

'But when are you coming home? You don't normally disappear with no warning. And it's awkward for the girls to go to school from Susan's house and what about your job?'

'Don't worry about us. We can manage.'

'Why did you go off like that with the girls, without discussing it first?'

'Why did you go off without consulting me?' Her voice had lost its coolness and sounded angry.

'I haven't gone anywhere. I'm here, at home. What do you mean?'

'Think about it, Will.'

Will didn't want an argument on the phone, especially with the audience that he envisaged standing around Anna as she was talking.

'Anna, please. I miss you. I love you and I want you to come home.'

'That's up to you. Look, I must go.'

'Can't I even speak to the girls?'

'No, because my mother's whisked them out to the corner shop. She's being tactful.'

'So you can talk now?'

'I don't want to talk. Another time, Will, when you're ready. Keep in touch.'

The dialling tone sounded in Will's ear. Anna had gone.

Chapter Six

Will put the phone down and wandered into the sitting room, switching on only a small side light. The emptiness of the house began to oppress him. Anna hadn't said that she loved him, but nor had she refused to speak to him and she had ended by saying keep in touch. He grasped at that last phrase, because for the present it was all he had. But what exactly had Anna meant by saying that he had gone off without consulting her?

He sat on the sofa in the gathering dark with the quiet house resting around him. Gradually he understood. Anna was talking about his visit to Christine on the previous evening. He had accepted the invitation without consulting her. Normally they were relaxed about doing things separately and it had seemed practical as well as appropriate for Will to have some meetings alone with his original family. Anna knew that, yet Christine was a source of tension between them and clearly Anna had minded his going to see her. She obviously felt abandoned or ignored by his relationship with his sister.

She didn't know how he felt about Christine, about the sexual attraction that had sprung up between them and that he was now aware that Christine felt as well, judging by her behaviour. At least, he had said nothing about it to Anna, but clearly, she had guessed. That was the trouble with Anna.

She always seemed to be one step ahead of him. He couldn't believe that this was happening. It had all blown up so quickly and now his marriage was in difficulties of a kind he had never experienced or foreseen. His wish to know his original family was taking him in an unforeseen direction, one that was fraught with problems.

What had she meant by keep in touch? Because she had refused to talk to him in any depth on the phone, it could only mean that he should get in touch when he had something to say, when the thinking had been done. Anna must mean him to get in touch when he had decided to keep a distance from Christine, rather than allowing her to cause jealousy between husband and wife.

An almost unbelievable thought danced into Will's mind. Was Anna saying that she had left him unless things were straightened out to her liking between him and Christine? After all, her parents had divorced, so she had been down that road before, if not for herself. She had seen it happen, knew the stages of separation and that life continued beyond it, however distressing it might be. Susan was always talking about relishing her independence. Will remembered what she had said during one Sunday lunch about men not being necessary as parents. She had repeated it on other occasions. Did Anna now believe that? She had grown up without a father at home, at least while a teenager. A household without men must seem natural to her.

Then there was her girls' night out. He had never asked her much about what they discussed, but she had mentioned conversations about equality with men, even independence of men. Some of the women in the group were feminists. Anna sometimes said that she was a feminist and she supported women's liberation. He wasn't frightened of the word. He liked strong, independent women, but there was a limit to independence in marriage.

Anna had told him that two of Susan's tenants had left recently and that their rooms were briefly vacant. There was space for Anna and the girls in Susan's house. Was she about to move in with her mother and had she already done so? Will had been aware since he first met Anna that she was close to Susan, a closeness that she always said had developed particularly after her parents separated and because she had felt protective towards her mother, once she was on her own. He hadn't realised at first how close they were, but he had become more aware of it over the years. Had she confided her distress about the events of the day before in Susan and been enticed away from home to the house where men were not allowed to live?

Yet he knew in his heart of hearts that it wasn't about Susan's attitudes or the views of the women in the girls' night out group. What was upsetting Anna was his relationship with Christine. For all that she said she wanted their children to have a normal family life, Anna was clearly not prepared to live with Christine's claim on Will's affections.

On the sofa in his silent home that was usually so full of life, Will began to see things from Anna's point of view. Had Anna married a selfish man, preoccupied with his past, who had swept her along in his quest with little thought for how she felt and who expected her to tolerate a sexually charged relationship with his new-found sister as if Christine were merely a family friend or a colleague of his at school? He wondered if this was the thinking Anna wanted him to do. If so, it hurt to realise that she was right and that he must make amends for his selfishness.

The anger he had felt on first realising that Anna had taken the girls away was overwhelmed by compunction. How could he have continued so blindly? He was grateful at least that things had not gone further with Christine. The clear invitation of her kiss could have led to serious trouble. It would have been much harder to row back from that.

He began to feel slightly sorry for himself. He could see now that he had allowed, even encouraged, the past to invade the present. Christine was affecting his life now because Florence had given him away as a baby. The mess he was in would have been avoided had he and his sister grown up together. They couldn't have done, of course, because Christine was only his half-sister, but if he and someone like Christine had grown up with Bill and Florence, all this would never have happened. He should have known better than to unpick the past, should have left it lying untouched. Anna had warned him off right from the beginning, in a general sort of way, when he decided to search for Florence, but he hadn't listened to her and even she had not foreseen what was happening now. The past was endangering the present, as he knew it often did. Who would know better than a history teacher how the past influences the present? Yet he had been unwary.

He had become so involved in his search for his original family and his wish for a relationship with them that he was neglecting his immediate family, displeasing his parents and, faced with the giddy, wild emotions that he felt towards Christine, was in danger of losing his way with his original family. If he wasn't careful, he would end up alone, separated from Anna, visiting his girls at weekends and regarded with suspicion by his parents and Frank. All the people who mattered most would be at odds with him. He shuddered at the thought.

In the late November dark, things were getting out of proportion. He stood up, turned on more lights than he needed and fetched his briefcase. There was nothing for it but to face the night alone. He sat at the dining room table and began to do some marking, from which there was no escaping. He found it hard to concentrate on essays about the First World War and caught himself on several occasions remembering nothing at all about an essay after he had read it. He took much longer over the marking than usual, even though there was no phone call that evening from Christine.

Later he made himself a sandwich and watched the television news at nine o'clock, feeling gloomy not so much because news was nearly always bad, but because of his own circumstances at that moment. He missed his family and felt even more sorry for himself, as he chewed on the sandwich. The bread was stale, the cheddar was more like concrete than cheese and the pickle he had added was vinegary. Anna was such a good cook. He liked cooking and he cooked for the family sometimes, but it was increasingly rare for him to do so.

Anna's precipitate action was a masterstroke on her part, like taking his queen in a game of chess or even checkmate. By absenting herself, she had made him think about her and want her in a more conscious way than usual. She had focused his attention on the effect of his actions. Even though she had made no demands about Christine, she was forcing him to give ground, with the implied threat of her continuing absence and that of the girls. It was inconsiderate of her not to say when she was coming back, but then, he had said nothing to her about how often or for how long he intended to see Christine. He didn't even know himself. Perhaps Anna didn't even know when she was coming back. That thought brought Will around again to whether he had lost her. He needed a masterstroke of his own to win her back.

Will had plenty of time to think that night, especially alone in bed and unable to sleep properly without Anna by his side. He tossed and turned, not enjoying the greater space of sleeping alone, but feeling the emptiness of the bed.

In the morning, with the noises of ordinary life around him, like the rattle of the paper coming through the letterbox, a shouted conversation in the street and the noise of traffic on his way to work, Will felt less inclined to beat himself up, but he was still determined to make amends. That day at school, he thought more, when he could, snatching moments between classes and during break-time, if nothing urgent claimed his attention. It was normally almost impossible to think about anything other than immediate matters when he was at school, where even break-time was often cut short by some demand or other. But his own actions and Anna's behaviour kept intruding on his attempts to work and he couldn't help thinking about his family. By the time that the school day had finished, he knew what he would say to Anna when he had the chance.

He rang her as soon as he arrived home and to his relief she answered the phone. It was embarrassing to have to contact her through her mother as if he were a teenager trying to persuade her out on a date. He spoke without any preamble.

'Anna, I've done my thinking and I hope you and the girls will come home straightaway.'

'I'm sorry, Will, but that's impossible. My mother has invited us out for a meal tonight and the girls are looking forward to it.'

'Tomorrow, then?'

'Let me see, tomorrow's Friday. Well, I'm not sure…'

'Look, I don't want to talk in detail on the phone. That doesn't seem to lead anywhere but into trouble,' Will said, thinking of his phone conversations with Christine. 'There will be changes, I promise you, but we'll talk when I see you. To start with, I'm inviting you and the girls to a meal tomorrow evening.' That was his return masterstroke.

'If you're sure that you will be different, then all right, we'll come back.'

Anna's voice sounded friendlier on the phone than the day before and Will sensed that the mood that had caused her to flee was changing. He hoped that she was encouraged by his promise and knew that he would have to fulfil it in a satisfactory way if he were to hold on to her. He slept better that night because he now had a plan that Anna had agreed to.

The following evening, Will went shopping on the way home for the meal which he was going to cook. He arrived home to find the lights on in the house and Anna and the girls back as if they had never been away. The girls gave him a tremendous welcome. They clearly had no idea about what was going on between their parents and Will was grateful for that. He didn't want them to know, because he would have found it hard to explain to them and anyway, it wasn't their concern. The real truth about his attraction to his sister would sound ridiculous to his little daughters. He could imagine that they would be upset or worse still, would make fun of him, if they even understood what he was talking about. Anna's greeting as Will entered the house was brief and he understood that much depended on what he would have to say to her later on.

He made a meal of pasta with a bolognaise sauce, followed by fruit salad and ice cream. The girls chattered unsuspectingly about their surprise visit to their grandmother, more excited about the rabbit who lived in a hutch in her garden than anything else and pleading with their parents for one of their own. The evening passed pleasantly enough except that Anna was quiet.

Will had work to do after the meal, so he sat in the dining room while Anna and the girls saw to the dishes. Later, the family watched television and Will found himself, for the first time, wishing the girls would leave the room so that he could be alone with Anna. They didn't seem to have a firm bedtime any more. Finally, Anna took them upstairs as he still had work to do.

When Anna came down again, they were alone together, but she hovered in the doorway, suggesting she would make a cup of tea and started to leave the sitting room. He stood up and crossed the room to her, taking her in his arms. She tried to wriggle away, but he held on to her.

'You're right, Anna. You're always right. What would I do without you?'

'You probably wouldn't survive for long.' She didn't step away, but she was stiff in his arms. 'That's not the point. What are you going to do about Christine? Where is all this going? I don't like it. Look, Will, I think you need to cool off a bit where she is concerned, before anyone gets hurt or upset.'

'Before you get hurt or upset, you mean?'

'And before you do!'

'I am fascinated by her. It's caught me unawares, I must admit. I had no idea that this was going to happen.'

'This attraction, you mean?'

'I suppose so.' Even now, he didn't want Anna to know exactly how he felt.

'I think I understand that. After all, you only knew of her existence recently. But you seem to have been bewitched by her. It's getting out of hand. You said at the beginning of all this that you wanted information about your past, to satisfy your curiosity, information that most people grow up with because they're not adopted. Fair enough. I've always supported you over that. But this thing with Christine is something else. I almost feel as if you're falling in love with her. Quite apart from the fact that she's your sister and so it's incestuous, it's upsetting me. I'm not prepared to have a husband who's running after some other woman, just like my father. Do you have any idea how horrible it was to know that he was always off with some other woman, leaving my mother to feel miserable? I promised myself that it would never happen to me. Where is it all going to end? What are you going to do about it?'

Anna was standing apart from Will and breathing hard by the time she finished. Will was taken aback by her open speech.

He hadn't thought that his feelings had been quite so obvious and he found her scrutiny discomforting. His marriage was on shifting sands and he had to move fast.

'I've been thinking since you've been away, as far as it's possible to think at school with so much happening all the time. All right. It's not going anywhere. I can see I've been selfish, just thinking of getting to know my new family and taking you and the girls for granted.'

'It isn't the family I mind about. Bill and the others seem fine to me. It's Christine. There's something greedy about all these phone calls and now you've started going to see her. My impression is that she's a clever woman who's a bit bored and neglected by her husband and rather than concentrating on finding a proper job or paying more attention to her family, she's turned her attention to you. And you've fallen for it, hook, line and sinker, because you think that you can make up for not being brought up by your natural family – either that or you've fallen in love with her and you've forgotten about me.'

'I'm not in love with her!' Will's denial sounded like a kind of admission to his own ears and he stopped, confused.

'What about all those phone calls and now you're going to see her on your own?'

'All right, Anna. I promised you some changes. I won't phone her again or go to see her as I did the other night. I hope you're not asking me never to see her again, but I won't phone her for a chat, one to one.'

'No, I'm not saying don't ever see her again. I'm just saying keep more of a distance and avoid the one to one. Think about the effect on me. You're making Christine into a rival to me. This thing between you isn't a brother and sister relationship at all, at least not like anything I've ever known, even though I don't have any brothers. 'And think about the effect on our family. I've been behind you all these years in finding out about your past, but there are limits and at the moment all you seem to do is think about your natural family rather than about me and the girls. I don't want to have to worry about what's going on between you and Christine. You haven't got the balance right. That's all. And the funny thing is that we think Florence has had a secret for all these years and now you seem to have one. A different sort of secret, I grant you, but a secret nonetheless. It's all a bit creepy.'

They were standing further apart by this time, flashing glances at each other.

'Anna, I'm sorry. I had no idea that it mattered to you so much. All this business with my family has been rather intense of late, I know. And you're right about Christine. I suppose I'm flattered by her attention. I didn't ask it to happen and it won't last because I won't let it. I'll take a step back from her. Nothing need be said. It's probably all a phase in getting to know a sister I had never met until a few months ago. And there won't be any secret.'

'All right. Now let's change the subject. It's wearing me out!'

'It's a relief talking to you,' Will said, ignoring her request. 'I've let all this thing concerning Christine happen without talking to you. I suppose it's because I sensed the tension in it, without properly sitting down and working out what it meant. I'm sorry, Anna. I'll make it up to you.'

'Thanks. There's no need, except by cooling it with Christine. That's all I'm asking for,' Anna said. He nodded and Anna went to the kitchen to make the tea.

Listening to Anna, Will regretted his actions recently. She was right. He had been taking her for granted, because she had always been his support in his family-finding. He wouldn't phone Christine again and he would be politely brief if she phoned him. They would probably only meet on rare family occasions in future, like weddings and funerals, because they lived in different parts of London and had busy lives. His attraction to her had blown up unexpectedly and it could just as easily subside. It would have to subside, because he couldn't allow Christine to threaten his relationship with Anna or his family life. He wasn't going to be stupid enough to allow the consequence of being adopted, because that's what the attraction to Christine stemmed from, to destroy his happiness.

Now that he had had time to think about it, indeed had been forced by Anna to think about it, he knew that the relationship he had been developing with Christine was unwise. It was teetering on the edge of the wrong way for a brother and sister to behave and it was causing tension with Anna. He had been so keen to get to know his new family that he had charged off in the wrong direction, allowing himself to be led by Christine.

He wondered if Tony, in Anna's position on the other side of the picture, was aware of Christine's interest in her new-found brother. Was he as jealous as Anna and if not, wasn't he a bit spineless? Or was he simply too lacking in powers of observation, too wrapped up in his job, to know what was happening? Or had he guessed and just didn't care? Will realised that he would probably never know and it wasn't his business, anyway. He had enough to do with putting his marriage back on track. He would think of some way of making it up to Anna, some special kind of outing for just the two of them. He would draw back from his sister and retreat to what he always had been, one of two brothers, himself and Frank.

That night, Will and Anna made love in a different way. There was an intensity to it that had been missing lately. Will was expressing his passionate love for her and she was saying that she had come back to him.

When Will and Anna moved house in 1980, a year or so

later, Will wrote both to Mrs Bradstreet and Paula Heron, giving them his new address. He had no real hope that Florence would ever contact him, but it was worth keeping a link, just in case.

- Part Five -

Flo

1986-1987

Chapter One

George died suddenly of a heart attack in his late sixties. It was a terrible shock. Even though Florence was not new to grief, she could hardly believe that George had disappeared so quickly from her life, with a massive heart attack that took everyone unawares. She had grieved for Bill, William, Rosie and later her parents. Now she was grieving for George. She wondered whether the pain of grief was as bad as it had been all those years ago when she had learned that Bill was dead and later had given up William. Those events had been unnatural and had brought an unnatural pain. Losing her parents had been nothing like as bad as losing Bill and William and her sister Rosie because her parents had both had long lives. Missing George now was painful, although she could see that his death was in the natural order of things, even though it had come too soon. In the end she didn't know which loss was the worst, but it was George's death she was living with now.

At night, her body would unconsciously search for him and she would wake in a panic in the small hours to find he wasn't there. Every night after waking, she lay for hours, willing sleep that wouldn't come. She didn't feel like getting up and doing anything, so she lay there, reliving the years of her marriage, amazed that it should all be over so soon when it seemed to be only yesterday that she had met George.

How little she had loved him when she married him, too soon after losing Bill, and with a kind of desperation, fearful that she was being left on the shelf after Bill's death and the loss of William. Yet how much she had grown to love him as the years passed, so that her grief now could not be greater. Towards morning, she would doze off and wake late, exhausted and guilty at finding herself in bed at a later hour than usual and with no one to get up for. It was a dreadful kind of freedom and felt like a dragging weight.

Florence dressed with care on the day of the funeral, in the half-light of the early morning, after a poor night's sleep. From her best clothes, she chose a white silk blouse, a black woollen skirt, a grey lacy cardigan and a moonstone necklace which George had given her on their tenth wedding anniversary. The clothes and jewellery were like armour with which to face the ordeal of the funeral.

The room in the crematorium was crowded. Val and her husband Dennis, Evelyn and her husband Colin, and Steve and his wife Lynne were there, with their children. Florence's sisters and brothers and their families and George's sister Carol and her family and some cousins of George's, whom she rarely saw, turned out in force. Monica, her employer and Doris, her main friend in Putney, had come. George's tennis partner, Sam, who lived nearby, looked sombre. He had been a good friend as well as a tennis partner and, as a single man living alone since the death of his mother, and without many friends, he had told Florence how much he would miss George. One or two of George's former colleagues from work stood together at the back.

Florence sat like an automaton through the service, looking at the coffin and then watching it disappear. She stood up and reached out a hand towards it as it went, but she was too late and failed to touch it. Her hand moved uselessly back to her side. Still numb inside, shaking hands with mourners, she moved like clockwork, thanking people for coming as they gathered afterwards at what she now had to call her house. She was grateful to Val and Evelyn for serving tea and cake and leaving her free to talk to people.

As the afternoon drew to a close, the faces began to blur around her. She knew she was exhausted, especially as she had slept badly since George's death. She sat as stiffly as a ramrod, fighting the tiredness. Val was solicitous and polite, more like a stranger than a daughter, she noticed idly, but then dismissed the thought as unfair. Evelyn was affectionate and moist-eyed and Steve kept offering practical help as if it would make everything all right again.

Doris, who managed to look dramatic rather than sombre in black, began to be bossy towards the end of the afternoon.

'Florence,' she said, as the number of guests slowly dwindled, 'you must give in. You're being too hard on yourself, so capable and managing. Let go and cry. It'll do you the world of good.'

'I can't today. I can't cry. I can't seem to unbend.'

'You will,' Doris said. 'Right now you're overtired and your life is not your own. But when all this is over' – she waved a ringed hand around the room – 'then you'll feel it. And don't be lonely, Florence. I'm here any time you feel like company.'

'No, I won't be lonely,' Florence said. She would always be lonely now, but was determined not to be openly sorry for herself. 'I have so many people to rely on. Thank you, Doris.'

She caught the roaming hand and gave it a squeeze, feeling a twinge of remorse for the times that she and George had laughed about Doris for her flamboyant style of dress and love of colour. George, a lover of butterflies, had called her the *Painted Lady* in private. Florence was going to need her friend now. However good they were at keeping in touch, her children all had their own lives to lead.

Everything would change now that she was a widow. She

tried the word out in her mind and disliked it. She felt too young, still in her sixties, to be a widow. It was an ugly word that made her think of spiders and weeds. She would need everyone more now, but would they want her? She had only her cat and the budgie of the day to look after and the cat liked to keep his distance most of the time. He hated being picked up and cuddled. He was nowhere to be seen now, because he avoided gatherings of any sort and was probably behind the sofa or under a bed somewhere. He would turn up when everyone had gone.

During the long days that followed the funeral, Florence pored over old letters and photographs, immersed in memories and only jolted back to the present from time to time by a phone call or a visit. Evelyn and Steve kept in better contact than Val, but that didn't surprise her. Even at this time, when she was grieving, conversations with Val usually ended in a disagreement of some kind. Doris plied her with food she didn't want, George's tennis partner, Sam, who had been devoted to his mother until her death, offered help in a bewildered way. Even they are treating me like bone china, she thought. Even Doris, my friend, who lost her husband, and Sam, who lost his mother, don't quite know what to say.

She cried on her own, because she didn't want to upset anyone and her grief felt private. One day, looking through George's clothes, she started to think about herself. What kind of life remained for her now? She was unused to asking herself this question. She had spent all her life until now looking after other people. She had nothing pressing to do. The shop felt further away than a short walk at present. Everything mattered less now that George was gone. She was grateful for her good health and had never much been troubled by illness. There was the house to run, but it wouldn't be too difficult. It was too big for her now that George wasn't there, but she pushed any idea of moving to the back of her mind. There was enough going on without that. There was her job. Monica had told her to take as much time off as she wanted to. At least she had somewhere to go on three mornings a week when she felt like returning to work and she wouldn't then be staring at four walls all day, every day.

In the small hours of one night, a few weeks after the funeral, she sat up in bed and switched on the bedside light. She knew she wouldn't sleep for hours. She tried to think of herself as others would see her. She was a woman in a nightdress, with a lined face and grey hair. She had always been careful about her appearance, thinking that she was only just on the pretty side of plain and therefore it was worth making an effort. She had never bothered with hair dye, though. She should have done – hair dye, make-up and colourful clothes would make her look younger. Then she would be less likely to become a victim of other people's ideas of what she should be doing. Since George's death, she felt more vulnerable to being pushed around by other people, especially Val.

She tried to see herself as a woman finished, life behind her, her passions spent, her flesh loose, her bones brittle, eyes dulled, chin quivering with indecision, teeth slipping out of place, even though she still had many of her own, hands trembling, skin wrinkled. She piled detail on unvarnished and exaggerated detail in order to be able to see herself from the point of view of someone else, someone younger and more part of the world than she felt now. She imagined the world would soon be thinking about putting her away, feeding and clothing her, letting her body continue and caring for it so that there were no accidents, but not noticing her, the character in the husk.

But she couldn't achieve that distance. The more she thought, the more she saw herself in her mind's eye. The wrinkles faded and there was a young woman called Flo, with brown hair glinting in the sun, eyes shining, clear, unlined skin, (often too pale from city life), the expression eager and curious. Somewhere within the husk that young woman lived on, as did Flo the young WAAF meeting Bill and losing him, then Flo, the mother of William, desperate to keep him but unable to do so, then Flo marrying George and bringing up three children, and the older Florence going out to work. Behind them all, little Flossie, with long, brown hair, wearing a frock, minding her brothers and sisters, sent out on an errand by her mother or going to school and escaping the housework. They were all there, invisible to everyone but her, yet to her so alive that the oldest woman of them all could barely shield the throng behind.

And then there was William. What was he doing now, a grown man entering his forties, possibly with his own children? Should she write to those people and ask if they could contact William for her? Now that George had gone, there wasn't the need for such secrecy as there had been. She toyed with the thought of contacting him, a thought she had tried to repel and that would not go away entirely. It seemed to have a life of its own and it was growing. Yet she couldn't contact William without telling Val, Evelyn and Steve about him and it was too much at the moment. She lacked the strength and the energy. It would be such an upheaval when she was learning to live with the loss of George.

What would her children think of her and of how she had deceived their father all those years? Val would certainly not lose a chance to be critical. Evelyn might decide that it was as bad as her husband's Colin's deception of her. Colin had deserted Evelyn not long after the birth of their baby, Sarah, when it became clear that he was having an affair. And Steve might judge her for destroying his one chance of having the brother he had always wanted. Florence's wish to see William was not as great as her wish to retain the good opinion of her children and some semblance of normality about her life, some blessed ordinariness, at least for the moment.

Monica went to an auction in Salisbury a year after George's death. It was partly a social trip because she had a good friend there. She left Florence in charge of the shop and Florence was on her own there the next morning when she received a phone call from the friend telling her in a tearful voice that Monica had been killed in a car accident. They had been on their way in the friend's car to the auction and a van driver had appeared without looking properly from a side road and ploughed into the car where Monica, in the passenger seat, hadn't stood a chance.

It was another shock, although nothing like as great as the shock of losing George. Even so, Florence had to sit down. She closed the shop until further notice as a mark of respect, putting a note in the window before she left, and went home to await events. It turned out that she was needed to arrange the funeral, because Monica's only relative was a cousin. The cousin rang Florence and said they would come to the funeral, but declined to help organise it because she and her husband were some distance away, in Bristol.

Florence could hardly believe it when a solicitor wrote one day to say that Monica had left everything to her – the property comprising the shop and the flat above, the contents of the shop and some capital as well. Monica had never hinted anything about a will and it never occurred to Florence to think about it.

By a stroke of the pen, she became the owner of a shop and the landlady of the flat above. Monica's cousin and her husband came to the funeral. When they questioned Florence over the flowers after the funeral service and understood that they would not be benefiting from the will, they were shocked.

'We've certainly had a wasted journey,' the cousin said, buttoning up her coat with jerky fingers, making it clear that she wasn't prepared to stay there a moment longer.

Her husband was blunter. 'You've done a good job of worming your way into Monica's affections,' he said, as they stood outside the Catholic church where Monica had worshipped every Sunday.

They both looked hard at Florence, who was feeling upset about the loss of her friend and employer and disinclined to take part in a dispute about the will.

'I'm sorry you feel that way,' she said, and wished them a safe journey home, before turning away to talk to someone else.

Doris was astonished when Florence told her the news.

'I expect the property and the business will fetch quite a bit,' she said. She stopped at the look on Florence's face.

'I don't want to sell. I want to carry on the business. Why don't you come in with me? We could run the shop together. I could pay you a proper salary from the shop, supported by rent from the flat if necessary. After all, you sometimes complain that you have time on your hands.'

'All right,' Doris said. 'Why not give it a go? We can be partners in crime. It's true that I haven't got much else to do and if it doesn't work out, you can always sack me.'

Now it was Florence's turn to teach. She willingly passed on all she had learned from Monica. She was in charge now. She had a shop to run and an employee, as well as a tenant. She was a businesswoman in her own right and she had finally, in her sixties, realised her ambition of a place in the world outside home.

She changed the name of the shop to Florence's Antiques, even though many people advised her to keep a name already known to customers. She wanted to put her stamp on the shop. She toyed briefly with the idea of calling it Florence's Findings because Monica had called her purchases findings and because it sounded good. In the end she thought that Florence's Antiques said more, even if the stock wasn't all strictly antique.

The shop front survived the renovation of the rest of the street. The window display was well set out. There was space around each object, just as Monica had arranged her goods. Antique might have been too grand a word to describe everything inside, but Florence stoutly maintained that it was not the junk shop Val was sometimes heard to call it.

Florence and Doris ran the shop together. They had a running joke that Doris, ten years Florence's junior, was young, a spring chicken no less. It had started after they first became friends when Flo was in her forties and Doris only in her thirties and had continued since then. Now that Florence was in her sixties and Doris in her fifties, the joke was in retirement but it still surfaced now and then.

After inheriting the shop, Florence decided to make her will. She told Evelyn about one provision, swearing her to secrecy. Evelyn was amazed by what she heard.

'You're leaving your house to me? That's going to set the cat among the pigeons. Val will be furious and Steve won't be too happy. I've never discussed it with them, but they must have expectations. I know Val will want the house because she's possessive about it, even now.'

'Val and Dennis are well off enough with that perfume factory in Croydon and in any case, I'm leaving Val a fair share, even though I hate to think of my money being swallowed up by Dennis. He's got no head for business. Steve is doing well as an engineer and Lynne is working.' Florence had little time for Dennis.

'I suppose so, and don't get me wrong. I'm delighted, but…'

'Don't worry about it. They're all much better off than you and Sarah. I don't think that Val and Steve will be so upset after all. I'm leaving Steve the shop and the flat above and Val will have the equivalent in money. Your father was a careful man and I'm a businesswoman who knows her trade. I've managed to put by a pretty penny over the years. It's best this way. It will help even things out. Don't forget that I was one of six and I've always been keen on equal shares.'

'I know, Mum. It just doesn't sound equal to me.'

'I've spoken to a solicitor and done the sums and it will be roughly equal. I've decided, but I wanted to tell you, so you have something to look forward to, as you're on your own. Now, promise me you won't mention a word to anyone.'

'All right. And I'm grateful because it will be a tremendous help. I just hope the family will still be speaking to me when they find out,' Evelyn said.

'And there's another thing – leaving my house to you means that one day Sarah will have it. I know Sarah's only a baby still, but I see myself in her,' Florence said. 'It's a family resemblance, if you like. You never knew me as a child, so it's hard for you to see. I want her to do well in life. She has a real spark, as I like to think I had at her age. I had to overcome a lot to get anywhere you know, and so will she, growing up without a father. I've always thought a child needs a father.'

'In an ideal world, maybe, but it isn't always possible, you know,' Evelyn said.

It wasn't long before Doris, an inveterate writer of romantic short stories, was writing about an antique shop owner who had fallen in love with a customer who was attracted to his antiques, but unfortunately not to him. And it was in the shop, on a summer afternoon in 1987, when customers were few and far between, that Doris told Florence a story from her earlier life. Florence listened intently. Every detail etched itself on her mind. Never had she heard a story that meant so much to her.

Chapter Two

Doris finished telling her story and silence followed. Florence was looking at her in undisguised amazement.

'You had a baby girl and gave her up for adoption before you were married?'

'Yes, why do you seem so astonished? Florence, don't say you disapprove. Times have changed, you know,' Doris said.

'It's not that. I mean, of course I don't disapprove.' Florence was unable to go on. She was overwhelmed by a desire to speak, by words stringing themselves together in her mind, but how could she utter them, after all these years, those forbidden, banished words which would tell Doris her own, similar story?

'I've met her once or twice. I don't think she wants to see me often, though,' Doris said. 'I've had to accept that she wanted to satisfy her curiosity about me, that's all. It's her birthday today and that's why I'm thinking about her, I suppose. I don't normally mention her.' She sounded calm, and accepting, then her voice rose with concern. 'Why, Florence, what's the matter? You're crying! Don't cry. I'm not that upset about it now. Of course, I didn't want to give her up, but I did it for her sake and she's turned out well.'

The struggle within Florence was expressing itself in tears, for Bill, for William, for deceiving George and her family and for herself, for all the years of self-imposed silence. Doris passed her a tissue and waited quietly.

'I had a baby, too,' Florence said, when she could talk. 'I gave him up for adoption and I've never met him, even though he wanted to meet me about ten years ago, when he would have been in his early thirties. And I never told George anything about it, and my children don't know either. But I've never been able to forget him.'

'I'm not surprised,' Doris said.

'Not surprised that I had a baby outside marriage? Or that I gave him up? Or that I never told George or the children?'

'Not surprised by any of it, but let's say not surprised that you gave him up, because in those days it was often the only choice. And not surprised that you've kept it a secret. And of course, I'm not surprised that you can't forget him. Now, if you want to talk about it, tell me. But you might not. It doesn't always help to stir things up,' Doris said calmly.

'Well…' Florence hesitated, but the relief of talking now, to someone who would understand what she had been through, was taking her over. She told Doris the story of Bill and William and of keeping William's existence a secret from her family for over forty years.

'I understand why you did what you did, Florence. It was different for me. My baby wasn't such a secret. My parents knew and so did my future husband. He accepted it and said it didn't matter; it was in the past,' Doris said, when Florence finished her story.

'I wish that had been possible for me. I don't know what to do now. Thank you for listening. I'm so glad to have told someone at last.'

'You don't know what to do about what?'

'I made things harder for myself by getting out of the East End. I mean, it helped to keep the secret, but I never had the relief of telling anyone until now, whereas I might have done if

I'd stayed there, if the family and neighbours, apart from Rosie and Jessie, that is, had known about William. But then George would have known and I might have lost him, so I had to do what I did. But George has gone now and I've been thinking lately that I could meet William. Only it's hard to break the habit of a lifetime and what would Val think, or Evelyn or Steve?'

'They might not think it's so terrible to have a brother,' Doris said.

'Oh, I don't know. I can't decide. One thing puzzles me about you. If your husband knew about your baby and she wasn't a secret, why have you never mentioned her before?'

'I think it's because she doesn't want to know me.'

Florence was reminded of William's request to see her and her refusal to have anything to do with him. If only Doris could receive a letter from her daughter asking to see her.

It was fortunate that no customers came in until later that afternoon. Tidying the shelves unnecessarily, dusting a little here and there, Florence enjoyed a lightness of heart that was unfamiliar to her.

Talking to Doris revived in Florence's mind a debate she had been having with herself since George's death about seeing William. He was forty-two now and might be a father. It was about ten years since her refusal to see him and he might still want to meet her. Wasn't it cruel, now that George had gone, to continue to refuse to see him? But what would Val, Evelyn and Steve think, on finding out that they had a half-brother their father had never known about? Would they think less of her? Florence was in a dilemma that seemed much sharper and more troublesome after bringing William to the surface of her mind by telling Doris about him, yet she still had not made a decision one way or the other.

Florence had not been able to forget William's wish to see her. While George was still alive, it had seemed impossible, but now that George had been gone for over a year and she was learning to live without him, there was far less reason to continue with her refusal. What mattered was more than her own comfort, more even than what Val, Evelyn and Steve might think, although those things were important. After all these years, she began increasingly to think that some thought must be given to what William might want.

She tried out her views on Doris in the shop one day when they were rearranging the window display. They had bought some framed prints of Victorian Putney in an auction and were placing them on the shelves of a bookcase that Doris had found in the back room and that fitted nicely in the window.

'It probably would help him and it would be a big day for you, after all these years, but don't expect it to lead to anything. He might only want to see you once,' Doris said, standing in the window. 'Of course, I'm thinking of my daughter who only wanted to meet me once. It might be different for you.'

'It's so difficult to know what to do for the best,' Florence said, handing her the last print to display.

'Well, yes, of course it is. It's breaking the habit of almost a lifetime. But I can't decide for you. You've got to make your own mind up.'

'I know. That's what I'm trying to do. I lie awake at night thinking about it. I want to be at peace with myself. You'd think that the older I get, the less I would think about it, but now George has gone, or perhaps because I'm getting older, I think about Bill and William much more.'

'It's because you feel there's something you ought to be doing now. I can be a listening ear, if it helps. Now, what would it be like, telling your children? What would Val say to finding out that she's got an older brother?'

There was no love lost between Doris and Val. Florence put it down to a certain jealousy she had noticed in Val concerning her friendship with Doris.

'That's easy. *But I've always been the eldest!* At least, she would say that at first. Then she might come round. I think Evelyn and Steve might rather like the idea. But we should have to wait and see what William is like.'

'It sounds as if you're making up your mind to see him.'

'Do you know, I think I am, after all these years. I've got to work myself up to it, but I feel as if I owe it to him. I must tell them all at the same time. If I tell Val first she'll lord it over the others and if I tell Evelyn or Steve first, I'll never hear the last of it from Val. I think I'll invite them round on Saturday afternoon, just the three of them and me. I'll make a cake for it today.'

'Well, if you're making a cake, that settles it. Oh, there's the bell,' Doris said, stepping out of the window, followed by Florence. The jangling of the doorbell announcing the entrance of a customer put an end to further conversation for the moment.

In any case, Florence felt decided now and the months of dilemma were over. She made a spice cake that evening. While it was in the oven, she rang Val, Evelyn and Steve. She invited them all to tea on that Saturday afternoon, but she wouldn't tell them what it was about, only that she had something important to say. Fortunately no one had an unbreakable appointment and they were all too curious about what Florence could possibly have to tell them to resist her invitation.

They all agreed to come and all arrived on time at Florence's house in answer to her summons. She had specified no husbands, wives or children, because she didn't want any distractions. Evelyn had prevailed on a neighbour with a child of the same age to look after Sarah. Her husband Colin had by then not only left her, but had become so thoroughly involved with his new girlfriend that his interest in Sarah had waned.

Val, Evelyn and Steve all crowded into the small sitting

room in Florence's house, the house where they had spent the later part of their childhood and which held many memories for them. The sitting room boasted an iron fireplace, with dark red tiles, its original features intact within a carved wooden mantelpiece, on top of which an old wooden clock sat ticking audibly. A small table in the bay window, flanked by two wooden chairs, displayed a blue glass vase and the rest of the room was taken up by a sofa and easy chairs with a pink floral pattern. Ornaments on every possible surface spoke of Florence's love of antiques and a cage with a budgie sat in one corner of the room.

The faint scent of the lavender that Florence always kept in the house could not compete with Val's strong scent from the factory which Dennis had inherited from his father. Florence didn't like the scent, which was too pungent and heavy for her. When it turned up among her Christmas presents, as it invariably did, she would pass it on to someone else. This wasn't always easy. Doris's dislike of Val, not helped by Val's tendency to refer to Florence's Antiques as a junk shop, extended to the scent. Evelyn didn't like the scent and nor did Steve's wife, Lynne. Florence much preferred the scent of the lavender from her garden that stood in vases around the house or lay in bowls that she filled every year with a fresh supply of the dried seed heads. She breathed in, grimacing.

Val and Evelyn were sitting as far as possible from each other. Her daughters had not grown up to be friends. Florence sighed, thinking briefly of Rosie. She still missed her sister, even more so since George's death. Val was bossy, while Evelyn was gentle by nature and not inclined to take the lead. Her honest, plain face often wore a puzzled expression as if life were slightly too difficult for her and she always said that Val had been too bullying as an older sister, when they were children, for them to be friends in adult life. Steve, on the other hand, was like his father, a straightforward, kindly man. Florence's only regret in his direction was that he was so busy with work and his young family that she didn't see him often, even though Sydenham in south east London, where he lived with his family, wasn't so far from Putney in south west London.

They waited expectantly, talking about their children, while Florence made tea and served cake. She was feeling tremulous, but was determined that she would not back out of her decision now.

'Come on, Mother! Tell us why you've summoned us. My curiosity is killing me,' Val said, taking a bite of cake and sitting forward in her chair. Her face was gleaming with anticipation.

Florence took a deep breath and told her story, much as she had told Doris, but also using words she had been polishing in her head ever since making her decision to tell Val, Evelyn and Steve about William. She described the missing parts of her life, the parts her children didn't know about and her growing feeling since George's death that she should respond, even ten years afterwards, to William's request to see her.

When she had finished, there was a silence, broken only by the twittering of the budgie. Steve spoke first.

'Fancy that, a brother after all these years of being bossed around by two older sisters! It's a bit of a surprise, Mum, but you know I've always wanted a brother. I hope I'll be able to meet William.'

Steve was looking pleased at the news and Florence loved him for the generosity of his response. It was true. She remembered Steve as a little boy asking for a brother, but she and George had decided to stop at three children.

'I hope so too, Steve. And thanks for taking it so well. I've been so worried about what you all might think.' She smiled at him with relief.

Evelyn, always more cautious, spoke next. 'So are we two brothers and two sisters? But it won't be the same because we didn't grow up with William and in any case, he might have other brothers and sisters in his family.'

'You're right. It won't be the same,' Florence said.

'You could have told us before, Mum. What a burden it must have been to keep a secret like that all those years. What made you tell us now?' Evelyn asked.

'I've been thinking about it since your father died, but it's partly because of Doris. She told me recently about a baby she gave up for adoption. We had a long talk when we were in the shop together one afternoon. Then I found myself telling her all about William. It just welled up in me, only a few days ago. Since then, I've been thinking harder about seeing William, but I didn't want to do that without telling you all about him first.'

'What a terrible time you must have had, being pregnant on your own and then having a baby. And no wonder that you like to tell me that a baby needs a father, as well as a mother. I thought it was just because I'm bringing Sarah up on my own. It wasn't easy finding a job and someone to look after her, with Colin walking out on me like that, even though you've helped out, Mum. Oh, what a shock. It's going to take a while to believe it, but I'd like to meet William too,' Evelyn said.

'Thanks, my dear,' Florence said. Two of her children were taking the news in their stride. Val's silence was unusual. She always liked to be the first to speak when the three of them were together, which was rare enough these days. Glancing at her elder daughter, Florence saw surprise and some distress in her face.

'I don't believe it. You had an illegitimate baby and you never told Father? You're making it up!'

Val sounded explosive, the way she often was with surprises. She was breathing hard and Florence was reminded of the steam train she had ridden on during a trip to Norfolk the previous year, with its huffing and puffing and its clouds of smoke.

Neither Evelyn nor Steve was close to Val. They tended to see her only on infrequent family occasions and eyebrows were raised and cheeks puffed out when her name came up in her absence. She was generally thought of in the wider family as something of a trial.

'Don't be ridiculous, Val! Of course I'm not making anything up. I've got letters from Bill to prove it. But I can see it's a shock for all of you and I do hope I've done the right thing in telling you,' Florence said.

'It's all so extraordinary. Imagine finding a new brother when you're in your thirties. It means rewriting the family story. I'm supposed to be *the eldest*,' Val said.

Florence could hear a reprimand in her voice. She had noticed the use of the word illegitimate, accurate but condemning, especially in the 1980s, when single parents were becoming more accepted and the word illegitimate was falling out of use.

'You're not the eldest anymore,' Evelyn said with a laugh and Florence could hear the satisfaction in her younger daughter's voice as she moved Val off the perch in the family tree that she had held all her life. Steve nodded in agreement.

'Do you know, I think it explains a lot…' Val said more calmly.

'What do you mean?' Florence asked.

'I think it explains a lot about why you and I have found it so hard to get along sometimes, Mother. Even when I was a little girl there were problems. I always felt I was the one who received the least attention. You were distant. Was it possible that you didn't love me because I wasn't William? Were you thinking about him all the time? You loved Evelyn and Steve all right. You were always cosy with them. Maybe you had got over losing William by the time that they were born. Thinking of it now, I was given short shrift by you as a child, even though I was the eldest. Well, I thought I was, but obviously not.'

'Oh, come on, now, Val, don't be sorry for yourself. Weren't you simply jealous of Evelyn and Steve?' Florence's tone was brisk, despite her feeling that Val might be right. She didn't want Val to gain an upper hand over the question of William.

'Of course I was, like any child faced with a younger sister and brother, but there was more to it than that. I always felt that you weren't looking *at* me, but *beyond* me. It was hard to get through to you, because you were was lost in your own world. I can remember being quite little and taking your face in my hands and saying look at me, look at me, and you would, but you seemed to come back from a long way away. I used to think you weren't completely there. Now I would say you were preoccupied. You must have missed your baby so much. I can't imagine the pain, especially if it was a double dose, losing Bill and then William. I've never had to deal with anything like that, as I've been lucky enough to have a family in the usual way. And to think I once accused you of being an ordinary woman! I can see now that I'm far more ordinary than you are. It must have taken a lot of determination to keep a secret like that and pass yourself off as someone different from the person you really were for the rest of your life.'

This time Val made being an ordinary woman sound decent and respectable, while not being ordinary was to be treacherous. This was in complete contrast to the teenage contempt of the ordinary woman that Val had once hurled at her, but Florence refrained from saying so. It would be too much of a distraction when she wanted to keep the attention firmly on William.

'You were always an observant child,' she said instead.

'Well, I think it's an extraordinary story. What would Father say?' Val said.

Florence felt the question like a blow, but did her best to remain calm. 'He's not here to ask, so we can never be certain, but I hope he would understand why I did what I did. Now we're having this conversation, I wish even more than I used to that I'd had the courage to tell him about William, but I can't do anything about that now. It always seemed like too much of a risk. I was afraid he would throw me over when we first met and, after we were married, it was harder and harder to say anything, because he might have felt I had married him under false pretences. I suppose we were both the product of the world we lived in.'

Val was silent and Florence was grateful for that. She had told her story and in their different ways her children had accepted it. An enormous sense of relief spread through her and something else, that she scarcely dared call hope. A hope that she might finally be able to say yes to William's request to meet her.

Chapter Three

In the lull which followed telling her story about William, Florence fell back on serving more tea and cake.

'What are you going to do about William?' Steve said, accepting a second slice of cake.

Florence was ready with her answer. 'I'd like to try to find him. I think the time has come now to get in touch with him.'

'Do you know how?' That was Evelyn. Val was sitting back.

'Well, I can't remember who it was wrote to me all those years ago and, of course, I didn't keep the letter because I was in such a panic. I could get in touch with the people I gave William to in the first place. I remember they were called the Waifs and Strays, something to do with the church. I've no idea if they still exist, but if I can't find them, the Citizens Advice Bureau would probably be able to help.'

'It might be difficult, though. William could have moved since he tried to contact you,' Evelyn said.

'He could have changed his mind, even if you find him,' Steve said.

'Yes, I do hope not, but I can't be sure he'll want to see me. It's likely that he will, though, as he wanted to before.'

'Isn't it all in the past? Why disturb William when he's lived to this age without you? It's one thing for us to know about him, but quite another to go looking for him, surely?' Val said with a hint of impatience. 'Who are you doing it for, you or him?'

'Both of us, I suppose. He wanted to meet me and I couldn't see him then, because I couldn't tell George about him, after all those years of marriage on a different basis, but I'm trying to do something about it now. It would be dishonest to pretend I'm only thinking of him. I'm looking for some peace for myself, to know that he's all right. I suppose I want to know it was successful.'

'I can't help being curious about a new brother, but it would be too much for all of us to meet him at once,' Val said. 'I suggest Mother and I see him first, unless of course, you want to meet him on your own, Mother.'

Florence could see that Val would not give up being the eldest easily and, depending on what William was like and what he wanted from them, she might not have to at all. She obviously wanted to be involved, despite her initial reaction of disbelief.

'Well, let's see if I can find him first, but I'd like one of you to be there and since you've offered, Val… If it goes well, you two could see him another time,' Florence said glancing at Evelyn and Steve, silently imploring them to accept the plan.

For Val to have offered to meet William with her was surprising and welcome. She knew by now that Val was much easier to get along with when she had something purposeful to do or was being allowed to take the lead than when she was being pushed aside.

The mood of their discussion changed after that. Florence's story had united her children in a way that nothing had done before. She spent the rest of the afternoon talking to them about her life as a young woman during the war on an RAF station and the difficulties she had faced after Bill had left and she had realised that she was pregnant and then learned of his death. There was a lot to say, a lot that she hadn't been able to talk about for years and she was surprised at how fresh it all seemed once she took the plunge into the waters of the past.

'How strange to think that none of us would have been born if Bill Martin had survived the war,' Val said, when Florence had come to the point at which William had left her.

'Unless something else had happened,' Florence said.

'What do you mean?' Steve asked.

'Oh, I don't know... supposing Bill's parents had threatened to cut him off if he married me? I never thought that would happen, but the letter from his mother was a nasty piece of work,' Florence said. 'Anyway, what matters is that I did marry your father and that you're all here. Of course, I was desperately unhappy when I heard what had happened to Bill, but I had to get over it. I loved your father and we were happy together. Things have turned out well.'

The way she had seen George as more as a refuge than a husband in their first years together was not something she would ever willingly discuss with her children.

'For us, but what about William?' Val asked.

'That is what I want to find out,' Florence said.

She felt lighter of heart after her confession to her children about William than she had done since George's death. She took the steps she had suggested and wrote to the Church of England Children's Society as she discovered the Waifs and Strays were now called.

17th September, 1987

Dear Madam,

I am writing about my son, William Haldon, who was born on 12th January 1945. I gave him up to you for adoption when he was three months old and I know he tried to contact me ten years ago. I said no at the time, but things have changed now and I should like to see him, if he is still of the same mind.

I should be most grateful if you could help to put me in touch with him.

Yours sincerely,

Florence Cruise (Mrs)

A few days after posting the letter, Florence had a phone call, making an appointment for her to see a social worker at the Church of England Children's Society and asking her to bring evidence of her identity. She wished she hadn't left William's birth certificate in Jessie's house when she moved out all those years ago, but she took her marriage certificate with her.

Arriving at the office, she saw a young man, Jamie Wood, long-haired and casually dressed. His unconventional appearance surprised her, but she liked his friendly manner. Once satisfied about her identity, he explained that William had been in touch with them some years previously, seeking information about his father. On the file was a letter from William giving them his new address and phone number when he moved, in case Florence ever contacted them.

'What a relief! I thought he might be hard to find,' Florence said. She had been feeling anxious on the way to the interview, but now she relaxed.

'Would you like me to contact him for you?' Jamie Wood asked.

'Yes, please. Just in case he's changed his mind,' Florence said.

Within a few days, Jamie Wood was on the telephone to Florence, saying that William had been amazed and pleased to hear from him and wanted to meet her. He gave Florence the address and phone number, adding that William was now known as Will, that he had a wife and daughters and was a history teacher in a secondary school. Florence was both pleased and nervous. She thanked Jamie Wood for his efforts on her behalf and she began to think of her first son as Will. Two days later, a letter arrived from Jamie Wood, confirming what he had told Florence on the phone.

Florence was relieved to hear that Will was doing all right; at least, he had a wife and family and a job. What would she have done if the news had been that his life was in difficulties, that he was a criminal or a drug addict or even simply an unhappy man? What if he had refused to see her, after her refusal to see him ten years ago? She was thankful that she didn't have to face that. Her path to Will was clear and open now and she didn't want anything to stand in the way of meeting him.

The question then became one of where and how to meet. Florence had been glad of Val's offer to take part and consulted her now.

'I know a pub near where I live which would be perfect for a first meeting with a stranger. After all, Mother, he is a stranger,' Val said. 'Also, I don't think we should let him know where you live, until after we've met him. Supposing he's angry with you and disturbed? He could become a pest, turning up at your house unasked.'

'Well, he's given me his address and yet I could equally be a pest, so I don't see why I should be so much more cautious. However, now that you mentioned it, perhaps somewhere neutral is sensible. It might be easier all round. I've been thinking about it and I've got somewhere in mind.'

'Where then?' Val pursed her lips and looked at Florence with the air of a nurse indulging an elderly patient.

'A hotel I know in Richmond.'

'But that's miles away from Hackney, where William, sorry, Will, lives! It's right on the other side of London.'

'Doris took me there once, to celebrate my birthday. It's perched high up on a hill with a wonderful view of the Thames and you can see the nearest cows to the centre of London. Believe me, it's a special place and worth the journey. And he'll find it. After all, we know that he's good at searching things out,' Florence said. 'And, by the way, the tea will be my treat. They do a good afternoon tea. Make that clear to him, Val, so there's no uncertainty at the time.'

Florence was grateful to her daughter for the care she was taking over the meeting with Will. Val confessed that it was helping to take her mind off trouble that Dennis was having at work. The perfume factory he had inherited was in difficulties and was probably going to be sold. Florence kept quiet about her opinion of the scent itself. Val was clearly worried about their future and criticisms of the scent would seem trivial beside that. Then it turned out that Dennis had accepted the offer of a job at the factory, under the new owner, so they would have an income after all, in addition to the small amount that Val earned from a part-time job now that their children were older.

Val gave Florence a ring as soon as she had spoken to Will. 'I've arranged the meeting, Mother. He's agreed to go to Richmond and offered to wear a red scarf to identify himself. He said it wasn't as far out as Epsom. He sounded nice. A friendly manner and pleased about the fact that you got in touch,' Val said.

'That's a relief. I've been worrying a bit about whether I did the right thing, disturbing him after all these years. But why Epsom?'

'I don't know. I didn't ask. You and I should arrive ten minutes beforehand, so we can find a table and be waiting when he gets there,' Val said.

'That's funny. My only connection with Epsom is that it's where Bill came from. Oh well, perhaps Will has relatives there,' Florence said. She agreed with Val's suggestion of arriving early. It was, after all, their meeting and they wanted it to go smoothly.

She lived through the last days before she met her first-born in a kind of dream. She kept making little mistakes in the shop or at home and apologising to Doris or anyone else within hearing for her absent-mindedness. Her nights were disturbed by dreams of Bill and of Will as a baby, in a way that hadn't happened for some years now.

She hoped that she had done the right thing in arranging to see Will and Val together. Val might be bearable for those who knew her, but could be a bit much to meet out of the blue. How strange families appeared to be when you held them up to the light of the outside world! And supposing, as Val had suggested, that Will was hard to like for one reason or another? He might resent being adopted or, like Doris's adopted daughter, he might want to meet his blood relatives only once to satisfy his curiosity. He would be perfectly entitled to do that. On the other hand, he might simply be pleased to meet his original family at long last and be looking forward to getting to know its individual members.

Florence had to be ready for anything and not expect more from Will than he was prepared to give. She would have to do a certain amount of giving herself because she owed him an explanation. He would want to know why she had given him away. She approached the fateful meeting with a mixture of excitement and trepidation and could not bring herself to think beyond it.

Florence and Val arrived at the chosen hotel by taxi from Richmond Station twenty minutes before Will was due. Florence had spent ages getting ready, unsure of what to wear to meet her forty-two year old son for the first time since his babyhood. In the end, she had chosen a light grey skirt and cardigan with a pale pink blouse, trying to look neither too formal nor too casual. She had pinned a silver brooch to her cardigan. Early that morning, she had visited her hairdresser and she surveyed her appearance in her bedroom mirror with some satisfaction when she had finished dressing. The brown tresses of her girlhood had long since given way to short silver waves and her face was lined, but she thought she looked pleasant and approachable. Light make-up added a finishing touch.

The mid-October day was mild and sunny, with most of the leaves still on the trees and a gentle breeze barely stirring them. This was the time of year over forty years ago, Florence recalled, that she had heard that Bill Martin was missing.

Dennis had taken the children out for the afternoon and said that he would meet Will another time.

Florence and Val secured a window table in the hotel tea-room. It was a sunny afternoon and the view below them of the winding Thames with fields around it, dotted with brown cows, was entrancing. Florence was pleased to note that Val was impressed by her choice of setting. They fobbed off requests from hotel staff about what they wanted to order. Val was wearing a belted dress with a shirt collar and was carefully made up and clearly restless. She kept getting up and then sitting down again, complaining of a knot in her stomach. Florence was nervous about meeting the stranger as well and was hoping that they would like him. It would be so difficult if they didn't and if he wanted to continue seeing them.

'Supposing he's angry about being adopted and he hates us?' Val was saying.

'We've already said we'll only see him again if we want to,' Florence said.

'Oh, I must stop fussing. I wish he'd arrive. It's the waiting I can't stand.'

'He's not late yet, Val. Remember, he probably hasn't been here before, so he's got to find his way.' Florence sounded calmer than she felt. She was glad of Val's presence, but her daughter's need for reassurance made it seem as if Will was coming to see her instead of his mother.

The hotel tea-room began to fill up just before three and

Florence was glad they had secured a table in good time. She looked around the room. It would be easier for them to spot Will, a man coming in on his own, than for him to pick them out from the tables scattered around the room, especially when he had no idea of what they looked like. She began to wish that they had exchanged photographs before meeting. At least Will had said he would wear a red scarf.

People were milling about and Florence wished them to perdition rather than have them obscure her view of the entrance to the tea-room.

It was a few minutes past three o'clock when a vigorous man with curly, dark hair walked in and looked around him with an appraising air. A number of tables were occupied by two women and he appeared to be uncertain about which table to aim for. Even at a distance of some yards, with her eyesight not as good as it had been, Florence was convinced that she was looking at Will. It wasn't just the red scarf she could see around his neck. Some resemblance to Bill or to her seemed to tell her that here, at last, was the son she had given away all those years ago. She caught her breath and laid a hand on Val's arm, unable for a moment to speak, but pointing with her other hand.

'There's a red scarf. I'm sure that's him. I'm going to ask,' Val said and stood up.

Florence waited at the table, her heart in her mouth. Memories of her baby from over forty years ago were swirling about her as she watched Val walk over towards the man who had just come into the tea room and saw him turn towards her.

- Part Six -

Will

1987

Chapter One

In the ten years that had elapsed since Florence's refusal to see him, Will had tried to forget about her or at least to consign her to the further reaches of his mind. Days, sometimes weeks, even months would pass without more than fleeting thoughts about her. Yet, even though he had respected her wishes and had never tried to contact her again after that first refusal, he had not entirely been able to rid himself of the hope he had carried with him since adolescence that one day they would meet. It was that hope that had led him to leave his new address with Mrs Bradstreet and Paula Heron when he moved.

Will had risen in the teaching profession to the position of head of the history department in a different comprehensive school from the one where he began his career. He and Anna had been married for twenty years and Susie and Lizzie were approaching school-leaving age. The family had moved to a larger house in Hackney than the one they had bought after Lizzie was born and they still saw a lot of Will's parents and Anna's mother.

Shortly after her outburst during the visit from Will in the late 1970s, when he had questioned his parents about what they knew about his original father, Marion had been diagnosed with breast cancer and had undergone lengthy treatment. Much to the family's relief, it had been successful and she had not so far had a recurrence.

Frank still lived at home and had never married. Marion often said that she was grateful to Will and Anna for allowing her to be a grandmother because it would be Doomsday before Frank produced any children.

Will and Anna had met Bill and Rowena and Gerry and his wife several times and become friendly with them. Will had even seen Christine again. He had been brief with her on the phone after his visit to her and she had soon stopped ringing him. He had met her once or twice since then, at Bill's house, but always avoided any suggestion of meeting up or telephoning and indulging in the teasing banter of their early relationship. Within a few months, his strong feelings for Christine had simmered down and he was surprised, looking back, at how powerful they had been at the time. These days he could scarcely believe what had taken him over in the summer and autumn of the year when he had first met her.

Christine had trained as a social worker and become deeply involved in her job. Tony continued to work long hours. Will and Anna rarely mentioned Christine and only wondered if Christine and Tony's children ever saw their parents.

Will opened the letter that was waiting for him after school one day without any thought for what it might contain. The plain brown envelope with his name and address typed on the front looked more like a bill than anything else. He was in the kitchen with Anna and the girls after school. The family ritual of many years' standing that allowed them all to catch up on the events of the day still continued, when possible.

19th September 1987

Dear Mr Tyler,

I am writing to tell you that I have been contacted by Florence

Cruise, originally Florence Haldon, your birth mother. I am aware from our files that you left your change of address with us some years ago in case she got in touch. She has expressed a wish to see you.

Please telephone me at the address on this letter if you wish to take this matter further.

Yours sincerely,
Jamie Wood,
Social worker

Will could hardly believe what he was reading. The ordinary afternoon retreated as the words hit home and he handed the letter to Anna.

'Florence wants to meet me! Either she's plucked up the courage to tell her husband about me or he's died or gone off somewhere and she feels free!'

His eyes were shining and all his old curiosity about his origins was bubbling up inside him, where for years, as far as Florence was concerned, it had been pushed aside.

Anna reached for the letter. 'So your attempts to track her down have paid off at last!' she said, after reading it. 'What a momentous year! There's Reagan and Gorbachev shaking hands over the end of the Cold War, Thatcher winning another election in this country and now Florence wanting to see you!'

'Don't mock,' Will said, but without any force. His mind was already on meeting Florence. He was in no doubt about his wishes. He snatched a moment at school the next day to ring Jamie Wood. He gave his permission for Florence to have his address and telephone number.

When the phone rang at home in the evening, a few days later, Will answered it, expecting the caller to be Anna's mother, who often rang at about that time. The voice at the other end was unfamiliar, not the confident and fluent voice of Anna's mother, but a voice with a lighter, cooler tone.

'Hallo, my name is Val. I'm Florence Cruise's elder daughter. She thought it might be easier if I rang first. Am I speaking to Will Tyler?'

'Yes, that's me. Hello... Val,' Will said. His searches at the Public Record Office some ten years previously had not taken him as far as Florence's children and so he had been unaware that Florence had a daughter.

'You're my long lost brother. All this must be a shock for you. It's a bit of a shock for us as well, because we, that is my brother and sister and I, didn't know of your existence until recently.'

'And I didn't know of your existence at all. Well, thank you for getting in touch. So I have two new sisters and a brother?'

'Yes. It must be rather amazing for you.'

'It certainly is. I had no idea. I've known Florence's name for some years now, but I had no idea about her family.'

'Mother says you asked to meet her about ten years ago, when the new legislation came in, but she refused to see you because my father didn't know anything about you. Well, he died last year and that seems to have brought everything to the surface. She invited us all round to tell us about you recently and now it's all out in the open she'd like to meet you.'

Even though he had read the letter and was expecting a phone call, Will was hardly able to believe what he was hearing. It had the feeling of a dream. Even so, he wondered why Florence didn't ring him herself. She was the one who mattered to him, not Val. Could she be afraid of seeing him or did she simply think it would be easier for him to talk to Val to begin with? He decided not to ask. He would doubtless find out sooner or later.

'That would be wonderful. I've always wanted to meet her.'

'If it's all right with you, Mother and I would like you to come to a hotel she knows in Richmond. I hope that's not too far?'

'It's not as far as Epsom,' Will said, before realising that Val wouldn't know what he meant.

'Oh, no, I suppose not. Anyway, Mother says the view is special and they do very nice teas there. You can get a taxi from Richmond Station. Would 3rd October suit you, say about 3 pm? That's this Saturday coming.'

'Hang on...let me check... Yes, that's fine,' Will said, opening with his free hand the diary that he and Anna kept in the kitchen, where he had answered the phone. They were a busy family, but fortunately that Saturday afternoon was blank.

'Oh good. I'll write to confirm, with the address and so forth. I've got your address. Well, nice to talk to you. I must say that I'm curious to meet you now.'

Will remembered his meeting with Gerry. 'I'll wear a red scarf, so you'll know who I am,' he said.

She laughed. 'Oh, good thinking. I'll look out for it. I might even wear one myself! I like red.'

She rang off, leaving Will feeling shaken.

Later that day, talking to Anna, he thought of something.

'As far as I know, Florence thinks Bill is dead. I'm going to have to tell her that he's still alive. It will be a shock for her,' he said.

'Unless she knows. She might have found out after you were adopted and not told the adoption agency. Why not ring him first and explain what you're going to do? She might want to write to him or even to see him.'

'Good idea. You always have such good ideas, Anna. Where would I be without you?'

'Oh, probably somewhere at the bottom of the sea!'

Since discovering that Bill was alive, Will had been aware that Florence might still not know that and yet her refusal to see him previously had meant that he had no way of telling her. The episode with Christine had initially swept his realisation from his mind, but even after it was over, there had been no way he could talk to Florence about Bill. Things were different now because she wanted to see him. He would have to tell her if he saw her. When he rang Bill, he explained what he wanted to do and Bill agreed.

Despite a feeling that his whole life converged upon this point, Will was certain of one thing; Florence could never replace his mother in his heart, just as Bill hadn't replaced his father. He didn't think that Bill was trying to do that and he himself wasn't trying to undo or deny his adoption. He didn't know what Florence's intentions were, but time would tell. His parents had brought him up, had put up with the boorish teenager who had disliked being adopted and veered off the rails, even if not far off, but they had never given up on him. By contrast, he and Florence had no shared memories to draw on, no store of knowledge of each other, no old jokes to revive.

He visited his parents to tell them about Florence getting in touch, because he didn't want any secrets and he knew that it would matter to them. In the years since Florence's refusal to see him and since his first meeting with Bill and Gerry, he hadn't needed to mention his birth family often to his mother. Instead, partly because of her illness, he had treated her with kid gloves. He and Anna had seen Bill and Gerry and their families occasionally and Will had mentioned them now and then to his parents, but there had been no need to mention Florence.

'You're going to see her? Oh, I thought you'd forgotten about all that years ago,' his mother said, while his father looked merely curious.

'No, I hadn't forgotten. I just wasn't able to see her because she didn't want to see me, but she's changed her mind now. Her husband died recently and I think that's why she can. He didn't know about me and she could never bring herself to tell him,' Will said.

The conversation moved on to other things, but later on came back to Florence.

'Funny that she's changed her mind now,' his mother said, even though Will had already explained why he thought it was.

'It's because her husband died and he never knew about me,' Will said, telling himself once again that his mother's dislike of his wish to meet Florence stemmed only from an unnecessary, but understandable, feeling of insecurity on her part.

'I'd like you to accept what I'm doing, Mum. Florence can never replace you. You've always been my real mother,' Will added, reaching across and patting her knee.

His mother sniffed. 'Oh well, that's all right then.'

Will knew that it would never be all right that he wanted to meet Florence. He could only hope that his mother would realise in time that it wasn't going to change things for her, that she wasn't going to find Will disappearing from her life, at least, no more than he had done already in growing up and leaving home.

On the appointed day, he borrowed Anna's red scarf, which fortunately she still possessed, and took the North London Line to Richmond. Arriving before 3 pm, he wandered around for fifteen minutes or so, rather than be early for the appointment. It wouldn't do to give the impression of being anxious. He wanted to be alone to meet Florence for the first time, although Anna, who was by now almost as curious to meet Florence as Will himself, had offered to come if needed and he knew that Florence would be accompanied by Val.

Taking a taxi, he arrived on time at the hotel, an imposing and handsome Victorian building. Within seconds he was entering a sunny tearoom full of small tables and with a superb view looking down on the River Thames, its banks edged by fields full of brown cows. It was quiet in the tearoom and the tables were set far enough apart to give a sense of privacy. Florence had chosen well. Then he noticed that several tables were occupied by two women, like the table he was looking for.

He was just trying to work out which table to approach, when a woman wearing a red scarf came towards him. When she spoke and he confirmed his name, she gave an exclamation and introduced herself as Florence's daughter, Val. His first impression was of a tall, confident woman with an engaging manner. She invited him over to a table where an older woman was sitting on her own. As they approached, the older woman stood up, a little stiffly, he noticed, and yet she stood up straight, smiling with both hands outstretched.

There was a silence while Florence and Val looked at Will and he looked at them, as if it were possible to make up in a moment for a lifetime of not knowing each other. Florence was a small, grey-haired woman, slightly built. He didn't notice what she was wearing. It was her face he looked at. She looked like… like him, he thought, with an odd jump in his stomach. Looking at the face he had imagined all his life, he felt a kind of recognition. He noticed her clear features and the brimming eyes looking straight at him.

In a silence too powerful for words, Florence enveloped Will in a hug, which he returned. Val followed, both of them embracing warmly a man they had only just met. Will felt there were only three people left in the world. Then they all burst into laughter, not far removed from tears, before words began to flow instead.

'You look more like me, although you have Bill's hair. How strange that is, when I've always thought of you looking like him,' Florence said. Will agreed about his resemblance to her, despite her much smaller size. He was both delighted and shaken.

'Sit down, both of you,' Val said 'and I'll order tea and cakes all round.' She went off to find a waitress.

Will turned to Florence. 'I'm so glad you can see me at last. I've always wanted to meet you,' he said, as they sat down. Florence looked at him and nodded silently. She smiled tremulously and looked as if she didn't dare to speak.

Then she said simply 'I need time,' and he nodded and they sat for a few seconds together in silence. The world did not stop for long. Val returned with a waitress who took their order. Nothing less than a full afternoon tea would do, Florence said, as this was a celebration.

'May I call you Florence?' Will said to her. She nodded and said yes.

Val took the lead in the conversation then, explaining that she was the eldest of Florence's three children, except not the eldest anymore, she added hurriedly. She mentioned Florence's other daughter Evelyn and her son Steve, as well as her own husband Dennis and Steve's wife Lynne and rattled off an account of all Florence's grandchildren. Will was starting to feel bewildered at all the names, and felt that he wasn't being given much chance to talk, but Val clearly wanted to explain the family to him.

'You know, until Mother told us, I didn't have the faintest idea that there was a baby before me,' she said as she finished.

The tea arrived and the waitress set everything on their table. It was a relief to focus on something else for a moment.

'I'll be mother. Help yourselves,' Florence said, pouring the tea.

Will waited until Florence had put the teapot down before he said what he had planned. 'There's something I must tell you. This might come as a bit of a shock.'

'Tell me,' Florence said, putting her hands in her lap and looking at him expectantly.

'You seem to think that Bill died in the war. Is that right?'

'Yes. That's right… he was killed in France, after the Normandy landings.' She looked sad.

'No. He was injured and has never fully recovered, but he's alive.'

Will spoke gently, then stopped, out of consideration for Florence. She was staring at him with amazement, her face pale. For a moment, he thought that she was going to faint, but she collected herself and took a deep breath.

'But his mother said in the letter… her loss of her son!'

'How strange… I don't know why she said that. He was shot in the lung and at first he was missing, presumed dead, so maybe she was assuming he was dead at that point. He told me the story. He got separated from the men he was with and then he was wounded. Apparently they couldn't find him, but he was rescued and taken to a French hospital. He was there for a long time, because he couldn't be moved and then he was sent back to England, first to a hospital and then to his parents' home. He wrote to you, but there was no reply and when he was well enough to come to Plaistow to look for you, he was told by a neighbour that I had been adopted and that you were serious about someone else. Because of that, he decided not to distress you by contacting you.'

'I never received a letter from him. Our house had been bombed and I was living next door, with Jessie. That's probably why I never heard from him. I wrote to his parents, because I thought he was dead. His mother wrote back and accused me of… of intruding on the loss of their son or something like that. I've still got the letter. I kept it because it told me what had happened to him. Oh, but how wonderful he wasn't killed after all! And so you know him? I can't believe it. Do tell me about him.'

Will did his best to tell Florence and Val about Bill, his wife Rowena and daughter, Christine and her family and Bill's brother, Gerry and his wife.

After that, Flo and Val seemed hungry, as if they had been working hard. They helped themselves to the crustless sandwiches, scones with jam and cream and small cakes that the waitress had brought. It was good to have something to do, given the occasion, although Will wasn't feeling hungry. His mind and heart were full and his stomach felt the same. He managed a sandwich and a scone, so that Florence shouldn't feel that her afternoon tea was unwanted.

'I've brought a photo to give you,' Florence said, opening her handbag. Will looked at the wartime picture she passed to him. There were young members of the armed forces, including herself. She pointed out Bill and added, 'It's the only picture of both your parents. I should like you to have it. I've had a copy made for me to keep. Oh, I can't believe he's alive!'

'Thank you. I can't tell you how grateful I am at last to hear from you,' Will said, rubbing reddened eyes as he looked at the photo. 'I tried to meet you, after the law was changed. Also having children made me think differently about life and I couldn't help feeling that you would want to hear from me.' He had turned towards Florence and was speaking just to her.

'I was curious to meet you, had always wanted to, even before I knew your name, but having children of my own made it all the more important, because I thought they would have questions about my past as they were growing up. I didn't want to have to say that I didn't know anything about my mother, but now I shall be able to tell my girls the whole story!' he said.

'I'm so glad we've met at last,' Florence said tremulously.

'I applied for a copy of my original birth certificate and saw that my name at birth had been William Haldon and that your name was Florence Haldon. Then I searched the public records until I found your married name. The Church of England Children's Society wrote to you on my behalf, to lessen the shock for you. You may have thought you would never hear from me,' Will said, looking questioningly at Florence.

'It was a shock. Even though I couldn't forget you, I somehow never expected to hear from you,' she said.

'You must have replied instantly because I heard almost straightaway. I was disappointed when your answer was no, but it was pretty obvious that your refusal wasn't about me, because you didn't know me. I assumed that you had a reason for refusing to see me. Of course, I didn't try to contact you again. I was left hoping you'd change your mind one day,' Will said.

'You're right. I did want to see you, but I'd never told my husband about you and I couldn't bring myself to tell him after all those years. I'm sure you know, in those days, many men wouldn't have married a woman with a child, so I kept your existence a secret. Even after my husband's death, it was too difficult for me, at first, when I missed him so much, to think about seeing you. I am so sorry, Will, to have made you wait,' Florence said, stretching a hand towards him, a hand he caught and held for a moment.

'That's what I assumed, but it's nice to hear it,' Will said. 'I know that you looked after me for my first few months. You didn't give me up immediately.'

'I would have kept you… if it had been possible,' Florence said. She was struggling to control her voice.

Will began to think that it was all too much for her, especially with the shock of hearing that Bill was still alive. He was just wondering if they should call a halt and meet another time, when Val began to speak.

'You see, when I was little, I don't think Mother was always happy. It was sometimes hard to get her attention. Even though she was obviously busy looking after the three of us, there were times when she seemed a million miles away and I think that was when her mind was on you,' Val said.

Florence nodded and looked more comfortable. Will was pleased at Val's words.

'So how did you meet your father's side of the family?' Val asked.

'After Florence wouldn't see me, I hesitated for a while, because I didn't want another rejection, but then I decided to search for Bill Martin's family. I didn't know anything about him, even his name, but the adoption agency were willing to give me his name and squadron number and told me that he had grown up in Epsom. They told me that he had been killed in the war…'

'I wanted that passed on, so that you grew up knowing that your father died for his country,' Florence said.

'My parents were never told,' Will said, continuing his story. 'I went to see the Commonwealth War Graves Commission and then to Somerset House, but there was no record of Bill's death. My wife, Anna, had the bright idea of advertising in the local papers in Epsom and Gerry answered the advert and told me Bill was alive. I met them in a café, rather like we're doing now. Their parents were dead by then. Bill's mother never told him about your letter to them. He only found it after she died.'

'I wrote to his parents out of desperation really, when I was trying to find a way to keep you. I had already written to him several times in Epsom, but I'd heard nothing. By the time you were born, I no longer believed Bill was alive or I would have written to him then. There wasn't any money for single mothers in those days, the way there is now. I'll never forget Bill's mother's reply. It was the worst letter I have ever received,' Florence said, with feeling.

'It must have been difficult for you, being on your own and thinking Bill was dead,' Will said.

Florence nodded and a silence followed. It was not uncomfortable, only the silence of people taking a short break from their conversation, while they watched Val pouring more tea and waited for more of the story.

Chapter Two

Will broke the silence by offering to tell Florence and Val about his life. Florence nodded eagerly.

'I was adopted by a young couple who already had one child, but had been advised not to have any more for health reasons. So I grew up in a family with an older brother, Frank. My parents were always grateful to me for completing the family, as they put it. They told me that I was adopted when I was about five, but it wasn't until I was a teenager that I thought much about it,' Will said.

'They didn't change your first name,' Florence said with satisfaction.

'No. I've still got the name you gave me,' Will said with a smile and Florence smiled back at him. 'They liked the name William. I was Billy as a little boy and then, as a teenager, I wanted to be called Will and I've kept to that,' he added.

'Just like me,' Florence said. 'I was Flossie as a little girl and then Flo and now I'm Florence!'

Will smiled in appreciation of the similarity. 'I knew nothing about Bill, so I suppose I directed my curiosity at you, Florence. I couldn't help having fantasies about you as a teenager. I used to want you to come and find me and take me away to live with you, but it was also a terrifying thought, because I loved my family. I had nothing to go on, so my imagination ran wild. Well, nothing that is, except this.'

He slipped a hand into his jacket pocket and came out with a small jewellery box. He opened it and took out a faded blue ribbon from which dangled a tiny silver object.

'It's the heart that I tied to your wrist from the charm bracelet!' Florence said. She showed Will the charm bracelet, which she had brought with her, with its boots, flowers and rings and its one heart dangling alone, while two were missing. 'I brought it today because I thought you might want to see where the heart came from, if you knew about it. I wasn't sure you would ever have seen it.'

'My mother said that it was around my wrist when I was handed over to her,' Will said. He had decided beforehand to refer to his mother as he always had. She, after all, had brought him up and she deserved the name of mother. Florence would be Florence, as she had agreed to that.

'I've always taken it to mean that you loved me, because it's a heart, and that you only gave me up because you felt you had no choice.' His voice quavered and he sipped at his tea to steady himself.

'I did love you. I desperately wanted to keep you, but it was impossible. I couldn't afford to and I thought it would be better for you to grow up in a family with two parents,' Florence said. Her voice was choked, but she recovered. 'I gave the other missing heart to Bill when he was going to France in 1944,' she added.

'Yes, he told me. He's still got it,' Will said.

'Tell us more about you and your own family,' Val said.

'I went to university after school and studied history. I'm a history teacher in a comprehensive school now. I'm married, my wife is called Anna and we have two daughters, Susie and Lizzie. My parents are still alive, in fact they have mixed feelings about this meeting today, but they understand that

I wanted to do it. My brother never married and still lives with my parents. He's a postman, just as my dad was until he retired.'

'So you now have two more sisters,' Val said, smiling in a way that told Will that she liked him and might even be making a place for him in her life. 'And you're a teacher,' she continued. 'My brother – your brother – Steve is an engineer and my sister Evelyn works in a dress shop, but I was a teacher before I had children and I'm thinking of going back into teaching soon. What a coincidence! And thank you for telling us your story. Now, would you like to see some photographs?'

'I'd love to,' Will said.

The next half an hour was spent poring over pictures, including a portrait taken by Bill Martin of Florence in her WAAF uniform, smiling at him. At one point, Florence took another photo of herself as a young woman out of the album she had brought with her and gave it to Will.

'I'll make copies of some of these photos for you, but keep this one, because this is the sort of age I was when you were born,' she said. Will thanked her and scrutinised it before slipping it into the top pocket of his jacket with the photograph of Florence and Bill.

'It's impossible to make up for a lifetime in one afternoon,' Will said at one point. He felt no need to suggest meeting again. It was so obvious that they would.

'I was afraid you might be bitter or angry about being adopted, but I couldn't see any way around it at the time. I've been thinking… did Bill's mother think he was dead, when she wrote to me, or could she have known by then that he was alive?' Florence said.

'I don't know exactly when Bill came back to England or when his parents learned that he had survived,' Will said. 'But I can find out easily enough. Bill knows I'm seeing you today and I said I would ring him later.'

'It's such a shock, hearing that he's still alive. It's wonderful, but I need time to think about it,' Florence said.

Will couldn't help wondering whether her decision to give him away had been the cause of regret, but it was long in the past. He didn't wish that she had decided differently. That would have been to deny his childhood with Marion, Joe and Frank and he was too fond of them all to do that. Besides, as Anna had once pointed out, he was partly what they had made him.

'Well, you've certainly tipped Val off her pedestal of being the eldest,' Florence said, adopting a lighter tone.

'Oh... I can give that up,' Val said with enough hesitation to tell Will that her position in the family was important to her, but that she had accepted him.

'That's generous of you, dear. I must ring Evelyn and Steve to tell them all about it,' Florence said. 'Oh and there's Doris of course.'

'Oh, Doris,' Val said disparagingly, as Will looked puzzled.

'Doris is my good friend, who also gave up a child for adoption. It was Doris I talked to about you after George's death. She helped me screw up my courage to talk about you. I'm so glad I did. I've had enough of secrets,' Florence said, with a relieved smile.

The conversation halted. Will felt satisfied for the present and he stood up.

'I'm so pleased to have met you. Now I'm going to go home and try to take it all in. But I do want to meet the rest of your... of the family another time and I hope you'll come to Hackney and meet my family one day,' he said.

'Yes, of course,' Florence said and added 'Come and see me at home first and I'll tell you the story of Bill and your first few weeks of life. That is, if you would like to know.'

'I'd love to,' Will said, with feeling.

Val promised to arrange a family gathering for Will to meet

Evelyn and Steve and said that Will would be welcome to bring his family.

They all hugged again before Will left. 'It sounds corny to say it, but I feel I've found a missing part of my life,' he said.

'I understand. I think we feel similarly.' Florence was smiling.

Before he left, Will gave Florence the silver heart on its blue ribbon that she had once tied to his wrist. 'Have it, Florence, because I don't need it now that I know you,' he said. 'Perhaps you'll get the other heart back one day, the one you gave to Bill and then you can complete the bracelet.' He wished that it were so easy to knit together his background now that he knew about it.

Will came away from the hotel in Richmond with his mind bubbling over with new impressions. One of the strongest was that he looked like Florence. It gave him a sense of connection to her, different from anything he felt about his parents. Sitting next to her in the hotel, he had wondered if anyone passing had thought, *oh, mother and son.* He remembered that he had looked down at her when they were standing. She was smaller than he was. That wasn't surprising in a way and yet he was surprised, perhaps because he had been thinking of the childish fantasies in which the then nameless Florence had been the size of an adult.

Mother as she was, she was a stranger, not a complete stranger, but he knew little about her even after one meeting. It would take time to catch up, if it were ever possible to do so and in particular to find out exactly why she had given him up. He felt that he still didn't know. Surely it wasn't just because she couldn't afford to keep him? Then he admonished himself. It could have been just that. The historian in him knew that the welfare state, as comprehensive as it now seemed in the 1980s, hadn't fully existed at the time of his birth. He had always said he wanted to satisfy his curiosity and this afternoon's meeting had gone a long way towards it, but he wanted to know more. He always wanted to know more and again he had the feeling that he had first felt on learning her name, that Florence receded as he drew close to her.

She was his mother in one sense. He had to divide the idea of mother into giving birth to a child and bringing up the child. Both were important in different ways. Yet, although she hadn't brought him up, Florence had featured, in her absence, almost throughout his life, because of his curiosity about her. He had sometimes wished not to be curious, to forget about her and absorb himself in the life he had been given, without yearning for more and seeking to go beyond the possible. He had never been able to relinquish that wish to meet her and know more about himself. Now at last, at the age of forty-two, he had found what he had been seeking.

He felt pleased to have met Florence after all these years. More than that, he was conscious of a kind of wild enthusiasm for what had happened during the afternoon. It was like giddiness and he was wary of it, especially after the experience with Christine some ten years previously.

Meeting Florence for the first time, after a life of searching one way or another, was amazing, but it wasn't everything. A new horizon had revealed itself now that he had reached the one of meeting her. It was about getting to know her, finding out how he had featured in her life. There was a kind of urgency about it, not only because she was no longer young, but also because he had a strong desire for knowledge about her, at least in relation to himself.

He was glad that he liked Florence. He still remembered the hard-looking and ill-kempt woman who had answered the door to Florence's old home and how relieved he had been that, after all, she wasn't the woman who had given birth to him. It would be so difficult to discover a birth family that was so full of heart-sinking problems that he would want to keep a distance from them. He couldn't see that his birth family presented any such problems. The greatest difficulty had been over Christine. It was because of different attitudes and because of poverty that Florence had given him away. He might later see under the surface of this first meeting and find a different story, but for the moment he felt joyous about the afternoon.

Florence was friendly, with an alert, responsive manner. She was obviously a woman of great strength of personality, someone who had experienced success both in her personal life and in her work. She was someone he would be proud to introduce to anyone as his birth mother.

He was looking forward to knowing Val better, to seeing himself in her, if he could find anything, but he wouldn't repeat what had happened with Christine. Then there was another sister, Evelyn, and a brother, Steve, not to mention all their families. He would take Anna and the girls to the family gathering that Val had said she would organise. He hoped it would be soon, although he didn't want to push his new family. If he had learned one thing in his quest for Florence and Bill, it was patience. Meeting the rest of the family would happen easily now that the link had been made.

For the present he was content to mull over the meeting with Florence and Val, to savour all its details, think about what it meant to him and what sort of future it might bring about. He was looking forward to telling Anna all about the afternoon in the hotel. It would be easier talking to her than to his parents because he knew now that she had nothing to worry about in his getting to know his birth family, nothing except perhaps that it might take him away from her some of the time, like a new interest. But then, he could include her in the relationships that he hoped would develop, even though it was too soon to say how much they might mean in future.

Will arrived home and let himself into a silent house. He was surprised at first. He had been so absorbed in his experiences that he had forgotten Anna planning to go with Lizzie to an art exhibition that afternoon as he would be out. He remembered what she had said, and that Susie had been meeting a friend, as the silence of the house settled around him. He was disappointed at their absence because he wanted them to be there, his family, to hear the story of his meeting with Florence and Val. He was reminded of the time he had come home to find that Anna had taken the girls to her mother, all because he was getting too close to his half-sister Christine.

This time was quite different. He didn't have long to wait. He heard the sound of the key in the door and then Anna and the girls, who had all returned together, surrounded him, full of their doings that afternoon. Will listened, although with barely concealed impatience, which was unusual for a man who normally loved to hear what his wife and daughters had to say.

When at last he had a chance to speak, he was rewarded by the attention of three faces turned towards him and drinking in his tale of the afternoon, keen to hear everything about it. Anna had always supported his wish to find his birth family and he appreciated her generosity towards him. She always said that he was gaining by hard work something that she had been given as a child – acquaintance with relatives and knowledge of family background, but she also liked to remind him that he already had a family of his parents and Frank and all their relatives. For his part, he tried to understand how difficult it must have been for her that her parents' marriage had broken up when she was a teenager. He wasn't the only one who had encountered difficulties when young. As the mother of two teenage girls, Anna liked to say that adolescence was a time in life when children needed their parents as much if not more than they did when younger, only in a different way. She was good now at listening to the girls and being company for them when they wanted it.

'But what is she like to look at? You haven't said,' Anna was asking now.

'Small and thin, but there's plenty of life in her. Her eyes are expressive,' Will said. 'I didn't notice what she was wearing, but her face… well, I recognised her, even though we hadn't met before. She looks like me, not exactly of course, but you can see a family resemblance. That's what struck me most of all when I first saw her.'

'And this recognition, was it because of the family resemblance or because of who she is to you?'

'I don't really know. I asked her if I could call her Florence and I was glad when she said yes. I wouldn't have wanted to call her Mother, because of Mum.'

'Blood isn't everything,' Anna said.

'No, you said that before and I think you're right, at least, I do now. I haven't always been certain of that, but Mum is my real mother, because she brought me up.'

Anna smiled in agreement.

Susie and Lizzie, now seventeen and fifteen, were fascinated to hear that they had another grandmother, another aunt and other relatives and asked if they could meet them. Will promised that this would happen before long and then turned to see Anna's disconcerted face.

'Oh, are you going to be seeing them again, then? I thought this was the big *finale* today,' she said. Will sensed a reservation, a milder version of Marion's disapproval. Because Anna was close to her own mother and liked Marion, she could easily see Florence as an intruder. She had obviously been hoping that the meeting with Florence and Val would be the end of something, whereas he now saw it as a beginning.

'Well, yes. The next thing is to see Florence on her own and hear her story and then Val is planning a family gathering. That's where you'll meet them all, if you would like to come,' Will said, going on to explain about Florence's other children, Evelyn and Steve and their families.

'I suppose your curiosity knows no bounds, but I understand you want to meet everyone,' Anna said.

She went off to make some tea. Will felt relieved that she seemed to accept his plan. He was experienced at this now and would tread carefully with Florence and her family.

Chapter Three

Arriving home one evening from work, Will recognised the handwriting on an envelope lying on the kitchen table, even though he had previously only seen it on Florence's letter to Bill's parents. The clear, upright, square style was unmistakable.

10th October 1987

Dear Will

It was a pleasure to meet you last week after all these years. I've never forgotten you and I've thought of you and dreamed of you ever since I had to give you up.

Please come and see me at home one day if you would like to hear more about what happened when you were a baby.

With love from Florence

Will was pleased. The note was only short but it told him how Florence felt, it made no demands on him and it offered a next step. A quiet conversation on his own with her was what he had been hoping for after sharing their first meeting with Val.

He wanted to know about her family, her life on the RAF station with Bill and her reasons for giving her first baby up for adoption. He wouldn't rush her. After all, she had climbed the mountain of telling her family about him and arranged the meeting in the hotel. The last thing he wanted was to overwhelm his new family with intemperate demands. Take it easy, he said to himself. Think of what it's like for them. Except for Florence, they had never heard of you. Except perhaps for Florence, they never had that yearning feeling, that desire to know, even if it changed and calmed down as time went on, that you have had since you were a teenager.

Despite his admonitions to himself, Will was eager to see Florence and he phoned her at home a few days after receiving her note, to accept her offer. She appeared to be perfectly at ease about it and they arranged to meet. He also spoke to Bill, to tell him about the first meeting with Florence. He remembered to ask Bill a question concerning his return to England during the war, a question that had been in his mind since meeting Florence.

Will crossed London from Hackney to Putney to see Florence at home one November day after school. He had arranged his visit for a time when she didn't need to be at the shop. It was his first visit to her home, but more than that, it was the first time that he would be alone with her since babyhood, which didn't count in a way because he couldn't remember it. On the journey, he felt as if he were moving from his everyday life into a parallel world.

The house wasn't difficult to find, although it was tucked away on a side street right by the underground, which ran overhead at this point. Florence opened the door and welcomed him in, pleased to see him. He had not been sure if it would be an ordeal for her to see her long-lost son a second time, not long after the first meeting, but without the presence of Val. Stepping into her house, he reminded himself not to tire her with all his questions.

In the narrow hallway, he was struck by a faint scent and

he asked about it. She explained that it was lavender. She grew it in her garden and then dried it and kept it around the house, in bowls or as part of displays of dried flowers that he could see here and there. She invited him to squeeze some in his hands for a stronger scent and he did so, but he didn't like it much close up. Unlike the scents that Anna wore, it seemed pungent and heavy.

'I've been baking in your honour,' Florence said as they sat down in her sitting room, surrounded by the many pictures and ornaments that spoke of her love of antiques and with a budgie twittering in a small cage. Will felt faintly disapproving of the presence of a caged bird. He liked birds to be free.

'I hope you like Dundee cake. It's made with fruit and nuts and it always suits a special occasion. This is our first chat together, so there's good reason for a cake,' Florence said.

'I love fruit cake,' Will said. 'I hope it's all right to say this, but I've been looking forward to seeing you on your own and finding out more about your life with Bill and about the time I lived with you.'

He chose his words carefully, not wishing to sound in any way critical of Florence. He wasn't critical of her at all. He could understand why she hadn't wanted to meet him while her husband was alive, he believed her when she said she had loved him as a baby and had wanted to keep him. He wanted her to tell him about Bill, about their relationship, their war, the circumstances of his birth and his adoption. Since first meeting her, his craving to know as much as possible had not abated. That knowledge, which other people built up over a lifetime, and could value or ignore at their pleasure, he must now acquire all at once and he wanted to acquire it quickly. All the questions he hadn't been able to ask, questions of the kind that Frank and his new half-brother and sisters had been able to ask at any time or even not to ask, but to have the freedom to lack interest in, were flooding into his mind. The meeting in the hotel had been important, but it had only skated over the surface.

Florence served tea in bone china cups with saucers from a tea set which she had bought through her shop. Will was more used to a mug and handled the delicate cup carefully, examining the colourful Japanese pattern with appreciation. She cut slices of the Dundee cake, served them on plates from the same tea set and then began her story. She talked about meeting and falling in love with Bill at RAF Burghfield, his departure for France, their letters, realising that she was pregnant and telling Bill about the baby, hearing that he was missing, presumed dead, her abrupt dismissal from the WAAF because of her pregnancy, her long journey home only to find that the house had been bombed and her mother was dead, the good fortune of being taken in by Jessie, meeting Betsy in the butcher's shop and having to admit that she was pregnant, being fearful of gossip, William's birth, writing to Bill's mother and the reply, her struggle to keep William, her exhaustion and the threat to her health and her eventual decision about adoption. She went on to say she had never forgotten him but had never thought she would see or hear from him again. She mentioned the letter that she had received saying William wanted to meet her, her refusal and later telling her children about William and her decision to meet him.

Hours passed. Glued to Florence's words, Will also managed to drink another cup of tea and demolish a second slice of the Dundee cake. It was deliciously moist and fruity and he was always hungry after work.

'I can't thank you enough for telling me all this,' he said as Florence brought her story up to the present day. 'You've given me a lot to think about, but one thing shines out. You loved me and tried hard to keep me.'

He tried to steady his voice, but it seemed to go its own way, so he stopped, reached across and squeezed Florence's hand.

He remembered then that something needed clearing up. 'Do you have the letter from Bill's mother?' he said.

'Yes, here, I've sorted out the letters because I thought you'd want to see them.'

Florence showed him the letter from Winifred Martin. He saw the date of 5th February 1945. One sentence leaped out at him: *How dare you write to us in the midst of our grief for the loss of our son with your story about a baby fathered by him.* The date on the letter confirmed the suspicion that had led him to ring Bill before seeing Florence. Something was badly wrong here and he needed to tell Florence.

'Bill told me that he was back in England by Christmas 1944. He was still weak from his wound and the loss of a lung. He spent some time in hospital and then was invalided home where his mother nursed him until he was as well as he was going to be. He gave up smoking after he was wounded, because he had to give his one lung the best possible chance.'

'He always smoked a pipe,' Florence said, with a smile, her memory of Bill with his pipe eclipsing for a moment what Will was saying. Then realisation hit her.

'So she knew he was alive when she wrote to me in February 1945 and yet she talks about the loss of their son as if he was dead. Do you mean she was deceiving me?'

'It looks like it. You told me, when we first met last month, that you had written to his parents after I was born and been told of his death. So I queried that with Bill, before coming to see you today, because I couldn't remember exactly when he said he came back to England from France. He assured me on the phone the other day that his parents knew he had been found alive while he was still in hospital in France. They came to see him as soon as he was brought back to England before Christmas 1944. By the time of Mrs Martin's letter to you in February 1945, she certainly knew her son was alive. He was there in the house with her.'

Florence's bright eyes were fixed on Will, drinking in every word and her hands were clenched.

'So she lied to me, a terrible lie. What an evil woman! To think that I believed her. She didn't want me marrying her son because she thought I wasn't good enough for him. She must have destroyed all my letters without ever letting him see them,' she said.

She twisted her fingers together in her lap. Looking at her, Will could see that she found the forty-year-old lie as fresh as if it had been told the previous day. She had believed Bill was dead, believed it because of that sentence in the letter which now lay exposed as a lie.

'I'm sure she did. It also looks as if she never posted his letters to you,' he said. 'When I began to think that Bill's mother had lied to you about his death, I asked him if he posted his letters to you himself. He didn't, because he wasn't well enough to go out. He gave them to his mother to post.'

Florence was speechless for a moment, staring at Will. A short bark of laughter escaped her and when she spoke her voice was high with astonishment.

'How extraordinary! But for her, my life would have been so different. I wouldn't have given you up for adoption and Bill and I would have married and brought you up.'

Will took a deep breath. 'It is extraordinary what that one sentence in her letter did,' he said. 'It's almost unbelievable because it changed your life and it changed mine. I've been thinking about it ever since I spoke to Bill and worked out what had happened. I can't quite take it in. There's more, though. Bill says he wrote to you several times after his return, to the address you gave him, but there was never any reply. In the end he came over to Plaistow. It was autumn 1945 by then, over a year since he had last seen you, but he hadn't been well enough to track you down on foot before. That was when he spoke to a neighbour and made his decision not to pursue you.

He asked the neighbour not to say anything to you because she told him that your baby had been adopted and that you were serious about a young man.'

'I wonder who Bill spoke to? Surely Jessie would have said something to me? A pity I can't ask her. It could have been someone else, though. That street was full of people who knew everyone else's business.'

'It's been a shock finding out not only that Bill is still alive, but that you were kept apart, hasn't it?' he said, after a short silence.

Florence gave a little shrug and seemed to return from long ago to smile at Will.

'Yes, it is, but I'm glad you told me. I always prefer to know the truth. You know, I can't bring myself to wish I'd never married George or had my other children. I can't even wish that your family hadn't adopted you, however much I missed you at the time and afterwards, because they clearly love you. Yet it's a terrible wrong, not only to me but to you as well.'

'I suppose I would have had a different life if Winifred hadn't told that lie,' Will said. 'But, as Anna once pointed out, I would have been a different person and I might not have met her! So I don't wish my life had been different either.'

Florence nodded. She was struggling to keep her composure and then she seemed to recover.

'I would like to see Bill, though. I've been thinking about it, ever since you told me that he's still alive. Just the once, to see that he's all right.'

'That's what he said, that he'd like to see you and that his wife understands that. He asked me for your address. May I give it to him?' Will said and Florence nodded.

Will was moved by Florence's story, especially her struggle to keep him. He was gratified to hear her say again that she had loved her baby and missed him terribly after he had gone. He pored over the flimsy, wartime notepaper of Bill's letters with care.

'What a hard time you had, with thinking Bill was dead and then having a baby without the support of his father,' he said.

'I thought of you often after you went, but I never expected to hear from you. It wasn't possible in those days.'

'What was it like, hearing from me after thirty years?'

Florence had already talked about that, but had more to say. She told Will about the morning ten years previously when she had been making a cake at home and had received a letter saying that he wanted to see her, explaining how shocked she had been and how she had not dared agree to his request because she couldn't bring herself either to tell George about her first son or to deceive George more than she had done.

In return, Will told Florence more about his discovery of Bill and his relationship with him since their first meeting in a café in Epsom.

Florence laughed with a sudden recognition. 'Of course, that why you said on the phone to Val that Richmond, where we met, wasn't as far as Epsom. It was because you were thinking of Bill,' she said.

'Oh, yes – of course I was. We meet Bill and his family once or twice a year, I suppose and we go over to Epsom because it's easier for him. He likes to think he has a son and even Gerry likes to say that I'm the closest he's ever come to having a son,' he said.

'They sound much nicer than their mother,' Florence said. 'Do you know, it might have been hard to be married to Bill with his mother as bad as we now know. And it's odd to think how desperate I was when I thought Bill had died and yet now I can look back on it all from a distance.'

'It was a long time ago,' Will said, adding, 'I was lucky to meet Anna when I did, with no war to tear us apart.'

Florence asked Will to tell her about his parents and Frank.

She had learned their names from him and was curious about them. She listened as he spoke.

'Of course, I'm only your mother in one sense,' she said. 'Marion is your mother in every other way. Did you tell her you were coming to see me today?'

'No. She knows about you, but she's uneasy about it all. I think she's afraid of losing me,' he said, feeling guilty, as if he had betrayed his mother by his admission.

'Maybe I can understand how she feels.'

Florence spoke clearly and calmly and Will felt that here was someone who wasn't going to try and cross boundaries. Florence would never try to undo her decision about his adoption, by trying to acquire a spurious closeness with him now. His mother was safe. He was glad to hear that Florence wasn't making any claim on him. It would have been confusing and unwelcome if she had made a bid to be a mother figure to him after all these years. Not only was he beyond needing a mother as a child did, but also she hadn't been a mother to him after his first three months.

'And you?' Will said. 'How do you feel now that you've told your family your secret?'

'I feel more at peace with myself now that I've met you. I only wish I could have told George, but it's too late to do anything about that now. I've put you through it as well, making you wait so long to see me. I did my best with it all, but I suppose I've made mistakes along the way.'

Will gave her a quick smile. 'Well, the main thing is that you changed your mind in the end. I was happy as a small boy and not troubled all the time as a teenager. I do feel it has all turned out all right, now that I've met you and there's no more mystery.'

It would have been difficult for Florence if he had been angry or resentful. His mind flashed back to the newspaper headlines twelve years previously when the adoption legislation had been going through Parliament. Florence had not been haunted by a fear of being pursued by her son. She had been surprised and shocked by his attempt to contact her, but she had dealt with it in the best way that she could at the time.

He told her about his idea of an angel or rescuer figure as a child, his rebelliousness as a teenager, meeting and marrying Anna and the help that she had given him over the years, his search for Florence after legislation made it possible for him to find out about his background, his disappointment when she refused to see him, his attempt to understand it all from her point of view and finally his joy when she had decided to meet him.

'My only problem now is that I might have too many relatives,' Will said, risking a light-hearted manner with Florence. 'There's my family and my parents, you and your family, Bill and his family. What am I going to do?'

She laughed at that. 'I'm sure you'll manage it all,' she said. 'Oh, and you mustn't let Val take you over, you know. She's powerful, but never entirely happy with herself. I don't really know why. Sometimes I blame myself because it took me time to love her. I was still missing you too much when she was born and I rushed into marriage and a family because I felt time was passing me by after the war and after what I thought was your father's death. But I don't know if that's why Val is like that now.'

'It could just be the way she is,' Will said, avoiding the idea of thinking much about Val. He had never quite forgotten those months with Christine.

As he left, Florence put her arms around him and hugged him close to her before releasing him.

'Thank you so much for seeing me. Will you be all right after all this talking?' he said as she opened the front door to let him out.

'Oh, yes. I'm so pleased to have had the chance to let it all out at last. And don't worry about me. I'll pop in on Doris. I told her you were coming today and she'll want to know how it went.'

'We'll meet again,' Will said, smiling down at her.

She nodded and smiled. 'You must come and meet Evelyn and Steve one day soon. I'll arrange something.'

'Of course and I'd like you to meet my family.'

More questions would probably arise, but they could wait for another day. Will was in no doubt that there would be another day. He didn't know what shape things with Florence would take in future, but having found her after all these years and liking her as he did, he was sure that they would remain in touch. He would like to see her again and meet her family. There was room for knowing Florence and Bill without upsetting things with his own family, with Anna and the girls and not forgetting Marion, Joe and Frank. There was no rush, because he could see that Florence already felt some relief from unburdening herself of her secret and his curiosity was satisfied for the moment.

Closing Florence's front gate behind him, Will couldn't wait to tell Anna and the girls about his visit to her. He began walking, but it was not enough and his feet moved faster and faster. Soon he was running to the station and the train home.

Acknowledgements

I am grateful to a number of people for advice and encouragement while I was writing *The War Baby*, in particular Margaret Briggs, Ruth Cohen, Sue Johnson, Alan Rushton, Hermione Sandall and Rachel Summerson. Julia Feast of CoramBAAF has given me valuable advice about adoption. I should also like to thank the team at The Book Guild for their efficient handling of the publication.